D0978763

# Trouble on the Books

# Trouble on the Books

A CASTLE BOOKSHOP MYSTERY

Essie Lang

CROOKED LANE

NEW YORK

This is a work of fiction. All of the names, characters, organizations, places and events portrayed in this novel are either products of the author's imagination or are used fictitiously. Any resemblance to real or actual events, locales, or persons, living or dead, is entirely coincidental.

Copyright © 2019 by Linda Wiken

All rights reserved.

Published in the United States by Crooked Lane Books, an imprint of The Quick Brown Fox & Company LLC.

Crooked Lane Books and its logo are trademarks of The Quick Brown Fox & Company LLC.

Library of Congress Catalog-in-Publication data available upon request.

ISBN (hardcover): 978-1-68331-981-8
ISBN (ePub): 978-1-68331-982-5
ISBN (ePDF): 978-1-68331-983-2

Cover illustration by Teresa Fasolino

Printed in the United States.

www.crookedlanebooks.com

Crooked Lane Books
34 West 27th St., 10th Floor
New York, NY 10001

First Edition: March 2019

10 9 8 7 6 5 4 3 2 1

# Chapter One

The third time Shelby Cox hit her head on the low-hanging gargoyle that morning, she was sure the entire castle could hear her yell. Fortunately, it wasn't yet open to the public.

She dropped the heavy box of books she'd been carrying, kicked at it, and then let out a string of expletives. When she'd recovered her composure, she glanced around, relieved no one had been following her in, heaved the box back onto her hip, and hobbled over to the trolley, where she deposited it on top of two others. Moving-in day at the castle.

"You break that gargoyle, you buy it." The disembodied voice belonged to Loreena Swan, curator of the exhibits and the heritage attraction that was Blye Castle.

*As if I could break a cement gargoyle.*

Shelby knew that Loreena wouldn't rush over to help her with her burden. She was probably too busy setting out and straightening her many brochures. Obviously, an autocrat in training.

"Grumble, grumble," Shelby hissed under her breath. "Witch."

"I won't tell her you said that. My lips are sealed."

Shelby turned to face Matthew Kessler, her face feeling like it had just been zapped by a heat lamp. She'd hoped no one had heard. "You'd better not, or I fear that my days in this place will be a living hell."

Matthew grimaced. "You just have to show her total respect and do a lot of butt kissing."

"Like you do." Shelby said with a straight face. She doubted it was true. As the caretaker of the castle and grounds, he was probably beyond Loreena's reach, reporting only to the owners. He also came across as someone who wouldn't be pushed around, someone you'd better not cross.

"We have an agreement. She knows I won't take any guff from her, and she also knows what she can do about it." He hefted one of the large boxes of books off the cart and in through the door that Shelby had just opened, into the bookstore.

Shelby had a moment's concern. Those boxes were heavy. One hundred percent books. And Matthew had to be at least sixty if he was a day. Before she could say anything, he'd put it down next to the antique desk that served as checkout for the bookstore. She flipped on the overhead light switch and sighed. It had taken an entire day to fill three-quarters of the shelves. Now the final books needed to be added before the official opening the next day.

"I hope you've got yourself some help putting out all these here books," Matthew said as he straightened and took a deep breath. He looked around the room, and Shelby followed his gaze. Three hundred square feet on the main floor of the castle, an odd protrusion from the side of the building when viewed from the outside.

"Help will arrive in a couple of hours on the launch. I wanted some time to myself to figure things out so that we can jump right in when she gets here."

"Well, then I'll just finish bringing the boxes in, then get on with my duties."

"Thanks so much, Matthew." She followed him back into the entrance hall and watched as he headed to the front doors, trying to make it look like a saunter. He looked the part of a caretaker, or woodsman even, in his worn jeans and red plaid shirt. She'd heard he'd been through a lot. She'd first bumped into him a couple of weeks ago when she'd visited the castle to get the lay of the land, or rather, bookstore. Her Aunt Edie had filled her in on some of his story.

"You have yourself a good day, Shelby, and just call out if you need anything," Matthew said as he pushed the final box across the floor and into the room. "Don't let the witch get you down. You just stand your ground. It's your bookstore, after all. I hope you'll like it here," he added and wandered off.

Shelby nodded and glanced around. This was her new life. Running two bookstores, the main one, Bayside Books in Alexandria Bay, and the seasonal one in Blye Castle on Blye Island, part of the Thousand Islands.

She had vague memories of touring the better-known Boldt Castle as a small child. It had then seemed magical and massive. Blye Castle, on the other hand, was smaller, only four stories tall compared to six. But the dark oak walls throughout the main floor were just as regal, as was the sumptuous staircase set toward the back of the grand hall, branching out into two circular sets of stairs after the first landing. It took her breath away. *Imagine living here.*

She went back into the bookstore and pulled out a feather duster, flicking it over the shelves even though she knew the space had been professionally cleaned the day before. She took a few seconds to look around the room and then smiled. The three hundred square feet allotted to the store was the only part of the castle that had been recently renovated, substituting large bay windows for the smaller casement ones that had originally been there. The area was now bright and light, ideal for two comfortable club chairs placed invitingly in front of the windows, tempting shoppers to spend some time looking through hopefully future purchases. It was just the sort of bookstore she herself would love to shop in.

*Back to dusting.* The task made her feel more like this was really her store. Or rather, half of it was. That thought still made her feel the need to pinch herself and make sure it wasn't a dream.

She was still an upstate New York gal at heart even though she'd been brought up in Boston. And she knew she'd made the right decision coming back to Alexandria Bay, even before she'd learned that she was a part owner of the Bayside Books stores. It also afforded her the opportunity to find out more about her mom, who had died when Shelby was a toddler. That was a definite plus.

She just wasn't ready to be knocking heads with Loreena Swan. But it looked like that might go with the territory. She'd have to get some advice from her Aunt Edie on how to handle the dragon. Although Edie had been sidelined by knee replacement surgery a month before, she was still more than ready and able to offer advice, or criticism, from the comfort of her home. And begging her niece Shelby to take a leave of absence as an editor at a small publisher in Massachusetts had been Edie's way of dealing with her own change in lifestyle.

Shelby pulled out the layout Edie had given her, showing how the books were to be shelved and, also, where the new chocolate section should be set up. She wished she had one of those delicious truffles right now.

It might help her deal with Loreena.

# Chapter Two

"You know, you have to bring in a whole lot more local books. That's what our tourists are looking for. And look at this, you have far too many mysteries," Loreena Swan dictated a little later in the day, swinging her arm in a circle to include the entire bookstore. It wasn't hard, since the store was so small.

"I'm working on it, Loreena. Thanks for the suggestion," Shelby answered in what she hoped was an assertive voice. She hated confrontations but knew she had to come across as strong if she was going to work with this woman. Her dad had often told her she looked stern, even when she was in relaxed mode. He said it was her dark eyes and thin lips. She knew it was because she often had to remind herself to smile. She might as well put it to use, she thought, and put aside the books she had been shelving to turn toward Loreena. Time to face the dragon head on.

Loreena looked the part, like she'd just volleyed a flame full of bad karma. She'd planted her feet in a wide stance, maybe for balance, Shelby thought, but more likely for emphasis. Her hands were firmly embedded on each hip, maybe to showcase her figure-hugging fuchsia top and skinny black pants, but more likely to look like she meant business. Her obviously-out-of-the-bottle red hair fit the flaming scenario. But her teeth were out of place. *More like a ferret.* Appropriate, since she seemed to work so hard at ferreting out negative things to say about everyone.

That thought made Shelby smile.

"What? You think it's funny? I also notice that you don't have any copies of *The Thousand Island Memories*, which is my guidebook to Blye Island and the Thousand Islands area." Loreena's right foot, encased in a two-strap wedge sandal, started tapping. "It's been written up in the media so much that a lot of people ask for it each year. In fact, I'd say it's the best known of the local guidebooks."

"It's on order," Shelby mumbled, although she wasn't sure what book Loreena meant. She hadn't come across Loreena's name as an author when restocking.

"It better be. It's a very popular book. That's obviously why it's sold out."

*Or maybe we never carried it.*

Loreena began pacing, inspecting the shelves. "Honestly, Shelby. I'd think you'd be trying really hard to impress your aunt if you want to stay on once she's back working. This just isn't good enough."

That did it. Time to practice being assertive. Shelby moved very close to Loreena and tried to look her in the eye even though Loreena had at least a foot on her.

"Your comments are duly noted, Loreena; however, this

bookstore belongs to my aunt and me, and we are leasing the space from the Alexandria Bay Heritage Society. That in no way gives anyone the authority to dictate what we will carry and how it'll be set up." She stuffed her hands in the pockets of her jean jacket to hide the shaking.

Loreena sputtered, looking like she'd like to choke Shelby or, at the very least, slap her. Shelby managed to stand her ground. Loreena took a deep breath and, in a voice to rival the Ice Queen, stated, "You had better take a look at your contract, Miss Cox. You cannot talk to me like that, and you can't, you can't . . . oh!" She stomped off.

*Can't what?* Shelby took a couple of deep breaths and then did some shoulder rolls to relieve the tension. *What a witch. An aging witch.* That thought made Shelby feel a bit better, although she'd always been taught to be polite to her elders. What must Loreena be? Fifty? Sixty? Close to Edie in age, anyway.

"Wow, that was quite the verbal exchange," Trudy Bryant said as she backed in through the door that Loreena had left wide open. She set the box she'd been carrying down on the floor and lifted out a cup of coffee, setting it on the counter. "I picked this up while waiting for the launch, so it's probably on the cold side now. Is the microwave set up?" She looked around the room, then reached down into the box again. "And I brought over the extra coffee maker from the store."

"That's great. Thanks, Trudy. Even cold coffee will do right now."

Trudy glanced at the door. "Loreena is overbearing and

hard to get along with at the best of times, although Edie always seems to ignore her, but I've never heard her sound so threatening. You don't think there's anything in the contract, do you? Edie would be heartbroken if we lost this spot."

Trudy and Edie Cox had been best friends since grade school and both had grown up in Alexandria Bay. Edie had decided to stay and make her future there, and when Trudy had returned many years later after her husband died, they had easily resumed their friendship. The fact that Trudy was Edie's second-in-command at Bayside Books meant that Shelby valued Trudy's opinions, but she wished she hadn't been there to hear what had just transpired.

"Please don't mention it to Aunt Edie." Shelby reached down and pulled her purse from under the counter. "I'll tell her, but I need to make sure we're all settled into the new season before that." She rooted around in her purse and found an elastic to wrap around her long, wavy, dark-brown hair, which she pulled back into a ponytail. Nothing worse than having her hair flying all over the place when she was trying to work.

Trudy nodded, her own short gray hair blowing slightly in the breeze from the small fan on top of the counter. "I won't. I don't like to upset her while she's recovering, but you know, she'll have some good advice on how to handle that battle-ax." She winked at Shelby.

Shelby smiled, feeling a bit better. "I hope there weren't too many people in the entrance hall that heard that."

"Just me and a few volunteers. I think Loreena has them

browbeaten though, so they're probably on your side. Now, what can I do?" She looked around. "It appears that you and Taylor got most things sorted before boxing them."

"We tried. She's a hard worker. I'm sure we'll make a good team over here. I just hope the staff at both stores aren't stretched too thin with the extended hours. Of course, since I'm just easing into all this, I totally trust your judgment."

"Speaking of which," continued Trudy, "I'm hoping many of our regulars will come over here for the grand opening for the season. I'm making sure to remind them all about it. We have a strong and loyal readership base. Of course, since we're the only bookstore in Alexandria Bay, that's to be expected. But it does go beyond that. Our customers like what we offer, the things they can't get online. Advice, discussions, gossip," she added with a wink.

Shelby nodded. There were so many details to be aware of when running a business. She loved books, but her retail experience had been limited to two summers during high school, working at a local dress shop. It had done wonders for her wardrobe but hadn't really added a lot of other skills.

"Are you going to be okay?" Trudy asked. "Don't let Loreena get you down."

"Thanks, Trudy. I am, or at least, I will be once I get some tips from Aunt Edie on ignoring Loreena." She gave the older woman a hug. "And please thank Erica for the chocolates. These will be a great start, and as soon as I see how quickly they sell, I'll put in a regular order. It must be a real treat having a daughter who's a chocolatier."

Trudy pointed to her midriff. "You can see just how tasty

it is. I introduced the store book club to them a couple of months ago, and Erica's sales shot up." She chuckled and finished off her coffee before starting to shelve the mysteries. "By the way, we're all hoping you can come to the next meeting and meet the gang, the Bayside Book Babes Plus One."

"I've been meaning to." Shelby shrugged. It was another one of those items on her list that she just never seemed to get around to doing. There was still so much about the book business to learn. "By the way, who's the 'Plus One'?"

"We have one male in the group. I won't call him a token male because he really gets into the spirit of things, but we thought we'd immortalize him in our name." Trudy smiled. "Our meeting is a week from this coming Wednesday, at my house. I'll send you an email to remind you, shall I?"

"Sounds great. Who came up with that name, by the way?"

"Edie. Who else!"

Shelby chuckled as she removed the small trays of assorted truffles and chocolates, carefully placing them in the new refrigerated display case that had been delivered the day before. She knew they would be a popular addition to the store. Just to be certain, she chose a chocolate ganache truffle and popped it whole into her mouth.

At that moment, the phone rang. Shelby eyed the ceiling and chewed far too fast, regretting not being able to savor the flavor. She glanced at the phone as she picked up the receiver. Her aunt. Had word traveled so quickly? She glanced at Trudy, who gave her a thumbs-up.

"Is everything all right with you?" Edie asked without waiting for Shelby to say a thing.

"Well, sort of. Why do you ask?" Shelby felt her heart beating faster.

"I just got a call from the president of the Heritage Society. It seems that Loreena Swan has registered a complaint against you and the store."

# Chapter Three

"Oh, Aunt Edie, I'm so sorry. I flew off the handle this afternoon. She was badgering me, complaining about the stock and how things were set up, even though I followed the plan you'd given me. She was just being a total jerk, and I tried to keep calm, but . . ."

Edie chuckled. "I'm not calling to add to your misery, Shelby. I just wanted to know what's going on over there. I have complete confidence in you, but I think you need to stay out of her way in the future. She's not one to easily forgive and forget."

Shelby sighed. "I did mention something about how it was our store and no one could tell us how to run it. And she said something about reading the contract. Did I do wrong?"

She could hear Edie shuffling some papers. "Not really. However, there is a clause in our contract about catering to the tourist trade. So, along with books covering the history and geography of the Thousand Islands, I've included anything that's local nonfiction. I've even stocked some books on castles, and as you're undoubtedly aware of by now, I've added some local fiction authors to the mix if they portray the sense of setting strongly in their books. So, what's her problem?"

"Loreena said we didn't have enough, but I think what really got her going—and she added this after the fact—was that we don't have her book on the shelves. I've never even heard of it, nor did I come across it when reordering the stock for the opening."

"Well, that's my fault and I'm sorry you had to be the one to face her wrath. We did carry it when it came out last spring, but it took most of the summer for five copies to sell, so I decided to put it on the special orders list. If someone asks for it, we'll get it in. In hindsight, that was an unwise decision, one I'll admit to having made after having words with her."

Shelby smiled. "Glad to hear it. I could have spent all morning browbeating myself if you hadn't told me."

"It's the Cox temper, although I think that, over the years, mine has evened out a bit. So there is hope for you. Maybe you should order a few copies in just to help smooth things over. Ask her to sign them, too. But don't worry about it anymore. I'll set it straight with the Heritage Society board. Just between you and me, aside from Andrew Truelove, the president, I don't think Loreena has too many admirers there either."

* * *

Before Shelby closed the shop for the day, she did a final walk-through, trying to put herself in the customers' place.

The dark oak flooring continued seamlessly from the main hall. But that's where the similarity ended. Instead of wood paneling, the walls had been painted something called Willow Wood, giving a fresh, outdoorsy feel to the room. The wall behind the sales counter had been the ideal place to hang an oil painting Shelby had brought in.

The books looked tidy, and numerous titles were appealingly placed face-out. Fiction took up the entire left-hand wall; mysteries were shelved on two free-standing shelving units close to the checkout counter; the right wall had a variety of seasonal nonfiction filed by subject; and the sunroom was bewitching, if she did say so herself, with five-foot shelving between each window and four comfy white wicker chairs decked in bright blue and green cushions and matching white wicker end tables. It was all very inviting for readers to stay a while and find the perfect book.

She found it fascinating that this recent addition to the castle had been built in 2001, when the Heritage Society in Alexandria Bay had decided to put Blye Castle firmly on the tourist map. Their intentions had translated into some creative and effective projects, as witnessed by the boatloads of tourists visiting the island every day during the season.

Tomorrow would be the big day. The first tourists of the summer would set foot on the island at ten AM, and Shelby felt certain she'd be ready for them. She'd preordered several boxes of mini-cupcakes to be served along with freshly brewed coffee. Hopefully, there would be enough for most of the day. However, she'd already been alerted to the fact that no food was allowed in the castle, so shoppers would just have to stay in her shop until they'd finished. She saw that as a major plus. She just had to remember to pick up the treats on her way to the boat in the morning.

Terry's Boat Lines had agreed to put on an extra sailing of their smaller boat, which was used to get the various staffers and volunteers to the island, an hour early. She felt a small knot in the pit of her stomach and wasn't quite sure if it was excitement or maybe a touch of dread. She shook her head and took a deep breath. Tomorrow would be a great day. Everything would turn out all right.

Shelby felt an intense pride of ownership, something she'd never experienced before, as she locked the door behind her. She also felt satisfaction in knowing that she'd made the right decision to move back to Alexandria Bay although she had agonized over it. When she thought about it, and that wasn't often, she did miss her job as an editor at Masspike House, and of course, her small handful of friends, but she doggedly kept her mind from expanding on that thought.

It really was for the best. A good decision. The right decision.

She checked the clock on the wall. Shuttle service had been provided that day in the morning, at noon, and at 4 PM. The last shuttle of the day would arrive in half an hour, and that was her ride back home. She just had time for a short walk around the island. She'd started exploring her first day on-site, a couple of weeks before, a few months after she'd arrived in Alexandria Bay.

She'd felt immediately drawn to the place. The castle, while not on as grand a scale as Boldt Castle or the other main attraction of the Thousand Islands, Singer Castle, had its own history and charm. Blye Castle was almost square in shape, aside from the protruding room where the bookstore was located. The gray stone facade was softened by elegant carvings in the masonry, marking the top of each level. Two turrets rose above the upper corners at the front of the building, and each was flanked by two gargoyles, larger cousins of the smaller one Shelby had done battle with earlier.

The double oak doors, ornately carved and sporting gleaming brass hardware, each had a small window up high and peepholes visible only to those who knew about them. Shelby half expected to see uniformed guards in red tunics and bearskin hats standing at attention on either side.

She'd realized right away why her Aunt Edie was so pleased with the location. It was a tourist magnet, mostly because of the castle and its eclectic history but also because of the lush grounds and the thick grove of trees providing the backdrop. She bet the sunsets were spectacular. Tomorrow she'd find out, but for today, she had just enough time for a quick saunter and then the boat ride back to Alexandria Bay.

She set off along the marked path behind the castle, keeping an eye open for Matthew Kessler and hoping she'd have a chance for a chat to get to know him better. Edie had labeled him gruff, but so far he'd been nothing but helpful and friendly, much to Shelby's relief. She could handle only one temperamental person at a time.

She picked her way down a grassy slope, looking for the entrance to the famed Blye Grotto, the cave where the illicit rum trade had taken place during Prohibition. It was currently out of bounds to visitors while new hand railings were being added to the pathway. Shelby saw the entrance up ahead and stopped to enjoy the view of the St. Lawrence River. She tried to imagine living there. So isolated and yet so beautiful. She'd heard that Matthew, the only person to live permanently on the island, liked the solitude, but she thought it must also offer so many moments of pleasure. She wondered how he managed over the winter, though.

She swung around at the sound of twigs snapping behind her in time to see a blur of red plaid disappear into the trees. She almost lost her footing, then shook her head and focused on where she was stepping.

It took her eyes a few minutes to adjust to the darkness in the cave. There was minimal light coming from behind her; the main source was the large but sheltered opening in the wall leading to the river. She could hear a boat motor nearby and wondered if her ride had come early. The boat must have passed fairly close by, because small waves lapped at the sides of the cave.

Shelby looked down at the water. It was dark, but not dark enough to hide the fuchsia cloth floating in it. The same color as the top Loreena Swan had been wearing the last time Shelby had seen her.

It took a few seconds for Shelby to realize that the screams echoing through the cave were hers.

# Chapter Four

Shelby leaned against a tree, shivering, trying not to think about what she'd just seen, waiting for Matthew to come back. He had heard her scream and come running. After taking a look inside, he'd tried to persuade her to go back to the castle. She'd shaken her head, not certain she could actually walk that far, and instead sat on a tall rock with a flat surface, waiting to be told if what she'd seen was real but all the while hoping it wasn't.

Matthew had rushed back to his cottage to call the police. He had also grabbed a blanket along with a bottle of Johnnie Walker and two glasses. He'd wrapped the blanket around Shelby and then poured out two portions of the whiskey, handing one glass to her.

Shelby still held hers after taking a sip that burned all the way down. She thought about the fuchsia blouse and took another, longer sip.

"Do you think it's Loreena?" she whispered.

Matthew walked back to her from the entrance to the

cave. He'd already downed his whiskey in one swallow. "It looks like it might well be."

"She's definitely dead, isn't she? What could have happened? Did she slip and fall in? Maybe she hit her head and got knocked out? Was it an accident?"

"Those are all questions I'm sure the police will be asking."

She wondered at the resentful tone of his voice. Had he had issues with the police in the past, the past about which Aunt Edie had said she'd someday share more information with her?

They could hear a large motor getting closer. Matthew turned to look toward the water. "And that would be them. I'll meet them at the dock and lead the way. You sure you don't want to come back up to the castle now? The shuttle has already arrived, but the police relayed strict instructions that it was not to leave."

"No. I'll wait here. She shouldn't be alone."

That thought sent a tremor through her body, and she pulled the blanket even tighter around her. Shelby had always had a healthy fear of water—why, she wasn't sure—but she could think of nothing worse than drowning, especially in such a desolate place. And even though she hadn't known Loreena well and knew there was no chance they'd ever have been friends, maybe not even on friendly terms, Shelby wouldn't have wished this fate on her.

Matthew patted her shoulder and headed toward the castle.

Shelby wasn't sure how long she sat there waiting for the

police, her mind toying with all the questions she'd asked earlier. She added a new one: *What was Loreena doing out here anyway?* The sound of footsteps making their way along the path alerted her that the police must be approaching. She took a deep breath and stood.

Matthew led the way, and he gave Shelby a tight smile as he walked past her. An older cop followed. The light-blue shirt of his uniform had a couple of twigs stuck to one sleeve, and he carried his hat in his hands. He nodded at Shelby as he walked past her and into the cave. The second officer was a woman about her Aunt Edie's age, wearing a dark-blue uniform with the Alexandria Bay Police crest on both sleeves. She hesitated and looked like she might say something to Shelby, but instead she continued walking toward the grotto. Shelby noticed another guy dressed casually in jeans, a black T-shirt, and a black windbreaker break away from the first two and make his way down toward the edge and the ten-foot drop to the water. Matthew stood like a sentinel, staring straight ahead.

Shelby wondered at the transformation in him. No acknowledgment of the police. No effort to assist in any way. In fact, he looked like he'd temporarily tuned out. Had the shock finally set in?

After what seemed like an unbearably long time, the first cop reappeared and walked over to her. He stuck out his hand. "Lieutenant Dwayne Guthrie, State Police. And you are?" he asked.

"Uh, Shelby Cox. I'm from the bookstore."

Guthrie nodded. "Kessler tells me you found the body. Tell me about it."

Before she had a chance to answer, the woman joined them. "I'm Tekla Stone, chief of police in Alexandria Bay." Her gaze was intense, but Shelby felt relaxed in her presence.

"Ms. Cox, you were going to tell me about finding the body?" Guthrie sounded irritated.

She desperately wanted another sip of the whiskey, but she straightened her shoulders and tried to sound confident. "I'd decided to take a walk before leaving today, and I ended up at the grotto, so I went in. And that's when I saw her. That fuchsia top . . . I remembered Loreena Swan had worn that color today. It is her, isn't it?"

Guthrie nodded. "Did you touch anything in there?"

"Like what? The wall, I guess, but mainly to guide me out."

"So, there was nothing lying on the ground?" His eyes seemed to bore into her.

"Not that I saw, but I didn't really look around. All I saw was the . . . the body."

He stared at her a few moments and then switched his gaze to the pathway. "Did you see anyone on your way over here?"

She started to shake her head, and then remembered. Chief Stone picked up on the hesitation.

"What are you thinking?" she asked.

"I'm not sure, but I sort of thought I saw a flash of a red shirt or something bright in the forest."

"Hm." Stone looked over at Matthew, still in his red plaid shirt. "But you're not sure?"

"No, I'm not. But I did hear a small motorboat while I was inside. It must have been close, because it caused a small wake in the grotto. That's when I looked down and saw . . . I saw . . ." She was seeing it again in her mind.

Stone looked at Guthrie and nodded. She placed her hand on Shelby's arm. "That'll be all for now, Ms. Cox. I'd like you to stop by the station later today or tomorrow. I'll need a formal statement from you."

"All right." Shelby stood there watching as the woman walked back to the cave. Somehow her brain didn't feel connected, and she wasn't sure what to do next.

Stone glanced at her, then finally said, "You can go now. I don't think you should stay any longer."

Matthew started toward Shelby, as if to follow her.

"You, Kessler, stay right here. I have some questions for you."

# Chapter Five

Shelby poured a cup of tea for Edie and was about to get the plate of chocolate chip cookies from the kitchen when Edie pushed herself up out of the straight-backed chair and, with the aid of her walker, worked her way over to the china cabinet, opened the top doors, and pulled out two glasses and a bottle of Southern Comfort.

"I think this will suit us better," she said. "We'll have the tea as a chaser."

Her long, multicolored tie-dyed skirt barely rustled, she moved so slowly. She'd said her right thigh felt stiff and that's what gave her the most grief at the moment, but after physiotherapy, which would start in two weeks, she was hoping she would be back to normal fairly quickly. And that would mean it wouldn't be long before she was back where she belonged, behind the cash register in the main bookstore on James Street in the village.

Shelby acknowledged a tiny twitch in her stomach at that realization. It was Edie's store, or stores, even if they were partners on paper. Edie was the history, but maybe

Shelby could be the future. That cheered her a bit. She admitted to herself that she was surprised by such a strong reaction. When she'd first returned to Alexandria Bay, she'd believed it would be for a short time, just until Edie was feeling one hundred percent and back to work full time in the bookstore. Now . . .

Edie deftly poured each of them a finger's worth and urged Shelby to down it. As the burning sensation trickled down, Shelby felt the tension easing. What a day. She noticed that Edie did the same with her own drink, even though she hadn't been there in person. Of course, she had known Loreena, and no matter how well they had gotten along, or hadn't, it would still have been shocking news.

"Do you know anything about her family, Aunt Edie?" Shelby asked. Even though she also hadn't felt all warm and fuzzy about the woman, she felt bad for whoever was left behind. She knew it wasn't easy to cope with the death of a loved one.

"Loreena's? She has a nephew, Carter, and it's an old family in Alexandria Bay, and that means almost everyone knows her or someone in her family. She always prided herself on her heritage."

Edie poured herself a drink and sipped it and then tucked some strands of long salt-and-pepper hair back behind her ears rather than taking the time to undo the barrette that held the rest of it back.

Shelby stared out the window, eyes focused on the backyard garden, Edie's pride and joy. Previously, the house had belonged to Edie's parents. It was the house Shelby's dad had grown up in, and that was part of the reason she'd come back to Alexandria Bay, to find out more about her family and especially her mother.

"You know, I'm feeling really terrible about the things I said and thought about Loreena earlier today. I mean, what if she was just having an off day and I've now fixed her in my mind as the wicked witch of the North?"

"Believe me, honey, from what you said, it wasn't an off day for the woman. It was a normal one. I told you there was no love lost on the Heritage Society board for her, except for the chair, who, as it turns out, is a cousin of hers. To Loreena's credit, she was passionate about her work. It's her people skills that were lacking. Now, I know it's not been a good start at the castle, and I also know this may sound a little crass at this point, but are you up to going through with the opening tomorrow?"

"I was wondering if they might postpone it?"

"No, I checked, and it's on as planned. Oh, the Society will do or say something fitting about Loreena before the doors open, I'd imagine, but they don't want to put off the tourist trade. I just know how upsetting this has been for you, and if you'd rather not go back this soon, I can make other arrangements."

Shelby sat up a bit straighter. "No, I'll be fine. After all, it's not as if her body was found in the bookstore, or even inside the castle. Oops, did that sound harsh?"

Edie reached over and touched her hand lightly. The three brass bracelets dangling from her left wrist made a light tinkling sound. "No, I know exactly what you mean.

I'm really sorry I brought you into all of this. I was hoping to hook you into staying on with the store. A body certainly doesn't help. Now, how about we tackle some of that aromatic food you brought."

Shelby walked to the counter, pulled two containers out of the oven, and dished out the lasagna she'd picked up at Tuckers Italian and Seafood Restaurant on her way over. It had taken only fifteen minutes to reheat.

"Oh my, that smells heavenly. Very thoughtful of you, Shelby."

"My pleasure."

They ate in silence that was occasionally disturbed by mumblings of food pleasure. Finally, after Edie had finished off the last bit of lasagna on her plate, Shelby asked, "Will you fill me in on more about Matthew Kessler's background?"

"Why? Because you think he's a suspect?"

Shelby wondered at the sharpness of Edie's voice. Had she hit some sort of sore spot?

Edie must have noticed Shelby's reaction, because she sighed and started talking. "Well, it seems most people have been wary of Matthew ever since day one. How about putting on some fresh tea and I'll tell you about him, although it's really not my story to be telling. So, don't let on to him that you know, okay?"

Shelby nodded, now thoroughly intrigued. She was relieved to have a different focus to try to calm the chaos in her mind. She busied herself with plugging in the kettle and rinsing out the teapot, then poured the near-boiling water over the tea leaves, waited four minutes, and poured the tea into their cups. She pulled out a tray and then carried them to the table along with a small plate of chocolate chip cookies that always sat on the counter and was replenished daily.

Edie blew on her drink and took a small sip. "Mm, I'm glad to see you know how to brew proper tea."

"Well, tea according to Dad, anyway. So, what's the scoop on Matthew?"

Edie batted away a long unruly strand of red curly hair. It had taken Shelby several days to get used to her aunt's appearance. The obviously dyed red patch of hair that framed the left side of her face seemed a beacon next to the remaining gray locks. However, it did match the brightly colored long skirts and tie-dyed tops she favored. Shelby had easily guessed that Edie was somewhat stuck in her hippie days. She hadn't dared ask just how far that extended, though she hadn't yet detected any telltale odors of pot around the house.

Edie hesitated a moment, and Shelby wondered if she'd changed her mind; then she pushed herself out of the chair and started pacing, as well as she could with a long skirt and a walker.

"Sorry, I have to get moving every now and then. Anyway, Matthew came to Alexandria Bay around seven years ago and right away got the job as caretaker on Blye Island. Old Hank Harvey had just retired and we were about to start the summer season, so Matthew was a godsend. He moved into the cottage on the island and was off and running. However, Matthew kept pretty much to himself, nodding to folks on the street but rarely saying anything. That didn't really go over too well. It turns out—and I heard this from one of the publishing sales reps—that he was a very well-known true crime writer, not exactly my forte, but I did carry a couple of his books over the years. I just didn't connect the name. It seems he gave up the writing when his wife was murdered."

"Murdered?"

Edie eased herself back into the chair. "Uh-huh. And he was the prime suspect, but they never got enough evidence to charge him. That's about when he moved here. I guess he liked what he found, and so he's still here."

"That's so sad. Was the murderer ever caught?"

"Not according to anything I've heard, even though Matthew spent a lot of time and money doing his own investigating. Unfortunately, our police chief always did think the worst of everyone. And even more unfortunately, her opinions carry some weight here in the village. She's convinced he's still a person of interest, or so I've heard said, so he hasn't had a very warm reception."

"How did you hear about him investigating and all?'

"I hear things. That's something you'll learn about the bookselling business. People love to talk. Sometimes I even feel like a bartender when the customers start sharing their problems."

Shelby sat back, knocking her elbow on the edge of the table and spilling some tea on her pant leg. "Drat." She righted the cup and blotted up the spill with a napkin. "I can't imagine first losing the person you love in a violent crime and then being accused of it. No wonder he's nearly a recluse. Today was really the first time we've carried on a conversation since I've been going over to the castle. He sure doesn't strike me as being the violent type."

"Love can make one do strange things," Edie said, adding quickly, "Not that I'm accusing him or even believe he did it. But I'm sure it adds up in Police Chief Tekla Stone's book, and this just proves what she's said all along, that he's a killer. So I'll bet he's the prime suspect in Loreena's death. And it doesn't help that they didn't get along at all."

"He didn't threaten her at any time, did he?"

"Not that I know of, but he looked even gloomier than usual whenever she was around and would only grunt out answers." She brightened. "So, you see how far you've come in such a short while? I understand he's communicating in full sentences with you."

"Huh. How long has Loreena been in charge of the castle?"

"Not 'of' but rather 'at.' Her job with the society is director of outreach, which is a fancy way of saying, 'Keep an eye on the volunteers and make sure the brochures are all on display.' She's also curator of the exhibits, but that's just another title, because our executive director does the real work. Chrissie Halstead is the PR person, and she's done all the creative stuff. The board is comprised of some of our most prominent citizens, including *moi*, and did include the previous owner of Blye Castle, who sold it to the society for one dollar. His grandson is still active in board business. The executive director is paid an honorarium, but all other positions are volunteer."

Shelby nodded and chose another chocolate chip cookie, closing her eyes as she chewed it. She could never get enough chocolate. "With all the politics involved and hoops to jump through, what made you want to expand with a second location in the castle?"

"Romance."

Shelby opened her eyes. "All right. You've got my attention."

Edie smiled. "The romance of the castle. Who wouldn't want a chance to spend time there, and so much the better if I made some money while doing so. You know its history by now."

"About Thomas and Millicent Blye emigrating from England, buying the island, and building the castle? I haven't read that book about the history of the castle yet, but when I took the boat tour of the islands recently on the day they did special trips for the locals, I heard a lot about them."

"That's the start of the story. They weren't spring chickens when they moved, unfortunately, so they only had about fifteen years there before it was too much upkeep for them. Luckily, they found a buyer."

"The gangster?"

"Exactly. Joseph Cabana. He found the island to be the perfect spot for his rum-running operation during Prohibition."

"But he died there, didn't he?"

Edie nodded. "His body was found in the grotto also. They thought at the time it was gang related and that's why his ghost hangs around."

"You don't believe in ghosts, do you, Edie?"

She shrugged. "I haven't had the opportunity to test it out. He's seldom seen haunting it, but then again, it's been closed half the year. Who knows what he does when he's there by himself. I wonder if he was a reader. Maybe he'll pop by the bookstore." She gave Shelby a wink.

# Chapter Six

The next morning, Shelby turned a bleary eye to her clock radio. Yes, it was time to get up. No, she didn't want to. She was usually an early riser, but today was different. She hadn't slept much due to a very active imagination that danced between bodies in the water and ghosts. Her worst fear was that Loreena Swan would come back to haunt her. She shook her head. That was way too flippant a thought at such an unnerving time. Besides, she had to be at the shuttle by nine if she wanted to have the bookstore open and inviting for the grand opening at ten.

She heard a scratching at the door as she walked into the kitchen after enjoying a long but reviving shower. That cat again. She hesitated. Did she really want to start something? Well, okay, she guessed she already had, since she'd fed the thing twice already that week. However, in her book, that did not translate to an open invitation to move in. But she had bought a few tins of a no-name tuna cat food, and she also had some pouches of dry food on hand. She sighed as she opened the door to the imposing amber-colored feline.

He sure didn't look underfed. She'd had no idea he came with the territory, although perhaps he didn't. She peeked out the door to make sure he hadn't invited any friends.

Her rental was a two-story thirty-six-foot houseboat moored at the docks reserved for pleasure craft. She loved the feel of the water gently lapping away and the sounds of fish jumping and seagulls crying. The owner, whom she had met just once, was a local guy who worked for the forest service. He had bought the boat two years earlier, hoping to make it his home until he'd learned, too late, that all boats went into dry dock over the winter months. So he'd opted instead to rent it out for the summers and recoup his investment.

Shelby had fallen in love with the place the minute she'd stepped on board, even though it meant that she'd have to find new digs at the end of summer. She knew her aunt had originally hoped she'd moved in with her, into the large family house that had belonged to Edie's parents. That was always a possibility, but Shelby was so used to living on her own. It had taken a lot of finesse to smooth Edie's ruffled feathers after Shelby had first arrived and declined the offer of a room. Thanks to Trudy Bryant, who had declared she would move in for as long as Edie needed care, Shelby was able to rent the houseboat, which seemed to be working out for everyone. And, since Trudy was in charge of the main bookstore while Edie was laid up, it meant that although Edie was housebound, she wasn't out of the loop.

The cat sat thumping its tail. She got it. Time to get the food going. After dishing out both types along with a bowl of water, Shelby set about making her own coffee. She glanced back at the cat, and a smile formed on her face. She really didn't want a cat, but what would it hurt to name it, even if it just stopped by occasionally? Its coloring was that of a tabby, but its size hinted at an unlikely coupling, maybe with a Maine coon or something. Now, what would be a proper name? A nonhuman name for sure. *Boots. Whiskers*? Too common. Oh, well, it would come to her.

Her Keurig delivered a cup of dark roast coffee quickly, and she leaned back against the counter as she sipped. She didn't even know what sex the thing was, and she wasn't in any hurry to check. The first time they'd met, she'd tried to pat him and retrieved her hand just in time to miss being scratched. Ingrate. *Claws* might be an appropriate name, but that didn't feel right.

"What do you want to be called?" Shelby asked, not expecting a reply. "Better still, what is your name and where do you come from? Do you have a home already and are just a greedy gut hanging around begging for food? Because you sure don't look like you're starving."

The cat stopped eating and eyed her indignantly, its green eyes framed by a bushy mane of golden fur. *You look like a lion.* That thought made Shelby feel slightly unsettled. She shook off the feeling and poured some granola into a dish, covering it with fresh blueberries and sliced strawberries. Fresh but not local. Not yet, but soon.

She had to get going. She ushered the cat outside and stood for a couple of minutes enjoying the scenery. Living on a houseboat had been a whim, but she'd discovered she really enjoyed looking out on the water and the islands beyond. She wondered if she'd get some more neighbors during the summer. She acknowledged the houseboat tied up between her own and the shore, still unoccupied. As part of her plan to become more outgoing, she'd decided to start saying good morning each day and would keep it up when there were actually people living on it.

One of the great things about Alexandria Bay was that everything was close to everything else in the town. Shelby could walk over to the boat shuttle in minutes, and she could also get to almost any place in the center of town in the same amount of time. The bookstore was even closer than that. She'd checked the weather already, and it promised to be a clear although not overly warm day. That's what jackets were made for. She went back inside and grabbed a lined red windbreaker from the coat rack next to the door, locking up behind her.

Shelby reached the boat dock at the same time as the store's part-time employee, Taylor Fortune. She'd been working at the main store for a couple of years but had asked to switch to the castle bookstore for the summers. Shelby had at first been uptight about meeting new colleagues and going through the whole bonding routine. But she had been relieved when she realized after the first couple of weeks working side by side in the main store that she and Taylor worked well together. Shelby even had great hopes they might become good friends.

"Good morning, Taylor. Ready for the rush?" Shelby said it jokingly, but deep down she was hopeful. "What are the flowers for?" she asked with a nod toward the two wrapped packages in Taylor's arms, obviously bouquets.

Taylor laughed. "I am excited and then some. Opening day is always busy, with a lot of the village people coming over for the celebrations. And the flowers are for the store, to bring the celebration inside."

"That's a great idea. I should have thought of it."

"Edie usually does, but I wasn't sure if that info had been passed along. I thought even if you had some, the more the merrier."

Shelby nodded. "Thanks. She surprisingly didn't mention it, although she did try to fill me in on every last possibility for today, or so it seemed. A really busy day is what I most remember her stressing."

"That's not surprising. The shuttle is free, thanks to the Heritage Society, in addition to the regular boat tours. And, you never know, with a fresh murder on the island, people might come in droves."

Shelby caught her breath. "You know that it really was a murder? Your husband is a police officer, isn't he? Is that what he told you? Have they done an autopsy already?"

Taylor had a look on her thirty-six-year-old face like a child caught with her hand in the cookie jar. "Oops, wasn't supposed to say that. Please don't tell Chuck that I mentioned murder. He'll stop telling me what's happening, and I do so enjoy getting the lowdown on everything."

Shelby chuckled. "No problem. He won't hear it from me. But do you think you could find out about that autopsy?

I'm dying to know what killed her. Oops, wrong choice of words, but you get the picture."

Taylor gave an exaggerated sigh, like she felt put upon, but her expression quickly changed to a conspiratorial one. "I'll try and find out. I'm really curious, too. I can't believe there's been a murder. It's just like in one of our mystery books, although I prefer the murder being on the pages, not in our backyard."

The sun caught and reflected off her short blonde hair. The pixie cut suited her. In fact, Shelby thought she'd make an ideal pixie in a stage production of *Peter Pan*. She thought back briefly to the version her dad had taken her to at Jordan Hall in Boston. That had been a very long time ago.

"Do you ever get in trouble at home saying things like that?" Shelby wanted to know. She was trying to imagine the dinner table talk in their home.

"We haven't had a murder before, not since I moved here, anyway."

"And when was that?" Shelby waited for Taylor to lead the way onto the boat.

"I guess I've been here about six years. I moved here one year before I met Chuck, and we got married one year after we met." She grinned.

"Wow. Sounds like a good move on your part."

"Was it ever. I also like to remind him that marrying me was a good move on his part," she said with a laugh, which tapered off as she looked past Shelby at the dock.

Shelby turned and followed her gaze. The State Police officer, Lieutenant Guthrie, was stepping onto the boat. He looked over at them and touched the brim of his cap, then followed one of the crew members into the wheelhouse.

"I wonder what the lieutenant is doing here this morning." Shelby said. "I wonder who's in charge, him or Chief Stone? I read a lot of mysteries, and there's always tension between the different forces when it comes to investigating a case." She looked expectantly at Taylor, hoping for some more intel.

Taylor whispered, "He's going to do some more snooping around on the island. Chuck said he'd also probably be questioning everyone again."

Shelby grimaced. What more could she tell him? She hoped he didn't have more questions about when and where she'd seen Matthew, or rather, the patch of red. She shook her head. She'd have to stop assuming it had been him. But who else could it have been?

They were pulling up to the dock at Blye Island when Lieutenant Guthrie reappeared. He made no attempt to talk to either of them as they left the boat, but she was aware that he was in the group of volunteers and staff as they followed the stone stairwell to the castle.

She looked around for Matthew as they entered through the front door and was a little disappointed not to see him. She did take a moment to enjoy the grandeur of the entrance hall. The bottom halves of the walls were red oak and gleamed in the sunlight shining through the stained-glass windows. The matching cornices and trim added that regal touch. Castle indeed. Shelby wondered what it would have been like to live there, but her imagination didn't stretch that far. No matter how hard she tried, she could not picture herself doing an elegant stroll down the curved formal stairway, the gracious mistress of the mansion. Standing at the bottom, holding the cloak for the mistress of the manor, waiting to drape it over her elegant shoulders would have been more like it.

Shelby shook her head to focus. No time for daydreams. Not today when there was so much happening. She'd have to be alert and, even more important, cheerful and welcoming, if she wanted the bookstore to make a good impression on the hundreds of visitors expected for the grand opening day. She just hoped she was up to the task. Her people skills were sometimes lacking.

By the time she had unlocked the door to the store and Taylor had started the coffee brewing, she'd forgotten about everything except the bookstore. She wandered around the shelves trying to picture what the shoppers would see. Everything looked in its place and maybe even enticing.

She had just started sorting out the cash drawer when Lieutenant Guthrie walked in. Shelby glanced at the antique-looking clock on the back wall above the windows. Twenty minutes until opening. She hoped he'd be brief.

"I hope you have time for a few questions," he began. "I won't take up much of your time, but I need to talk to you while yesterday's events are fresh in your mind." He glanced around the store as he took off his police hat and laid it on the counter. His hair was much shorter than she'd thought, almost an old-fashioned buzz cut. Maybe he had some military background. "I thought you'd prefer doing it here rather than taking time out this morning to come in to the station. Even though I know you have capable staff." He ended with a smile, and Shelby couldn't help but relax and smile back.

"That's fine, but you do know we open at ten." She quieted her hands, hoping not to sound or look too perturbed.

He nodded and pulled out his notebook. He looked much like he had the day before, hat in his hand and dark-brown hair with obvious graying at the temples. There was no smile, either. The notebook looked like the pages were slowly detaching from the spiral binding. "I just wanted to clarify the times yesterday. You say you went for a short walk around the island before the shuttle was due to arrive at four PM?"

"That's right. It usually gives a long toot as it's getting close to docking, so I thought I'd have time to hurry back when I heard that. Of course, you know all about the horn, don't you?"

He didn't answer but came back with his own question. "Tell me again about the walk. Where did you go? What did you see?"

Shelby thought back, wanting to make sure she included all the same details she had yesterday, and more if they came to her. "I walked out the front entrance and took the stone walkway to the left, hooking around the castle and leading down the hill on the side. When it intersected with the path from the dock, I turned left and followed it into the woods. I'd been on it a couple of minutes when I heard a branch snap, and out of the corner of my eye saw a flash of red off to the left. Nothing else happened, so I continued walking to the grotto, and that's when I heard a boat engine, so I glanced out to the river but didn't see a boat. Inside the grotto, there were waves splashing along the sides as the wake from the boat came in. I looked down and saw Loreena. I backed out screaming and Matthew came running over shortly after."

"How did you know it was Loreena Swan? She was floating facedown."

"Because I recognized what she was wearing. It was the same blouse she'd had on earlier in the day."

"When you had your run-in with her?"

Shelby swallowed hard and nodded. How did he know about that? She was certain it hadn't been mentioned yesterday.

Guthrie was eyeing her closely as she nodded. "Okay. Can you be more specific as to how long it took Matthew Kessler to reach you?"

She thought carefully, reliving it in her mind. "No more than a minute, I'd say."

Shelby definitely felt uncomfortable under his gaze, but she couldn't think of a thing to add. Or say. Finally, he flipped his notebook shut and stuffed it into his shirt pocket.

"Thank you, Ms. Cox. I'll be working out of Chief Stone's office for today, and I do need you to come by after you finish up here today to make a formal statement."

Shelby nodded. "Not a problem."

He nodded as he stuck his hat back on and left.

Taylor joined Shelby at the counter.

"I hope you didn't mind my sticking around. I do tend to get a bit nosy."

"I've been accused of that myself. By my dad." She took a deep breath. "Did I look as scared as I felt?"

Taylor looked startled. "Not in the slightest. Why were you scared?" She opened the box of cupcakes that had been set on a small table temporarily placed next to the cash register to hold the food offerings for customers.

"I don't know. I guess it was like being sent to the principal's office as a kid."

"I can't imagine that happened to you too often," she said with a warm smile.

Shelby shook her head, returning the smile. "Not often, but my dad made sure I learned my lesson from it." *Tell her more,* a little voice at the back of her head said. *She could turn into a friend.* "My dad had high expectations of me in the behavior department."

"What about your mom?"

"It was just Dad and me. My mom died when I was three."

"Oh, gosh, I'm sorry. That must have been hard, growing up without a mom."

Shelby hesitated. She didn't usually talk about herself so much, but she had made the decision to be more open to making new friends. "At times, but my dad did his best to play both roles. It must have been tough on him," she continued with a wistful smile. "He died three years ago."

"So now there's your Aunt Edie and you. Any other siblings?"

"Yes and no, in that order. I haven't seen much of Aunt Edie over the years because, although I was born here, we moved to Boston when I was young, but I'm hoping to make up for missed time. And I'm an only child."

"Edie's pretty special. I really appreciate that she offered me a job even though I had no retail experience. And even better, that she allowed me to choose my schedule." She paused, looking thoughtful. "I do love reading, though."

"I'd say that's a top priority in this job. To tell the truth, I don't have a retail background either."

"You don't? I guess I assumed that since you're part owner, you had been in the business. What did you do before moving here?"

"I was an editor at a very small regional press, Masspike, in Lenox, Massachusetts."

"Wow, I'll bet that was fun. So, you've got the literary background, anyway."

"Same as you."

Taylor smiled just as the horn on the tourist boat sounded. "Guess we're open for business. The first hour will probably be the busiest once the tourists check their gift bags and find a certificate from the bookstore. It's really clever of the Heritage committee to hand out a gift bag to everyone on the first boatload on opening day."

"I'm tempted to ask for one myself, just to make use of some of the bargains that the village stores have contributed," Shelby said, then quickly added, "But don't worry, I wouldn't do that."

Taylor laughed. "I've thought about it too, in the past. It's about that time. I'll check on the coffee and open the door.

Shelby took a deep breath. "Bring it on!"

# Chapter Seven

The first hour had been staggeringly busy, as Taylor had predicted, and Shelby felt she needed a breather once the crowds had dwindled. She checked with Taylor, who assured her everything would run smoothly for however long Shelby stepped out. It was just the encouragement she needed. She left through the front door of the castle and slowly walked down the wide stone stairs, focused on what lay in front of her.

The lawn had been decked out in streamers with helium balloons strung from the trees. Several white tents, their sides rolled up, had been staged at various intervals near the gazebo, the Sugar Shack, and the upper patio. These all had small square tables for four and chairs, begging merrymakers to stop a while and enjoy the scenery and the food. A couple of the tents showcased fresh baked goods and small takeaway meals prepared by businesses in Alexandria Bay. And those who chose to take a break, along with a drink and some food, would be treated to the breathtaking view of rolling green lawn and the somewhat choppy river surrounding Blye Island.

For those with good binoculars, there were glimpses of the surrounding islands, some with mansions visible, and of course, the mainland with its array of hotels and green space. Shelby realized it all took her breath away. But not as much as the castle itself did.

She could hear the string quartet, which was located on the patio. They were playing Vivaldi's "Spring," appropriate for sure. At least she thought that was what they were playing. Titles, except those on books, had never been her strong point. Later she planned to take a walk to the Sugar Shack, the outdoor coffee and snack shop down by the wharf. When she'd first spotted it on the island, Shelby had wondered who'd come up with the name. Maybe Edie, she'd thought, chuckling to herself. Of course, the CDs being played were all from the sixties, with the shop's namesake, "Sugar Shack" as sung by the Fireballs, popping up at least a couple of times an hour. The first time Shelby had heard the song, she'd been delighted and had looked it up on the Internet. Definitely a sixties free spirit at work there, which added to the fun feel of the place.

There was a nineties rock band scheduled for later, after the string quartet finished. And, although she couldn't hear them, she could see the four singers, a four-part group thrown together from the local theatre group, as they wandered throughout the grounds. She knew this was a daylong event and wondered, hoped really, that they would be spelled off at some point. From her own short stint in a community choir in Lenox, she knew how taxing a couple of hours of singing could be.

She made her way around to the back, where an outdoor games area had been set up, courtesy of the Alexandria Bay recreation department. The tents that adorned the area had a medieval flare, with spired tops and flags waving in the breeze. Kids of all ages would find something to try, and the prizes had all been donated by the villagers.

Shelby felt the little kid in her bubbling up, wanting to get in line and give the ring toss a try. She'd always been good at that. Or maybe she should sign up for the crokinole tournament starting at noon. She knew one of the prizes for an adult player was a massage at the spa in town. Now *that* would be a treat. On the other hand, as a sort-of staff person, it might not be kosher for her to win prizes meant for the guests.

Although she had been given an agenda for the day's activities, Shelby found she was quite unprepared for the sight of the occasional couple or group of women wandering around in their nineteenth-century dresses and suits. There were even children dressed in bloomers and breeches, spinning yoyos, running with hoops, and down on their knees shooting marbles. She'd known, but she hadn't given it much thought beyond deciding that, in the bookstore, they'd be wearing everyday contemporary clothing for the big day. It wasn't that she was against costumes or dressing up; it's just that she wasn't comfortable doing it. There had been no Halloween costume parties for her as a child. She'd also had to find her own outfit each year for trick-or-treating. Usually they were quite bland and easy-to-put-together affairs.

She sat on one of the many stone benches placed strategically around the island and watched two couples, one pushing a stroller, stop for a chat. The hoops under the women's dresses guaranteed there was some distance between them. When she glanced to the side, she noticed the official party, the mayor of Alexandria Bay along with some notables from the Heritage Society, making their way from the shuttle toward the castle. The guards in their blue tunics, white breeches, and long rifles were a dead giveaway. Tourists made way for them and joined in behind, following this new-style Pied Piper to the side patio that had been set up with a podium and sound system, awaiting the speeches.

Shelby was keen to hear what they had to say but decided to skip the ceremony and get back to the bookstore, where there was always something that needed doing. She took a deep breath as she gave a final look around and realized, *This is what happy feels like.*

The only downer was the sight of Lieutenant Guthrie threading his way across the lawn. A stark reminder that today's festivities contrasted greatly with the horror of the day before.

# Chapter Eight

Midafternoon, Shelby stretched and did a couple of neck rolls, finally deciding that what she needed was another infusion of fresh air and exercise. She'd chosen to work right through lunch, but she needed a short break before Taylor left early on the two-thirty shuttle—something about a family picnic if her husband could be torn away from work. Fortunately, Cody Tucker, the high school student who worked part-time at the main store, would be coming in to help out even though both locations would be feeling the retail rush that day. Most stores in Alexandria Bay were also celebrating the official start of the tourist season, and the main bookstore would feature refreshments and specials.

Shelby chose to walk through the castle, enjoying the excitement buzzing from the crowds and out the side door leading from the music room, with its massive grand piano that was roped off to protect it from inquiring hands, to the wraparound terrace.

She could see Matthew in the distance, down on his

knees, digging in one of the hundreds of colorful flower beds on the island. She was not a plant person, but she knew that whoever had arranged the mixture of short green shrubs and taller bursts of color knew what needed to be done. She wondered if it was Matthew or a professional landscaper. She must remember to ask, at some point. She nodded and smiled at some tourists and made her way down the stairs and in Matthew's direction. This would be a good opportunity to ask some questions that had been niggling at the back of her mind since her talk with the lieutenant.

"Hi, Matthew. You're one of the lucky ones, being able to work outside on a beautiful day, but in the shade." She was watching a couple of young men applying a coat of sealant to one of the small gazebos overlooking the water. She'd thought all that type of work was supposed to have been finished before the tourists arrived. She mentally shrugged. It wasn't her problem.

Matthew followed her gaze as he pushed himself off the ground, wobbling a bit on one knee before successfully standing up. She wondered about his age. He looked like he might be in his mid-sixties, like Edie. He pushed up his New York Rangers ball cap a bit and squinted.

"It's what I do best. Now, what can I do for you?" he asked, the original look of annoyance on his face giving way to a friendly smile. "Do you need any heavy lifting done today?"

She wondered if that might be a safe way to put him at ease. There were always boxes to be moved, and then she could ask him some intrusive questions, but she decided on the straightforward approach. It was odd how comfortable she felt with him. Then again, having grown up with only a man in the house most of the time, she often found it easier to talk to men.

"I know this is none of my business, really, but since I was there yesterday and found the body, I think I deserve some answers." She hurried on before he could react. "Was it you I saw hurrying through the woods as I walked toward the grotto?"

She hoped he would answer, but his face gave away nothing, and he took his sweet time before saying anything. Finally, his shoulders seemed to relax, and he took a deep breath. "It was me. I heard the boat motor and I was rushing back to my place to get my binoculars. I'd been hearing, on occasion, smaller motors coming close to the island, and I wanted to start tracking which boats were getting too close and watching what they were up to."

"What do you think they're up to?"

"Possibly looking for an easy landing spot where they can tie up and get onto the island. We don't allow that, you know. Terry's Boats and the proper Thousand Island Boat Tour companies are the only ones who have permission to dock here."

She thought about what he'd said. It made sense, but then again, if this was a concern, why didn't he have his binoculars with him at all times? As if he read her mind, he answered, "You're probably wondering why I didn't have them with me. I did when I started out that morning, but they must have dropped out of my pouch somewhere along the way. I have spare ones at my cabin."

She eyed the dull-green canvas pouch slung from one shoulder across his chest and resting on his hip. It looked like the fisherman's pouch her dad had used in his days of fly-fishing.

"Look." Matthew sounded exasperated this time. "I know what they say about me, especially Chief Stone, but I'm no killer. Wasn't before, and I'm not now. As much as I disliked Loreena Swan, she was more of an annoyance, like a fly that you swat away rather than a mosquito that you squash."

Shelby shuddered at the very real picture that presented. She had to refocus on what Matthew was saying.

"Although I wouldn't be surprised if she did some blood-sucking from time to time. Mean disposition along with a feeling of entitlement."

"Entitlement to what? Just because she was a director in a volunteer organization?"

"I see your aunt has been filling you in." He grinned. "Now, there's one fine woman."

"Yes, she's been filling me in on the background of the castle and the bookstore, but she doesn't know anything about what's currently going on. Do you? Why would someone kill Loreena? Or did she just slip and fall? And if so, why are the police back again today asking so many questions?"

Matthew snorted. "You're the one with a lot of questions, I'd say. I heard the cops talking yesterday, and apparently they're going with the theory that she was murdered. That gash on the back of her head? I assume you saw it." He watched as Shelby struggled not to visualize it. "Well, if she'd slipped and fallen, it wouldn't have been quite so high up, meaning the killer was taller than her. Also, there was a depression in the wound that couldn't have been made by the rock siding inside the grotto. In my opinion, that is."

"You sound so professional," Shelby said. "You sure you were never a cop?"

His face darkened, and she saw the pain in his eyes. She wished she could retract the statement and give herself a good kick at the same time. He turned away from her as he said, "I've had some practice with police speak. I'd better get back to work. I guess you've taken the river cruise. You know the Ivy Lea Bridge? This garden is much like that. The minute you finish tending it, it's time to start all over again."

Shelby had heard the story about it taking forty years to manually paint the Ivy Lea Bridge. You couldn't use a spray gun on those spans without covering everything in sight. She'd been one of the first to take the Uncle Sam's boat tour that season and had soaked up the local history and that of the River, as they called it in Alex Bay, as the locals referred to the village. She knew a lot of the jargon, which helped make her feel at home, or at least on the road to reclaiming her birthplace.

Shelby started her climb along the stone pathway to Blye Castle.

She heard the boat horn from one of the tour boats and knew that a fresh crop of eager sightseers would be shortly pushing through the doors. That was her cue to stop daydreaming and get back to work. She hoped Cody would be on that boat, too.

She took a final moment to enjoy looking at the store through the open doorway. It truly did look inviting, like someplace a tourist would be drawn into in search of more reading material about the castle. That's what she hoped, anyway.

* * *

By late afternoon, Shelby was totally exhausted. She hadn't realized how much energy it would take to talk to customers and dash around the store, pulling out books to recommend. Of course, it was the schmoozing that felt the most overwhelming. In her old job, she'd been left mostly to herself and spent most of the time at her computer or reading, her desk tucked behind a pale-green baffle in a medium-sized room where noise was muffled by a thick carpet and low ceilings. She'd never stopped to wonder whether she was an introvert or extrovert. She liked people, but she fiercely guarded her privacy. She'd learned that from her dad. But at the bookstore, she had to be pleasant and inviting, hoping the customers would relax and spend money. Of course, that wasn't her only concern. She was a book person, first and foremost, and she knew she was in the right job now, matching readers with authors they would love.

Cody, on the other hand, was in his element. He had an easy, friendly style that kept shoppers talking and buying, perhaps a bit more than they'd intended. With his dark hair, worn a bit on the long side, tucked behind his ears and held there by his thick-framed glasses, he looked more like he was in grade school than finishing his year of high school this year. It was the bow tie—a trademark, she guessed, because every time Cody had come to work he'd been sporting one—that gave him the appearance of having an older soul. Today's was a cheery statement of red polka dots on a navy background. She'd once seen him in a knit vest that was the same combination. Maybe that too was a signature look of some sort. And he was tall, which gave Shelby an eye-level look at those bow ties whenever he stood in front of her.

Shelby wondered briefly what they'd do when he finally went away to college. By then, she hoped, they'd have more part-timers on staff, but Cody really knew his books and, she'd noticed, had a real way with people.

"I'm glad you didn't mind switching over to the castle today, Cody," she said as they were straightening things up at the end of the day.

"Happy to, ma'am, I mean Shelby. In fact, any time you want me over here, just let me know. I'm really into old things, you know, and this castle has a cool history. Did you know that when Joe Cabana owned it, he had a smuggling operation working from here?"

Shelby nodded, hiding a smile at his enthusiasm. "I'd heard."

"I've got a couple of good books about the castle, if you'd like to borrow them." He looked momentarily embarrassed. "Of course, you've got a lot of books right at your fingertips here."

"I have been known to borrow some from the shelves,

but I'm a careful reader and no one would ever know I'd read them. That's our secret, okay?"

He grinned. "'Kay."

Shelby looked at the clock and suddenly felt all the fatigue of the day. Between the two of them, she and Cody managed to get all the tasks done quickly, and after he'd dashed off to meet up with some friends who worked in the gift shop, she treated herself to a truffle. It had been an excellent idea to include the chocolate section in the bookstore. And the fact that they were locally made was a huge selling point. Besides, they tasted amazing and she knew word would spread. Sales had been brisk, and she'd have to be sure to pick up some more the next day on her way in. She sent Erica Bryant a quick email to place an order, which she intended to pick up on her way to the shuttle the following morning. She probably would have stopped by anyway, just to touch base with her new friend. Whenever she thought of Erica, she felt happy they'd bonded so quickly. She hadn't really had a chance to meet many other women her age since arriving.

She waved to a couple of volunteers who were placing new stacks of brochures in the racks as she left. Part of her plan to become the friendly colleague. She'd hoped to say goodbye to Matthew but saw no sign of him.

She sat on one of the wooden benches, leaning back, facing the late-afternoon sunshine, and felt herself dozing as the horn blasted her to attention. First that stop at the police station, then a quick trip to the main bookstore. It would be closed by then, but she wanted to have a look around. Not that she didn't trust the staff to make sure everything was just right. She just needed to see it and almost reassure herself that all this was happening. Then she'd head home and have a relaxing glass of wine. Day one, over and out.

# Chapter Nine

After supper, Shelby took the cup of coffee she'd left chilling in the fridge all day and added a scoop of vanilla ice cream to it, then climbed to the upper deck. She settled onto one of the two mesh outdoor chairs that faced the river, the best view to enjoy the sunset. She'd just taken a sip and set her treat down on the wooden outdoor table when she heard footsteps approaching along the dock, followed by a knock on her door.

She stood and went to the railing and looked down at the man, but all she could see was the top of his ball cap.

"Who are you? What do you want?"

He stepped back and looked up at Shelby. He was wearing a New York Yankees cap, jeans, and a checkered black-and-white shirt with the sleeves rolled up to his elbows.

"Who are you?" she asked again.

He flipped open his wallet and waved his ID at her. "Special Agent Zack Griffin, CGIS."

"What is that? I've never heard of it."

"It's the U.S. Coast Guard Investigative Service."

"Never heard of that, either. Can I see your ID again?"

He pulled the wallet out of his pocket and flipped it open. "I have a few questions about what happened on Blye Island yesterday. May I come on board?"

"How do I know that ID is real?" she asked, even though he sort of resembled the guy who'd tagged along with the cops to the murder scene. She hadn't gotten a good look at him, though, so she couldn't be sure. "I've never seen one before and you're not in uniform, which seems odd if you're trying to question me."

"Really?"

Shelby was struck by his deep bass voice, very masculine but also somehow soothing, but she wasn't about to give in that easily. "Yes. As far as I know, there could be a murderer running around the Bay. I wouldn't be very smart if I let every stranger on board, would I?"

"Why do you say a murderer? It could be an accidental death. Look, I'll give you a number you can call and check me out."

"How do I know the number is legit?" She stood blocking the top of the ladder, just in case.

He widened his stance and stared at her. "You've got to be kidding."

She shook her head.

"All right, why don't you call Chief Stone and ask her? Do you have a cell phone handy?"

"I do and I will." Fortunately, she'd added the police to her contact list on her phone just after arriving in case there was trouble at the store. Or elsewhere. She punched it in and then spoke briefly to the chief, who was working late. "All right. Thank you, Chief Stone. Sorry to have bothered you."

She hung up but hung on to the phone. "Okay, you're approved." In a quieter voice, she added, "She was laughing at me." She stood back, gesturing for him to climb the ladder.

Griffin was grinning when he stepped onto the deck. "Not at you, at me, Ms. Cox. She loves it when I'm not believed."

"You've dealt with her in the past, then?"

"She likes to remind me of some of my antics during my misspent youth. My family has a summer place here. And, yes, we have also had the odd professional standoff."

"She won, I take it."

"Got it. She did start out as a teacher, I'm told, and that training made her a tough interrogator with the desire to win. Now, if I could just ask you a few questions?"

Shelby could see he'd wanted to add more, possibly something sarcastic, and gave him points for self-control. He looked around and Shelby's eyes followed, wondering what he thought of her place. *Why does that matter?* "I guess I do recognize you. You were at the castle yesterday, along with the police."

He nodded but didn't offer any further details.

"Would you like something to drink? I don't have any more iced coffee, but I can make it hot or give you a dish of ice cream or both." She felt a moment's panic but wasn't quite sure why. The fact that he was a police officer of sorts shouldn't have bothered her. She had nothing to hide.

His sandy-colored hair and blue eyes were a combination she secretly found hard to resist, although it had been a while since she'd had any romantic entanglements. His eyes were what really held her attention though. Crinkly at the edges, they seemed to be smiling even when the rest of his face looked serious. And he was the perfect height, maybe two inches taller than her. *Oh man, what am I thinking!*

He shook his head. "Maybe I'll take a rain check," he said, so softly she almost missed it.

Also, it took her a few seconds to realize what he was talking about. She'd been so lost in thought, she'd forgotten her question.

He motioned her into one of the two mesh lounge chairs, then sat on the other one. "I need to talk to you about the body you found on Blye Island."

"How did you know where I live?"

"It's not a secret, is it?"

"Uh, no. But why would you be questioning me? Does the Coast Guard also investigate murders? I thought that would be more a matter for the local police, not that I have any experience with this."

He looked like he might smile but said instead, "It may be related to something we're working on."

"Okay." She'd think about that later. She did have another thought first, though. "Did you know Loreena Swan, personally, I mean, since you spent a lot of time in the area over the years?"

"I'm the one asking the questions." His voice still sounded stern, but the corners of his mouth twitched. "And I did know who she was, although that has no bearing on my questions to you," he continued. "Now, may I get back to my questions?"

Shelby nodded. "Of course." She had an intense desire to trace the webbing on the arm of the chair but knew that fidgeting would put her at a disadvantage.

"In your statement, you said that you'd heard a boat engine close by just before finding the body. A small engine, I think you said. Tell me more about that."

"I don't know how small because I'm really not a water person. I've lived in Boston most of my life, and we never even went on one of their ferries, but judging from the sound of Captain Terry's shuttle and the large tour boats, it sounded quieter and smaller."

"And there was backwash in the grotto? How high up did it rise?"

"Not much. It was more like little splashes."

"And the motor sounded very close?"

She nodded again. "What's this all about?"

"And you didn't see anything of the boat?"

"No. Now I'm getting curiouser and curiouser, as Alice said. You know, *Alice in Wonderland*."

He shook his head. "Thanks for your time, Ms. Cox. I'll see myself out." He grinned at the last bit and walked over to the same ladder he'd come up, although she was sure he'd noticed the stairs.

"Wait a minute." She leapt out of her chair. "You're not going to tell me anything, like what's happening with the investigation and why you're talking to me?"

"Afraid I can't," he said, holding her gaze for a few seconds before climbing down. "I'll probably be getting back to you if I need more information."

She watched him leap off the boat to the dock and walk away, his cell phone held to his ear.

*What a frustrating man.* But she did hope he had more questions. It might be nice to see him again.

# Chapter Ten

Before heading to the store on Tuesday, Shelby rushed through her morning tasks at the houseboat, washing the breakfast dishes and straightening anything that looked out of place. All the while, her mind ran through her agenda for the day, things she'd noted down on Sunday during a quiet period at the store. The excitement of the opening weekend had continued, and she'd been happy it was Taylor's Sunday to work. Shelby couldn't imagine handling that crowd on her own.

Her final morning chore was placing a dish of cat food from a freshly opened can outside the door. That cat was making its own hours, but Shelby didn't want it to go hungry, even though part of her brain said the regular feeding routine was a bad idea. It was definitely an open invitation to move in. She glanced around as she locked the door, then sprinted along the wharf to the parking lot. She checked her watch. She had time to walk, if she was quick. The car would stay parked again today, as it had most days since she'd moved to the Bay. She made it to the shuttle just in time and settled onto one of the benches near the front of the boat, hoping to be left alone to collect her thoughts.

Edie had persuaded her when she'd first agreed to take over the running of the castle location that she'd need a day off, and Monday would be the quietest day of the week. She'd readily agreed and had spent the previous day doing housework, finishing with a visit to any house within a short walk asking if they owned her new companion cat. She'd shown the photo she'd taken, and although many said they'd seen the cat, no one knew the owner. She wasn't quite sure how she felt about that news, but she did give the cat an extra treat that morning.

The shuttle ride was colder than she'd expected, and Shelby spent most of it with her coat collar turned up, huddled next to the cabin. She'd challenged herself to stick it out on deck no matter the temperature. If it rained, she'd head inside. That made her feel somewhat virtuous.

It didn't take Shelby long to figure out, as she made her way up the walk to the castle, that the voices she could hear arguing belonged to Matthew and Chief Tekla Stone. She slowed her pace, hoping to overhear some of the conversation but not wanting to appear nosy if spotted.

The chief's final words reached Shelby just as a young couple started walking toward her.

"There are many eyes watching you, Kessler. You're not going to get away with anything this time," the angry chief said.

Shelby cringed and picked up her pace, nodding at the couple as they passed. Fortunately, they seemed oblivious to what was going on around them.

*Poor Matthew.* The chief really seemed to have it in for him. As she entered the bookshop, Shelby nodded at Taylor, pleased to note that Taylor not only had gotten to the bookstore first but also had the coffee going and the dust cloth tucked away.

By the time she had stashed her purse under the counter and poured herself a cup of coffee, customers were arriving. Shelby smiled at an elderly couple and then noticed that they were followed in by Chief Stone. The chief paused at the doorway and looked around the room, then adjusting her belt, walked over to where Shelby was standing at the counter, slicing open a bubble mailer that contained a book for their inventory.

"Good afternoon, Shelby. Do you have a few minutes to talk?"

Shelby's heart started pounding. Was she in trouble? What did the police want with her? She'd given her statement. She nodded while saying, "Sure."

Tekla pointed to the door, and Shelby, after making sure Taylor noticed what was happening, followed the chief out into the hallway. They ended up at the window seat next to the indoor garden. Shelby's heartbeat sounded as loud as the indoor fountain, and she focused on it, telling herself to breathe slowly and relax.

Tekla sat in one of the hunter-green wicker chairs and waited until Shelby had done the same, then said, "Take me through the minutes before you found Loreena's body again."

Shelby stared at her. What was she getting at? Was the chief trying to trip her up? Was she now a suspect? Oh, well, she'd already made her statement, so she'd just repeat what she'd said then.

"And this all happened within a time period of, what, ten minutes?" the chief asked when Shelby finished her retelling.

Shelby thought about it and nodded. "At the most, I'd say."

"And Matt Kessler could have come out of the grotto before you arrived there?"

Uh-oh. "I don't know where he came from. I didn't see him."

"But you saw his red plaid shirt on one of the trails. Which could mean he'd come from the grotto?"

"I don't know what you want me to say. Or maybe I do, but I can't because I have absolutely no idea where he was before I saw him." She folded her arms across her chest and sat back in the chair. No way was she playing this game.

Chief Stone leaned even farther forward as she asked her next question. "And how long would you say you were in the grotto before you screamed?"

*What?* Shelby's mind raced through a variety of scenarios. *Does she think I had time to commit murder?*

"I . . . I'm not sure. It was probably only a few minutes, but it felt like a lifetime." *Dumb thing to say.*

The chief smiled, but Shelby didn't feel the love.

"What are you getting at?"

"Just checking my timelines," Stone replied. "I'm a stickler for the details, you might say." She stood. "Thanks for your time, Ms. Cox. We'll talk again."

She nodded and focused her attention on the group of volunteers at the bottom of the stairs. Shelby slipped away before the chief had a chance to think of anything else.

Taylor sat relaxing in a chair when Shelby slid in through the open door. Shelby debated sharing what had just taken place but decided it would be better not to. She took a closer look at Taylor.

"You looked wiped, Taylor. I hope everything's okay. You're welcome to leave early today if you want."

"Thanks, Shelby, but I just got here." She chuckled. "I didn't sleep well, that's all. I'll get to shelving those books you brought back from the store and then maybe take a walk. That should wake me up." She went over to the counter, pulled out the box cutter Shelby had been using earlier, and was about to slice the top of a box when she suddenly put it down and looked up at Shelby. "I have two things to tell you."

*Uh-oh.*

"First," Taylor went on without waiting, "I asked Chuck about the autopsy. If he thought it was odd that I asked, he didn't say anything. But he did tell me Loreena had a 'laceration to the back of her head'—those were his words—but the cause of death was drowning. So, according to Chuck, she could have slipped and fallen into the water accidentally, hitting her head as she went in. However, the bruising on her shoulders was made when she was forcefully held underwater."

Shelby felt suddenly chilled to the bone. "So, she was murdered?"

Taylor shrugged. "I guess."

"Huh. Well, thanks for finding out, Taylor. I hope he's not suspicious about your asking him."

"Actually, he's got other reasons to question some of the things I'm doing these days. I've been meaning to tell you my news."

Shelby felt another *uh-oh* in the pit of her stomach. She hoped it wasn't bad news.

"I'm going to have a baby," Taylor said, her face beaming.

"A baby. I had no idea. Well, of course, why would I? I mean, how exciting. I'm happy for you, Taylor." She hesitated a moment, then gave Taylor a hug. "Is everything all right?"

"Oh, yes. I had some difficulties with my last pregnancy, though, so the doctor is keeping a close eye on me. I may need more time off."

"Don't worry about it. When are you due?"

"The end of September or early October."

Shelby couldn't help clapping her hands. "That's so exciting. Wow, that'll be quite a difference in your lifestyle." Would she need to look for a new employee?

"I haven't allowed myself to go there yet. I've been so worried, but now I'm feeling more comfortable that things are on the right track."

"Is it a secret, or can I tell Aunt Edie?"

"For sure, I'd like her to know. Trudy, too." Taylor paused, and it looked like there were tears in her eyes. "Thanks, Shelby. I'm relieved now that I've told you and that you're okay with everything."

"Of course I am. And don't be hesitant to ask if you need anything. Please."

Taylor nodded and dabbed at her eyes as she opened the box.

Shelby hadn't really been close to anyone who was pregnant. Would this be an emotional time for them all? she wondered.

"I take it the chief had some more questions."

"She did, but I don't think she liked my answers."

# Chapter Eleven

Shelby decided a short break after a couple of hours of intense hand-selling would be a good idea, even though it was getting close to closing time. She was surprised at how many tourists were actually visiting the castle for tours but happy they were including the bookstore in their stop.

She bought a double-scoop vanilla ice cream cone at the Sugar Shack, and then wandered around the grounds for ten minutes. She realized, on her way back to the bookstore, that she'd been hoping to see Matthew and maybe find out what he and the chief had been arguing about. Tactfully, of course. She figured he must be busy on the opposite side of the island, but there was always tomorrow.

Shelby was back in the bookstore and had just finished ringing another purchase through the cash register when the phone rang. She noted Edie's number as she answered.

"Hi, Aunt Edie. What can I do for you?"

"Oh, Shelby. I want you to come straight here after you close tonight, if you don't mind." She sounded panicked.

Shelby was instantly alert. "Sure, I'll be there. What's up?"

"I'm sorry, I'm too upset to talk right now, and besides, Trudy just arrived. I'll tell you when you get here."

"Are you okay? Are you in pain? Did something happen to you?"

"No, no. I'm sorry, I didn't mean to alarm you. I'm just not thinking straight. I'm perfectly fine. But I do need your help."

"Okay, I'll be there as soon as I can," Shelby said. She heard the click of Edie hanging up before she had a chance to say goodbye. This didn't bode well.

She brooded about it the remainder of the afternoon but was hesitant to talk to Taylor about it. She needed to find out what the problem was before she alarmed anyone else. She suggested they close the shop a few minutes early, and they both made the five o'clock shuttle back to the Bay.

She debated about stopping in at the Mango Lagoon for some takeout—she loved their mango coconut curry—but decided she could get the food after, if need be. When she arrived at Edie's house, she was out of breath from fast-walking up the hill. She took a few seconds to calm her racing heart before knocking and entering.

Edie called out to her from the sun-room in the back.

Shelby found her sitting in her usual chair, a cup of tea on the side table. Trudy had obviously already left.

"What's wrong? What happened?" Shelby asked, hurrying to her side.

Edie looked at her, and Shelby could see the anxiety in

her eyes. "It's Matthew. They've taken him in for questioning in Loreena's death. I know he's innocent, Shelby. I just don't know what to do."

"If he's innocent, the police will find out. That's why they're questioning him so thoroughly." She didn't really know how the police worked but thought it sounded good, and it might put Edie's mind at ease.

"No. You don't know Tekla Stone. She works with horse blinders on, and once her mind is set, there's no changing it. I told you she had it in for him."

"But she's not the only law enforcement involved. The State Police are working on it too. They might not be thinking the same thing. And then there's the Coast Guard Investigative Service, although I'm not sure how much involvement they have." She straightened. "Unless it's tied in to something they're investigating, which is what the agent suggested. Maybe something like smuggling."

"Well, that would be all too easy to tie Matthew in to, I'd think, if that's even the case, since he lives on the island. We have to do something, Shelby."

"Like what?"

"I want you to drive me over to see Tekla." Edie grabbed her cane and struggled to stand.

"What? We can't just stop in and ask about Matthew. The police won't tell us anything, for starters."

"Maybe not, but I've got to talk to Tekla. I think there's a lot more going on here than Matthew being a handy suspect. I think it's time to make the attempt to clear the air. Then she might start focusing on what's happening now rather than what happened back then." Edie's eyes were pleading.

"What do you mean, clear the air?"

"We don't have time to talk about it right now. We have to get over there right away."

Shelby didn't feel convinced. It might just make Tekla dig her heels in more. From what she'd seen and heard, she was one cold woman. But Shelby knew that Edie probably wouldn't take no for an answer. Talk about an immovable force.

"Fine. You realize at this hour there's probably nobody there." She looked at Edie, hoping for a change of mind. What she saw was a set line to her mouth. Shelby nodded. "Okay, we can go now if you like. I'll just go home and get my car."

"No, we can take mine. It needs a drive, although it's not a very long one. Maybe you should take it home with you and on your next day off take it for a long drive. Maybe to Clayton. I don't think you've been there yet, have you?"

"We'll see. Okay, are you ready to go?"

Edie nodded as she grabbed her sweater from the back of a chair and hobbled toward the door.

Shelby couldn't help wondering if they were making a mistake. From what she'd seen, Chief Stone was a thorough investigator. And the State Police were also involved. And what if Matthew Kessler really was the murderer?

# Chapter Twelve

The door to the police station, situated at the side of the municipal building on Walton Street, was locked just as Shelby had suspected. She knew the police station wasn't open twenty-four hours a day and that there was a phone number to call instead. But after hours that number connected to the Jefferson County Dispatch Center. She wondered what Edie would suggest next as she walked back to the car. The old Chevy Impala had a small dent on the right front bumper and hints of rust along the wheel wells, but aside from that, it seemed reliable, and it was easy to maneuver.

"It's closed," Shelby reported.

"I thought as much, but it was worth a try. Sometimes she works late if she needs to. We'll just go to her house. Turn left and go back again the way we came until Bolton Avenue, then take another left. She lives on the other side of Church, right near the end."

Shelby wondered how Edie knew where Tekla Stone lived. Obviously *not in touch* didn't mean *not in the know.*

Edie signaled for her to pull up in front of a two-story light-blue clapboard house, much the same as the one Edie lived in. A black-and-white police SUV was parked in the driveway, and they could hear hammering in the garage as they got out of the car.

Shelby led the way, walking slowly and wondering what to say to the police chief. Maybe she'd just let Edie do all the talking, since it had been her idea in the first place. The side door of the garage had been propped open, but there was a slight ledge, so Shelby knocked first, then walked in and turned back to help Edie step over and into the garage. The hammering had stopped and Shelby was hesitant to turn around.

"Tekla," Edie said.

"Edie," came the abrupt reply.

Shelby turned and noted that the chief was standing at a worktable about waist high on which an Adirondack chair had been placed on its side. The blue paint had chipped in many places, and one of the arms sat askew on top of the frame. Chief Stone, dressed in a plaid shirt and jeans, held a hammer in her right hand. Her hair was tucked under a faded black ball cap with the town logo, equally faded, on the peak.

"Shelby." The chief acknowledged her, then turned her sights back on Edie. "What do you want?"

Shelby glanced around to see if ice crystals actually hung in the air.

Edie took a few steps closer. "I want to talk to you about Matthew Kessler."

"Ha. It's none of your business, Edie. I'm police chief here, and you know nothing about police business. So I suggest you leave."

"I will not leave until I say my piece."

Shelby noticed Tekla stiffen, but she stayed silent.

Edie must have seen it also and took it as her cue to continue. "First of all, he couldn't have done it. He's not the kind of man who would kill. Anyone."

"And you know that how?"

"Because I know the man. And I also know that you've had it in for him since he got here." She paused to take a deep breath. "Now I'm thinking you might also have heard talk that Matthew and I are good friends. And if that's the case, it might have put you in a mind-set to finally get even with me."

Tekla dropped the hammer on the bench, and Shelby flinched. She noticed that Edie stood her ground.

"You, as usual, don't know what you're talking about, Edie. That's water under the bridge. I haven't given it a thought in years."

"Oh, yeah? So, why do you go out of your way to avoid me? And if you can't totally avoid me, you just give me that phony smile and say whatever needs to be said, but only if someone's watching. I can understand you not wanting to have any contact with us while Jimmy was alive, but he's been gone a while now. Surely we can be friends again, or at least share some pleasantries. It's a small village, Tekla."

Tekla looked like a stone maiden to Shelby. No sign of emotion. Not even anger, whereas she could hear the strength in Edie's voice turn to pleading. She looked at her aunt, who seemed visibly shaken.

"You don't know what you're talking about," Tekla finally said after a few minutes, which felt like an eternity to Shelby. "Now, please leave."

"I'm actually begging you, Tekla, to put old grudges aside. For Matthew's sake and for yours and mine."

Tekla turned away. "You're trespassing, Edie."

Edie stood staring at Tekla's back for a few moments, and then her shoulders collapsed. She shook her head and slowly turned to leave.

Shelby stood feeling lost. She couldn't think of a thing to do or say to help these two women, so she followed Edie out the door and back to the car.

Edie sat in silence on the drive home, and Shelby didn't push her into talking. Besides, she was too busy trying to absorb what had just gone on and what it all meant. That there was no love lost between Tekla and Edie was no surprise. She'd heard about it before, after all. She knew that Edie had been married to Jimmy Birch, but he had died when Shelby was in her early teens, according to her dad. He'd also said Edie had never changed her last name—something to do with being a feminist, he'd added with a shake of his head.

The shock was that, knowing how Tekla felt about her, Edie would want to approach her about Matthew. What did it mean? The most obvious reason was that Edie had feelings for Matthew, deep feelings. So why hadn't Edie just out and told Shelby about it? They had discussed Matthew several times. She must have her reasons, but Shelby was now determined to find out more.

Edie exited the car and hobbled into the house in silence as soon as Shelby stopped the car. Shelby felt almost like she was the one being punished. However, when she entered the house, she found Edie with the teakettle on and a jar of soup on the counter. Shelby sat down at the kitchen table and watched while Edie emptied the soup into a saucepan and then started slicing bread that had been stored on the counter.

Finally, Edie asked, her back still to Shelby, "You'll stay for supper?"

"Yes, thanks." *You couldn't keep me away at this point. Too many questions.*

Edie first made the tea, poured a cup for each of them, and, after serving Shelby, went back to stirring the soup. When it was finally heated, she prepared a bowl for each of them and brought everything to the table.

"Let's eat first," was all she said.

Shelby nodded and dipped her spoon into the soup. Celery. She knew it was homemade; Edie prided herself on her soups, but this was so thick and creamy it tasted and felt like comfort food. Edie needed comforting and Shelby felt that was her job. But she'd let Edie lead the way.

After supper, they took their refreshed tea into the sunroom and sat looking out at the backyard. The sun hadn't yet started to set even though Shelby felt like the last few hours had been twice that amount of time. The sunlight played on the multiple bird feeders that Edie had spread throughout the garden. The colors of the flowers, too many to name, were a cheery backdrop to the neatly mown yard. Shelby had been relieved to find that Edie had someone to do the outdoor work for her while she was recuperating. Shelby had been worried it might be one of her tasks, and her outdoor skills were nil. She now found herself wondering if Matthew was the one responsible for the picture-perfect yard.

Finally, Shelby could hear Edie take a deep breath, but she kept her eyes straight ahead as Edie started speaking.

"I guess you have questions about me and Matthew."

"I am wondering." *And about you and the chief.*

"Uh-huh. Well, there's not really anything going on, so I didn't feel there was a need to talk about it until now."

Shelby turned to face her. "I'm listening."

"We're good friends. He often brings his skiff over and comes for supper, or during the winter months, he would sometimes stay over if there was a bad storm or something." She looked at Shelby and added quickly, "I have several guest rooms, as you know."

Shelby tried to keep from smiling.

"We've talked a lot. It took quite a while, but eventually he told me all about his wife and her death. And what it's been like for him since then. That's why I'm so certain he's innocent. I know how he abhors that anyone would commit a violent act against another human being. And death? Well, he's written about true crime for a long time, and that was part of the reason. He wanted to gain an understanding of why one person would kill another. When it happened to his wife, he was totally crushed until he fought back and tried to use his research skills to find the killer. Unfortunately, it hasn't happened yet. But he hasn't given up, and that's what keeps him going."

*And now he has you*, Shelby thought, looking at Edie. But she stayed silent.

"He just wouldn't do it, Shelby. I'd stake my life on it."

A shiver ran down Shelby's spine. "So, now what?

Edie continued, "I have to get Tekla on board. She's so stubborn, when she has an idea, she can't be shaken. But she's wrong, totally wrong. We have to figure out a way to convince her."

"We?"

"Yes, you and me. You like Matthew, don't you? Surely you must have realized what a gentle man he is."

"Well, yes. I like what I know of him. He's been kind and helpful to me, and I can see he means a lot to you."

"Okay, that's a start. I've been thinking about this a lot. There's not been much else for me to do but read. So, I've decided I'll start talking to the folks I know in the Bay who might know something about Loreena."

"How can you do that? You're still recuperating."

"By phone, of course, and email."

Shelby dreaded asking the next question but knew it had to be done. "And what about me?"

Edie leaned closer, a conspiratorial tone in her voice. "You, my dear, need to poke around the castle and talk to everyone who's worked with Loreena. Find out more about her personal life if you can and, in particular, what they know about her nephew, Carter."

"I doubt anyone at the castle knows that much. I think they were all as afraid of her as I was."

"Ah, you haven't gotten to know Mae-Beth Warner very well, have you? She runs the workshops, although these days, it's purely an organizational role. She'd been there even before Loreena. She has a keen eye and a sharp mind, even though she's well into her eighties. Just pay her a visit and ask some questions. I'm sure she'll be forthright. And also, we'll need to talk to the other police officers involved, since Tekla's so stubborn."

It sounded like Edie had given it a lot of thought. So Shelby wondered why she suddenly felt so uneasy.

# Chapter Thirteen

Shelby tried to relax. She'd arrived home while it was still light out and decided to try to cozy up with a good book, *A Floating World*, by local writer Paul Malo. It had been recommended to her because it supposedly gave a credible feel for the history of the Thousand Islands, and she'd started reading it when she'd first moved to town. Now she was determined to finish it but also looking at it with an eye to finding out more about all the smuggling that had happened during Prohibition.

She'd also managed to pick up a book on the topic at the local library over the weekend. Cody had tweaked her curiosity, and she wanted to find out more about the possibility, remote as it might be, that some type of smuggling could actually be taking place using the old scenario from Joe Cabana's days. And, if so, if that could have led to Loreena's murder. Although how to make that connection eluded her, but she assured herself that she was just beginning to look into things. She also readily admitted that she was really curious about why the Coast Guard was involved in the investigation. It seemed to make sense that the two might go together.

She realized at one point that she hadn't gotten very far with her reading and that she was occasionally looking over toward the dock. She wasn't hoping for a visitor. No, she was not, although she did wonder how Special Agent Griffin spent his evenings. Then she wondered why she was wondering. She'd never been on the hunt for Mr. Right, like so many of the women she knew. Of course, there'd been Kerry in Accounting, but he'd backed off when she'd made it clear she wouldn't recommend they publish his manuscript.

As an only child, she was used to being on her own, with only a father as her guide. And he hadn't been the social type either. He'd warned her to be wary of relationships, and she'd eyed boys with caution when she'd reached dating age. From what she could see and remember, he'd never dated anyone himself, nor did he have many friends who dropped in to visit them. Maybe the occasional colleague from college. As a botanist, he was at his happiest traipsing around through nature, or taking refuge in his library of books. She'd been happy to go along on the weekend treks, more to be with him than because of any interest in plants and trees of her own.

If she stayed in Alexandria Bay, and she saw no reason why she shouldn't, since she had such strong reasons to do so, she'd have to look into some cooking classes and try to meet some more people. Or maybe join the community center and take some fitness classes. She looked down at her figure—she wasn't overweight, but she was a long way from svelte, and a couple of months of Erica's truffles hadn't helped. She'd so fallen in love with those truffles. Definitely, fitness classes were a requirement.

For now, she was happy that she and Erica had become so friendly so quickly. And then there was Erica's brother, Drew. An impressive guy whom she'd met a total of two times, both at Erica's place and for very brief periods. He had made an impression, though. Still in his thirties, he already owned his own restaurant, where he was also the chef, turning out an eclectic menu but known for his Italian dishes. Or so she'd heard. She'd definitely have to give it a try and sometime soon.

And now there was Aunt Edie, of course. Not her mother but an older woman, some female family, in her life. And, of course, the Bay was where she'd been born and where her mother had died. She wanted to find out more about her.

She had many reasons to enjoy living here. Except for the murder, of course. That thought quickly sobered her. Was she really a suspect in Loreena's murder? She couldn't wrap her head around it. Although it didn't seem too likely, she should probably pay Chief Stone a visit after work the next day and just flat out ask. And then there was her aunt's plan to investigate. It wouldn't do any harm, she figured, to ask a few questions around the village and find out how well Loreena had been liked. Or hadn't.

What she needed was a plan. She thought about it some more and decided to put her skills as an editor to work for her. She needed to look at the murder as part of a larger story. What was the plot? Who were the major players? What were the possible motives? And, of course, who had the means and opportunity? She had edited only a couple of murder mysteries, but she'd read hundreds more, so she knew what went into writing them. Now, the question was, what came before the murder? After all, she knew what came after. She'd never talked to so many police in her life.

* * *

The first customers into the bookstore Wednesday morning were a harried-looking elderly couple with three preschoolers running circles around them.

"I'm so sorry for these scallywags, but we'll try to be quick," explained the woman. She looked to be in her seventies, maybe even early eighties. Shelby would have been the first to admit she was terrible when it came to guessing ages. In fact, had she not known Edie's age, she would have taken her to be in her early fifties. Of course, that could have had something to do with her aunt's eclectic outfits.

"May I help you with something?" Shelby asked. She noticed that Taylor was enticing the children toward the small table set up with a Jungle Play and Train apparatus. It seemed to be doing the trick and was keeping them entertained. Shelby sighed inwardly. Although she had nothing against kids, she'd been unfortunate enough to have the mischievous kind in her bookstore before, the kind that delighted in pulling books from shelves while the parents, and Shelby, were busy.

"Yes." The woman looked at her husband, who rooted through the pockets of his red windbreaker and finally found a scrap of paper, which he handed to her. "I'd like this book, if you have it in stock. It was recommended by a staff member when we were here last year, but you were out of it at that time."

Shelby looked at the title. Loreena Swan's book. And she could just bet who had recommended it.

"We do have a copy," she was pleased to say. Trudy had managed to find one at the main store after Loreena's tirade.

"I'm so pleased. I don't see the woman working today, though." She glanced toward the main hallway.

Shelby wondered if she should pursue this line of conversation, which would mean mentioning the murder. Perhaps not. "Everyone is on shifts here. Now, would you like a bag?"

"Oh yes, dear. And here's my credit card." She watched the children as Shelby finished the transaction, then signed the receipt. "Thank you so much. We come here every year when we visit our family in Clayton."

"Where do you live?"

"Oh, we're Canadian. We're from Perth, a small town in Ontario. It's about an hour-and-a-half drive from here. Well, thank you, dear. I'm so pleased to see the bookstore is still in business and that you had the book this year." She held up the bag with her purchase as proof.

As the satisfied customers and their three small charges left, a noisy group of six, all adults this time, filtered in. They paid her no attention, so she was content to let them browse. Taylor also stood back and just watched.

It turned out to be a good strategy. By the time they left, they'd each bought one of the local-interest books. Shelby was starting to love tourists.

Just before noon, a woman not much older than Shelby walked in and went straight to the local books section. Shelby knew she wasn't a tourist. No one wore a clingy designer-looking tunic, leggings, and three-inch heels to go sightseeing, especially to wander around the island. But she was at a loss as to who this woman could be. Before Shelby could engage her in conversation, an equally non-touristy-looking man joined her. After a couple of minutes, they joined Shelby at the counter.

The woman stuck out her hand. "I'm Chrissie Halstead. I'm in charge of marketing and promotion for the Heritage Society, and this is my fiancé, Carter Swan."

Shelby hastily covered her surprise. *Loreena's nephew.* "I'm Shelby Cox. It's nice to meet you." She didn't attempt to shake Carter's hand, as he didn't offer it. Instead, she said, "I'm so sorry about your aunt."

He nodded. "Yes, it was a shock, and a tragedy. This castle and the village were her life."

Shelby couldn't decide just how much shock he was in. He didn't sound too upset, but she didn't know him, so it would be unfair to judge. He looked to be unscathed, though, in that *I just parked the Lamborghini and am waiting to play tennis* way. Somebody that good looking couldn't be real or touched by sadness.

Chrissie added, patting his arm, "We're so very upset about it. Loreena was so very kind to us both. I don't know if you've heard, but I've been put in charge of the volunteers until someone new can be appointed. This is my first visit of the season to the castle, so I wanted to be sure to meet you. I hope your aunt is doing well."

"Yes, she's recuperating just fine but, of course, too slowly for her liking."

Chrissie chuckled while Carter looked like he wasn't paying attention to their conversation. He just stood staring out the bay window at the back of the store.

"I do notice that while you have an excellent selection of local books, Loreena's isn't among them." Chrissie sounded pleasant enough, but Shelby wasn't taking any chances.

"I know. In fact, we just sold the last copy this morning, but I've placed a reorder, so it should be back in stock shortly."

Chrissie smiled. "I'm glad to see you're on top of it. Well, we must get back to the village. There's so much going on today, and we like to show our support for all the events. So nice to meet you. I'm sure we'll be seeing a lot more of you."

Shelby nodded. "Enjoy your day."

Carter honored her with a small and fleeting smile. If there had been some warmth in his eyes, Shelby might have even found him attractive. She'd always had a thing about guys with dark hair and eyes. As it was, he seemed a bit of a cold fish. She was glad when the pair left.

What was his problem? Surely he couldn't be mad because Shelby had gotten the job Loreena had intended for him. Maybe he was always a bit standoffish. Snooty, Edie would probably call him. She couldn't wait to fill her in on this meeting over dinner. Of course, maybe he was deeply upset by his aunt's death. Shelby knew that she sure would be in his shoes. She decided to give him the benefit of the doubt, even though he hadn't seemed all that upset when she had extended her condolences. *Everyone has their own way of dealing with things*, she heard her dad's voice whispering in her brain.

For now, she concentrated on becoming even more familiar with their local books so that she could actually recommend and hand-sell them. When she next looked at the clock, it was half an hour until closing. It had turned out to be a slow day, just as Taylor had predicted. Which was why Shelby had let Taylor leave early. Besides, she hadn't felt well. Shelby wondered if morning sickness could also turn into afternoon sickness. None of her friends had ever been pregnant, so Shelby had no idea what to expect. She hadn't even ever held a baby. Well, maybe once as a teenager, but she couldn't even remember the circumstances any longer, it was so long ago. The thought of being asked to babysit at some point caused the stirrings of a small anxiety attack, but Shelby reasoned that Taylor and her husband must know tons of people in Alexandria Bay. Lots of potential sitters.

Shelby couldn't imagine a mad rush at that late hour of the day, so she started counting the cash and doing the closing report. That way, she'd be able to just grab the money and run when she heard the final boat whistle.

She looked up in surprise when she heard someone enter the store, thinking she'd conjured up the customers she'd thought wouldn't show, and was unsettled to see Zack Griffin. She didn't know why she reacted in that way. She had nothing to hide. She wasn't guilty of anything, except maybe a desire to skip out early.

"Hey, are you here to buy some local history?" she asked.

He chuckled. "I got enough local history during my

summers growing up, thanks. I'm playing tourist today and thought I'd check out all the attractions on the island, so here I am. I know it's getting close to closing, so don't worry, I won't make you stay open late."

"Staying open late isn't possible here. I live by the castle regulations and also the strong desire not to miss the last shuttle back to Alex Bay. I didn't take you for the tourist type."

He shrugged. "I actually came over in my own boat. That's one of the perks of carrying a badge, getting to tie up almost anywhere. It gives me more flexibility."

"It might also help you figure out some of the details of the murder?"

He shrugged again. "It can't hurt. So, tell me, have you had any more thoughts on what happened? Anything come to mind that you didn't think of right away?"

She looked at him closely before answering. Was this a trap to find out if she'd been poking around the grotto again or just polite conversation?

"I thought it was the first forty-eight hours that were the most important and that's when any information would be fresh."

He chuckled. "You've been watching TV. And while that is true, it can also work the other way. After a few days, the shock wears off and the mind settles down to dealing with daily routines, which is when anything you didn't want to deal with at the time might surface. Not that this applies to you. But it's always good to ask."

"Huh. Well, if it did apply to me, I would have told Chief Stone right away."

"Good. That's good. And I'd appreciate it if you would let me know, too."

"Why? Doesn't the chief share with you?"

He grimaced. "Let's just say she likes to take her time."

"Ah. Well, you should know that Aunt Edie has asked me to sort of check on certain aspects of the investigation."

"You mean snoop."

"I mean, if I happen to remember anything or to stumble across something that might be useful, I'd be happy to tell you directly. And I hope you would do the same, if it's not classified information, that is." She held her breath, not sure if he would get angry or be amused. She was hoping for the latter, wanting him to humor her and maybe let something slip. Although he didn't seem the type to let that happen.

Zack held her gaze for a few seconds, then glanced at the clock. "Interesting offer. I need to get going, but I'll see you soon. And I'll probably have some more questions."

Questions? Well, so did she. The only problem was that she had no idea whom to talk to next.

# Chapter Fourteen

The warmth of the late-setting sun and a fresh breeze lured Shelby down off her upper deck patio on the houseboat after dinner. She wanted to check out the cemetery on Walton Street. She'd already driven out to the Barnes Settlement Cemetery a few weeks earlier in her quest to find the final resting place for her mom, Merriweather Cox. The one on Walton was closer to home, so she decided to listen to her body, which had been telling her lately that she needed more exercise and to leave the car at home. She figured it best to do the hard stuff first, walking uphill, and then she could coast on the way back down. Not that it was such a steep climb.

She set out full of enthusiasm and energy, but she had to admit to feeling winded by the time she finally spotted the cemetery. She definitely needed to get out and exercise more.

She stopped to catch her breath and thought about her mom. Merriweather, or Merrily as Shelby had once heard her called, hadn't been mentioned much when Shelby was growing up, and each time she asked her dad some questions, he'd quickly shut her down by switching topics. She figured it hurt him too much to talk about his young wife who had died when Shelby was only three years old. In fact, she knew that was why they had moved away not too long after that. He had been running from his memories.

Shelby had seen only one picture of her mom, a small 4×5 unframed black-and-white that she had found in a shoebox under his bed and pocketed. She'd been so worried he would realize she'd taken it and had tried to come up with excuses as to what she'd been doing checking the box to begin with. But she'd taken it out every night from her own hiding place and thought about how pretty her mom had been. She'd wondered if they'd looked anything alike but decided not. She had the small mouth and freckles of a Cox. Neither of which she thought of as pretty.

Over the years, they'd returned to Alexandria Bay only a couple of times, at Edie's request. One time had had to do with the final settling of their parents' estate, which had sat in limbo while a financial claim against it was being investigated. It had turned out to be bogus, and the two remaining Cox siblings had finally split what was left of their parents' savings after lawyers' fees had dwindled the value. She knew her dad had been upset by that, also. Another reason to stay away.

But now Shelby was back and she had a lot of questions for Edie, but it just didn't seem the right time to ask them, and whenever she had, Edie had resorted to her father's old trick of deflection. Out of loyalty to her brother? Or something else?

There were at least five cemeteries listed in the area, and Shelby planned to visit each one until she found what she was looking for. She doubted that Edie would tell her where her mother was buried even if she asked. No, she'd do this on her own and keep Edie as a last resort. She decided to wander methodically from left to right, although there were no straight rows to follow. Then she headed back toward the first side, checking the names on the tombstones. She stopped to admire an ornate crumbling marker from the late 1800s and felt sad when she counted the number of children in one family that had died within months of each other. That was the last straw. She couldn't look anymore and decided to go home before the darkness settled in totally. She'd be back another day.

She could see a runner approaching from her left when she reached the road but couldn't see his face. She didn't think to be worried until the man started to slow down. She thought about crossing to the other side of the street and then felt silly.

"Shelby. Twice in one day. I didn't expect to find you up here." Zack Griffin slowed even more until he stopped in front of her. He actually looked pleased to see her, or so she thought.

"Well, that makes two of us." She felt her heart rate drop back to normal.

He grinned. "I like to get out running at least once a day."

"Do you live close by?"

"My place is overlooking Casino Island Park, on Sisson,

the house with a red door and trim. It has a great view of the water."

"I'll say. That's an impressive location."

He chuckled. "It's the old family vacation place my grandfather bought when prices were much cheaper. Then, after he passed, it was left to my dad, and I rent it from him. So it's technically still the family home, and any family members get to stay with me when they visit. Fortunately, that doesn't happen too often these days."

She didn't quite know what to say to that. Choosing to ignore the personal stuff, she said, "I can't imagine not seeing the river every morning, now that I'm living the life."

"Views are important, but having a houseboat, that would be the dream," he admitted. "Don't tell me you did the self-guided cemetery tour."

"And why shouldn't I tell you?" She realized that her response had come out a bit terse. She added a smile as she finished, "I find them quite fascinating."

"Meet anyone you know?" He jogged slowly in place while he was talking.

"No, unfortunately. I was looking for my mom's grave site. Is there an office or something around here?"

"Not that I know of. I think the main office is in the municipal building. How old were you when you left Alex Bay?"

"I was three."

"And you haven't been back since? No desire to find your roots?"

"I had my dad. And my job. And my friends," she hastily

added. She didn't want him to think her life had been uneventful, even if it was true.

"You're lucky to have such a great aunt." His smile seemed genuine, and why wouldn't it be? Everyone loved Edie. *Well, almost everyone*, she amended, thinking of the chief.

"I didn't know you knew her that well." Shelby knew she sounded surprised.

"Oh, I do. She was always the most exotic person in town, with her long colorful skirts and vests, and always with flowers in her hair."

Shelby smiled. "I'd heard about her hippie origins. My dad could not have been further removed from that lifestyle."

"Conservative?"

"Yes, that's a good word for him, I guess, plus he was a bit uptight when it came to meeting people. Of course, when we were doing things together, he was an entirely different guy. He could be a lot of fun." She stopped, embarrassed by how much she'd shared with Zack. "How's your investigation coming along, by the way?" she asked, changing the topic, subtly, she hoped. "You didn't really share any information this afternoon."

He shook his head. "You don't stop, do you? I'd invite you to my place to talk about it over a drink, but that would involve my showering first, and that would make it a late night and the neighbors would talk."

She glanced at his face. He was worried about the neighbors? Apparently not, by his smile and the amused look in his eyes.

"Huh, that wouldn't be good for either of our reputations," she agreed, getting into the spirit of it. "Well then, enjoy the rest of your run."

She started to walk away when he caught up to her. "I wouldn't mind a rain check on that drink. I'll give you a call. That's a promise."

He didn't wait for an answer. He also missed the wide smile on Shelby's face.

# Chapter Fifteen

Shelby was going to have to hurry if she was going to have time to stop by Erica's coffee and chocolate shop, Chocomania, the next morning. She'd slept in, much to her chagrin, and realized with all that had been going on, she was probably a tad stressed and might need to start setting her alarm for the next little while. She hurriedly got dressed and tossed some fruit into the blender, topping it off with almond milk. Her smoothie went down fast, but she realized as she was finishing it that there was no cat around. She called out, but nothing happened, so she sprinted up the stairs, only to spot the cat curled up on the foot of her bed. Shelby had been in such a hurry, she hadn't noticed it; nor, apparently, had she even disturbed the happy feline.

She made sure to fill the cat's food dishes and then, with a quick look at the clock, grabbed her bag, pulling the door shut behind her and locking it. The cat would spend the day indoors. She just hoped he wouldn't repay the gesture by clawing something, like the couch that wasn't hers. At least there was now a litter box stashed under the stairs.

Shelby headed straight for Chocomania, almost at a sprint. She pushed the door open, knowing the chimes it had set off would bring Erica out of the back room. She appeared almost immediately.

"I'm sorry, but I'm in a rush and badly need my caffeine. I slept in." Shelby scrunched her face and realized she hadn't done a quick check of the mirror before running out. "Do I look put together, or is something glaringly not matching? Or even worse, missing?"

Erica laughed. "Trust me, I know how frustrating that can be. You look just fine; in fact, perfect. Here, I've got your truffles ready." She reached under the counter. "There you go."

Today, Erica also looked a bit tossed together, in Shelby's estimation at least. Her shoulder-length curly auburn hair, usually worn up, had tendrils that had escaped all over the place, and small white patches of flour, or so Shelby guessed, dotted the sleeve of her red T-shirt, not to mention the cream-colored bib apron that sported the caricature of a harried cook.

They both looked over at the door as a boy and girl in their late teens, both wearing the bright-red T-shirts of Uncle Sam's employees, walked in.

"Looks like they're in need of a caffeine boost also."

Erica nodded at the newcomers and then poured a coffee for Shelby. "Your usual. I'll put it on your tab. You'd better get a move on or the shuttle will leave without you."

"Thanks. And please tell me your secret to being so perky in the morning. I know you've been up much longer than I have."

"If there is a secret, that's it. For me, it feels like midmorning, so I'm completely awake now. Had you come in when I did a few hours ago, you'd have found a very different me." She smiled and winked.

"I'll take your word for that. Thanks for this." Shelby grabbed the cup and took a quick sip. "See you later."

Shelby continued her fast pace to the dock, then took a deep breath before stepping on board the shuttle. The harbor looked like a postcard. She wondered, in fact, if anyone had captured this exact view and marketed it. The water sparkled as the early-morning sun shone on it, not a ripple to mar the picture. That meant there was no wind, and Shelby hoped the entire day would continue like that. Although she'd never gotten seasick, she was not a happy traveler when there were waves, even for such a short distance. She knew she had to get a move on when a couple more castle volunteers tried to board. She followed them, found a place to stash her goodies inside the cabin, then went outside again and leaned on the railing, enjoying the slightly chilly breeze.

Her mind was on another, less pleasant, track as she walked up the stairs to the castle. That murder. She knew that's what had brought on all the stress. A small part of her wondered if the killer might strike again. But that was silly. Wasn't it? There was no reason to think there was a plot to sabotage the castle by doing in its staff. No serial killer on Blye Island.

Another part of her wondered if the police might be hard at work at that very moment, looking more closely at her and Aunt Edie. She knew they had nothing to hide, nothing to be worried about, but that's what happened when a murder hadn't been resolved. It was all too easy to let one's imagination run wild.

And then, of course, she'd promised Edie she'd do some investigating of her own, to help Matthew. What a useless idea that had been. What did she know about sleuthing, aside from what she'd read in her pile of mysteries?

But what if it was one of the volunteers who'd done it? It had to have been someone on the island, right? And, therefore, someone she worked with. That made sense. Shelby had heard Loreena tear into a couple of the other castle volunteers that fateful day, and she could imagine what it had been like for them during training sessions. But why leave her body in the grotto? Unless someone had followed her there and then done her in on the spot. She wondered whom to ask for a list of names, and then she wondered what she'd do with it if she had it. It had been a long time since she'd lived in the area. She didn't know anything about relationships and possible feuds.

But she did want to find out more about the town and the people who lived there, especially since she'd decided to make this her home. If she happened to solve the murder while she was at it, so much the better. She knew she had a lot to learn on both counts.

* * *

Shelby felt keyed up when she got off the shuttle back in the Bay at the end of the workday, so rather than going straight home, she decided a walk through the village might help.

She first stopped in at what had quickly become her favorite spot for retail therapy, Driftwood and Seawinds. The bright and breezy white-and-blue interior made Shelby think about summer vacation homes, although she'd never had one of those. But if she did, these would be the colors she'd choose. On her last visit the week before, she had spent forty minutes meandering through the store that must have been all of six hundred square feet. It just felt so relaxing to be in there, and although small in space, it had a lot to admire and look at. She'd left happy and not feeling the slightest guilt about her purchase: a wooden statue of a French chef with an armful of baguettes and a glass of wine in his hand. She'd named him Marcel, and it was her "welcome back home" gift to herself.

Today she made a vow to window shop only. Her salary, which had never been that large while she worked at the publishing house, was even less these days. She'd lucked into renting the houseboat at a very affordable monthly rate, although she'd wondered if Edie'd had a hand in that. Shelby would try to find out, because she didn't want to be indebted to anyone, not even her wonderful aunt.

Fortunately, the two Noland sisters who owned and ran the shop were busy with other customers, so Shelby wouldn't feel obligated to go nuts shopping that day. Of course, there was never any pressure. Maybe that's why she always felt she *should* buy something every time she visited. Shelby wandered, adding a couple of items to her wish list—a battery-operated pepper mill with a light and a small watercolor of lemons that would look great on the kitchen wall.

Shelby didn't hear Peggy Noland walk up behind her and was startled when Peggy said, "I hope you don't mind my saying this, Miss Cox, but just seeing you standing there, so engrossed by that painting, you reminded me of your mother."

Shelby turned in surprise to face Peggy, one of the owners. "You knew my mom?"

"Not well. She was younger, of course, but a good customer for a while."

"Can you tell me anything else about her?"

Peggy eyed her quizzically. "Not really. The person to ask would be your aunt, of course, or maybe even Izzy Crocker. They chummed around, I hear."

"I'm not sure who that is."

"She's a member of the Garden Club and the library board. Quite a bit of money in that family. Oh, excuse me, I have someone ready to pay for her purchase." She gave Shelby a broad smile and hurried back to the counter.

This Izzy Crocker was obviously someone Shelby had to track down, and soon. She went next door to Chocomania after, suddenly craving another truffle. That brought the day's count up to two. Tomorrow she'd start jogging. *Yeah, right.* She was pleased to see that it was still open. The bell above the door tinkled as she pushed it open.

"Hi, Erica. I hope you don't mind a late customer."

Erica looked up from her computer. She still looked fresh, even though her hair was even a bit more unkempt. "Customer? You want to eat some more truffles today?"

"What do you mean, more? The ones I picked up this

morning were for *our* customers. Well, maybe I had one. But that's all. Quality control, you know." Shelby smiled.

Erica laughed. "So do you need more already?"

"Just one for the road. It's such a long walk home, you know." Shelby waggled her eyebrows. "How was your day?"

Erica shrugged. "Business is starting to pick up. I'll bet this weekend will be a good one with the warm weather forecast. What about you?"

"Busy enough. Blye Castle makes for a great second location. I hope you're finding that to be the case too. I seem to be replacing your truffles a lot."

"You bet. I'm so pleased you thought to add them to the store. It wouldn't have been worthwhile for me to add a second location, not with having to bring in more staff. Plus, the gift store at the castle already has a big candy selection, doesn't it?"

"Candy, yes. But nothing can top truffles. I'll need to pick up some more tomorrow, by the way."

Erica grinned. "Lovely. Any more word on the murder?"

"No, but I meant to tell you, I got a visit the other night from Coast Guard Investigative Service Special Agent Zack Griffin, and I bumped into him again last night. Do you know him?"

"Of course I do. He spent a lot of summers here, and you know, the big-city boys were a big deal for us small-town girls. He's a nice guy and a good customer these days. Why? Interested?"

"Me? No. Well, maybe. I was just surprised he wanted to question me about the murder. I mean, since when do they do that? I thought they were all about immigration and smuggling. And, of course, incidents on the water. But then Cody Tucker started talking about the possibility of a smuggling operation being run through the grotto again. And, I have to admit, I think it makes sense, what with Zack Griffin being involved in the investigation and all."

"You mean like in Joe Cabana's day? Well, if it *was* happening, it wouldn't be booze, that's for sure." Shelby appreciated the fact that Erica didn't laugh at her speculation. "Drugs, maybe?" Erica shuddered.

"That's a sobering thought. I'd hate to think of anything drug related happening in the Bay."

"I have no idea other than wondering if it could be happening again. Do you think Loreena might have surprised some smugglers and they killed her?"

"Do you? Well, I think that's something you should wait to hear about, not go looking for answers on your own. You have this gleam in your eyes, and that's sort of unnerving to me."

"Well, it would be better if that's what it was, a professional smuggling ring or maybe a mobster family at work, rather than Matthew Kessler or one of the volunteers. Or even me," Shelby added as an afterthought. She shuddered.

"I doubt Chief Stone would believe there's organized crime in the area, and I'm certain she'd never believe you're a murderer."

"Why not? I had that argument with Loreena the day she died. But surely she must realize that would be a really flimsy reason to kill someone."

The front door opened as Shelby was speaking. Trudy Bryant answered before her daughter Erica could. “Tekla Stone can be one of the most stubborn women I know, next to your aunt that is, but she’s not stupid.”

“Good to hear. Thanks, Trudy.” Shelby glanced at her watch. “How were sales at the store today?”

“Pretty good, I’d say. You can tell it’s the start of the tourist season. I think Edie will be pleased.” She walked behind the counter and helped herself to a double-chocolate truffle and left two one-dollar bills beside the cash register.

Erica sighed. “It’s on the house, Mom.”

“You’ll never get rich that way.” Trudy popped the truffle whole into her mouth.

Erica pretended to look hurt. But Shelby could see the twitch at the side of her mouth. “Maybe I should get going.”

Erica laughed. “I’ll survive the verbal abuse.”

Shelby felt a pang. The bond between a mother and daughter. That’s what she’d been missing. She pushed the thought aside.

“By the way, Shelby, you’re still on for the book club next Wednesday?”

“For sure. But I’m curious, what did you mean about the chief, Trudy?”

“Well, have you ever seen Edie and Tekla when they’re in the same room?”

“Yes, and there’s a lot of tension there. But Edie hasn’t really told me what’s behind it.”

“Well, don’t tell Edie I told you anything, but they grew up together and were close friends until sophomore year of high school, when Tekla accused Edie of stealing her boyfriend, Jimmy Birch. And then Edie and Jimmy got married right after high school. Well, we were all shocked, more by the fact that Tekla thought she had a boyfriend than by the rest of it. But that story stayed with Tekla all these years, so she's not exactly harboring any good feelings for your family."

"That's silly. After all these years?"

Trudy shrugged. "That's just what I'm assuming because Tekla sure doesn't talk to me. Oh sure, she's nice in a fake kind of way when we meet on the street, but I know that's just for appearances. She has it in for me too because Edie and I are such good friends."

"I don't know how those two think. But I do know that Tekla Stone was tickled pink when Loreena Swan protested at the town council meeting after Edie announced she had asked you to come back and run the stores." Trudy looked momentarily abashed. "I guess I shouldn't have said that, but you know, Loreena thought Edie should promote one of us or hire someone from the community, you know, with an Alex Bay pedigree, like her nephew, Carter Swan."

"Seriously? To step in and temporarily run a family business?" Shelby couldn't believe it.

"I never said Loreena made a lot of sense most of the time. She just had a bee in her bonnet about it. Anyway, Edie stood right up at the meeting and told Loreena to stick a cork in it. You know how Edie can be. Or maybe you don't. But that's so typical. Loreena had steam coming out of her ears as she stormed out. The whole village saw it or at least heard about it the next morning."

Shelby thought about it for a few minutes while she savored the truffle Trudy had handed her. Trudy picked up her original payment and put a five-dollar note down instead.

Finally, Shelby said, “If the whole village and the chief know that Edie and Loreena were at odds, that could be a reason to add Edie to the suspect list.” She frowned, but then immediately let out a small laugh. “But, of course, she couldn’t have done it. She can’t even get out of the house, much less over to the grotto. Who else in the village has had a run-in with Loreena?”

“Who didn’t might be a better question,” Erica answered. “She usually had to stick her nose into everyone’s business. Like the time the sisters had a new awning installed at Driftwood and Seawinds. Loreena thought it should be bright blue to fit in with the others on the block. The only thing is, there’s only one other awning, so their choice of green worked quite nicely. Loreena didn’t really push it too hard though, possibly out of respect for their advanced ages.”

Trudy snorted and looked surprised at the sound. “Sorry. You know, I don’t think she knew that word, honey. Respect.”

Shelby took a closer look at Trudy. Although she and Edie were the same age, Trudy seemed to positively ooze vitality. Maybe it was her hairstyle. Shiny silver hoop earrings peeked out from under the natural silver-gray hair that was cut in a straight bob falling just beneath her ears. Shelby had noticed she was less flamboyant in her clothing, too, sticking to a lot of black with pops of color in her discreet accessories. *Opposites attract.*

“Well, it seems to me there’s an overabundance of

possible suspects around. That should keep Matthew Kessler off the hot seat."

"What makes you think he's in that position?" Trudy asked. "I know it hasn't been exactly easy for him since he moved here, so I hope they leave him alone. And I can't imagine any of the volunteers doing it. What would be the motive?"

Shelby shrugged. "I don't know, although I do know that he and Loreena were often at odds. Chief Stone seems to have her sights set on him." Surely Trudy must know how her aunt felt about Matthew, but if she didn't, it wasn't Shelby's place to tell her.

"That's another of Tekla's faults. She wears blinders most times, and since Matthew comes with a bit of a reputation, she's bound and determined to make him into the bad guy when one is needed."

"Now that's really too bad. Edie seems to think well of him," Shelby ventured.

"Most of us do. Now"—Trudy leaned across the counter and patted Shelby's arm—"I wouldn't worry too much about all this. Tekla Stone, underneath it all, is one smart cookie, and besides, I've heard that both the State Police and Coast Guard are involved. That should keep things moving along the right path."

Erica nodded. "And I don't think you have anything to worry about."

"Have you ever heard Loreena ream someone out?" Shelby asked. "She can be quite vicious. I still shudder to think about it. That just could lead to a motive for murder. By the way, Trudy, do you know Izzy Crocker?"

"I do, but not as friends. You cannot live in this village without knowing the Crocker name. Why do you ask?"

"It was suggested I talk to her about my mother. Do you know where she lives?"

"Here, I'll write down the address," Trudy said, grabbing a small pad and pen from the counter. "From what I hear, she's not out and about as often as she used to be. You'll probably find her in her gardens most times, but it might be wise to call first."

Shelby nodded. "Thanks."

Finally, someone who might actually give her information about her mom. Now, if she could just find someone to tell her all about the killer.

# Chapter Sixteen

Shelby spotted Matthew the minute she stepped off the shuttle the next morning. He was wearing the same red plaid shirt from the other day with a ball cap pulled low over his forehead as he trimmed back the natural greenery that had grown into a wild mass over the spring. He made eye contact with her but gave no other sign that he'd seen her. She wanted to talk to him again but didn't want to cut into his work time, so she followed the others up the walkway to the castle. Later. Besides, she had her own work to get started on.

Taylor had asked if she could come in an hour late because of another doctor's appointment, and Shelby had readily agreed.

By the time the first of the tourist boats pulled up to the dock, Shelby had the coffee going and was enjoying her second cup of the day. She looked up expectantly as she heard the first visitors exclaiming when entering the castle. It had that effect on everyone. *Oh*s and *ah*s and *look at that*s emanated from the entry hall as those who were seeing it the first time took in its splendor. By the time they'd recovered, the volunteers would be handing out maps and brochures, offering to answer any questions.

Shelby had been alerted, as seemed to be usual on Fridays, that there'd be a school visit of twenty-five ten-year-olds coming on the second boat from the Bay. She doubted many would be wanting books, although chocolate truffles might be another matter. If she was lucky, Taylor would be in and working by then.

The first shopper through the door was a well-dressed woman sporting an unnaturally blonde French twist and a thick southern accent. She wore a peach-colored sweater set and cream linen pants and carried a straw hat with a wide red, white, and blue scarf wrapped around it. Shelby thought she looked about Edie's age, even though the man who followed her in looked much older. His hair was totally white and he carried a cane, although it looked to be more for a dapper look than any actual function.

The woman walked straight to Shelby, hand outstretched. "You must be Shelby Cox. You look so much like your mama, I'd know you anywhere. I'm Priscilla Newmarket, but everyone calls me Prissy. I'd heard you were back in Alex Bay, and I just had to come around to see you." She had grabbed hold of Shelby's hand and was holding it tightly. "We live in Clayton, y'know."

Shelby was at a loss for words. Finally, someone who had known her mom, but from what an unexpected quarter! She wasn't sure what to say. She felt so overwhelmed by this larger-than-life southern lady. Shelby could actually picture

Prissy in a long skirt with a hoop at the bottom and matching bonnet.

"Now, do tell me what you've been up to all these years since your papa whisked you away. This is my dear husband, Jefferson, by the way." Prissy paused and took her first look around the bookstore. She focused back on Shelby. "So where did you go and when did you come back? And where is Edie? I'm really upset with that woman. She could have told me you were coming back, but instead I had to hear it on the grapevine. Now, where were we?"

Shelby thought it easiest to answer in reverse order, and besides, she'd already forgotten what the first question was. "My Aunt Edie is at home recuperating from knee replacement surgery, so she asked me to come and run the stores until she's back at it." She wouldn't fill in too much info until she had a feel for the woman. In fact, even then she probably wouldn't share her life story. It really wasn't her style.

"Well, I am just so tickled to see you. What are you now? Thirty? And how is Edie doing? Do you think she'd like visitors? Should I send some flowers or a fruit basket?"

Shelby took a deep breath, hoping to calm Prissy, who talked a mile a minute. She herself chose to answer at a slow, measured pace. "I'm twenty-nine, and although I'm sure Edie would enjoy seeing you, it's best to call ahead. I think fruit would be a good choice."

Prissy clapped her hands. "Oh, goody. I'll do that. Now, you must be wondering who I am. It seems your mama and I married ourselves Yankee boys and moved to Alex Bay at the same time. I'm from Raleigh, North Carolina, so we didn't know each other until we moved here, but we became close friends. My Beau was born around the same time as you, and then we moved to Clayton, where Jefferson was hoping to construct a large hotel, but it turns out his business partner wanted to do it in Alex Bay. But we weren't about to move back here. So, here we are, still in Clayton after all these years. It's only a twenty-minute drive, after all."

"And did they build a hotel here?" Shelby knew there were several and wondered which it might be.

"Sadly, no. The partners had a parting of ways. Jefferson wanted to take Alex Bay back to its glory days of wooden boat building and elegant living, but his partner was more a speedboat man. In the end, Jefferson decided to retire, so now I have him all to myself." She looked over at him and gave him a huge smile.

Either he had hidden radar or he was used to responding periodically to his wife. He looked up from the book he was holding and smiled in return.

"Now, I'd love to stay and chat all day with you, dear, but we want to hop the next boat and attend to some business in the village. I just had to come over and say hey to you. I want to have you over to visit us real soon at our place. We have a gorgeous view of the water, y'know, and we'll get all caught up." She gave Shelby a big hug before turning to her husband.

"Are you buying that, Jefferson?" Prissy asked.

He looked over again and seemed surprised they were leaving. He put the book down, much to Shelby's regret, nodded at her, and followed his wife out the door. Shelby realized she hadn't been able to get a question in edgewise but hoped to make up for it one day soon, now that the contact had been made. She wondered how hard it would be to find Priscilla Newmarket in Clayton.

Taylor arrived, as promised, and along with her, a handful of book browsers. She handled questions on the floor while Shelby kept an eye on those needing to make a purchase. It turned out, even without the school kids, to be a busy day, much to everyone's surprise. Tuesdays, especially Tuesdays in early May, were rarely overwhelming.

Once everything had settled down, Shelby left Taylor in charge and finally went in search of Matthew. She found him in his workshop, gathering some tools for what looked to be a repair job, if the hammer, nails, and saw were any indication.

"Hey, Matthew. How's it going?"

He looked startled. She could have bet he didn't get many visitors back here.

"Good, I guess. Nothing unusual happening, anyway. I see it's a busy morning in the castle, though."

"It is, and I'm relieved."

"Oh, yeah? Why so? I mean, I thought everything was going well with the store."

"It is, but I just want to have dynamite sales, every day if possible, to impress Aunt Edie."

He chuckled. "Oh, I'm sure she's just fine with how things are going under your watch. You know you have nothing to prove."

"Just that I can actually run a store or two."

"And you think Edie isn't quite sure about your capabilities? Is she always phoning to see how things are going? Does she expect reports every night? I don't think so. Just relax, kid. You're doing fine."

"Thanks, Matthew. I needed to hear that." *Time to get back on track.* "Do you get a set break time or anything?" She thought she might treat him to a coffee from the Sugar Shack and they could have a chat at the lookout by the grotto, mainly because few tourists knew about the spot and they were unlikely to be interrupted.

Matthew grunted. "I run by my own schedule, Shelby. As long as it looks like everything is being attended to, I do what I want and when." He held up a hammer. "Time to replace that missing board on the picnic bench in back. Why do you ask?"

"I just was hoping I could treat you to a coffee break and we could have a little talk."

"Hm, you've got a lot of questions on your mind, I'm betting."

"You could say that."

He stared at her a moment before answering. "Okay. Coffee would be nice, and we might as well get this over with."

She waited while he put his tools back and locked the shed door, then took the lead along the narrow path to the Sugar Shack. She felt some guilt because of his reaction. He must be thinking she was going to query him about his past. Although she was dying to know the details, she'd wait until he felt comfortable enough with her to make the decision to share. If it ever happened. She paid for the two coffees and then led the way to the grotto lookout.

"This is a great vantage point to watch the channel," she began. "Why is it out of bounds for the tourists? Or is that just because of what's happened?"

Matthew pointed downward. "No, it's not recent. It's too dangerous. We can't have families up here with kids running amok. If someone went over, that would be it."

Shelby eyed where he was pointing. "I get that."

Although a variety of greenery, including all sizes of deciduous and evergreen trees, seemed to frame the edge of the lawn, Shelby knew there were no fences to block off a downward trajectory to the rocks below. She couldn't even begin to estimate how far such a fall would be, but she knew it wouldn't be pretty.

"Why don't they just fence it off?"

"I've never heard. I guess they just figure that some areas are best left to nature rather than as another tourist lookout. And they still won't let tourists into the grotto."

"I saw that. I wonder how the investigation is going," she commented as casually as she could.

He shrugged. "They don't tell me anything. Just ask questions. And I'll bet you have some, also."

"I don't really know what to ask, but it's bugging me that all this is going on around us and we're kept in the dark."

"Why does it matter to you? Just let the police go about their business."

*Interesting, coming from you. And, obviously, he knows*

*nothing about Edie's desire to help him.* "Because I keep hearing about people who had connections with Loreena, one of them somebody I care about, who had possible, well, tenuous really, motives."

He looked at her sharply. "Like who?"

"Well, my Aunt Edie for one, although like I said, it's tenuous at best. And then there's me, also tenuous, I admit. But Loreena and I did have that argument the day she died. And Loreena's nephew was in the store the other day, and I got to thinking, what, if anything, does he gain from her death? And then, there's you." There, she'd said it.

The look on his face shouted surprise. "Me?" he snorted. "I'm always in someone's bad books and expect I will remain there. Don't you go giving it another thought." His expression turned serious. "Although I do appreciate your concern, Shelby. Now what's Edie on the hot seat for?"

"Oh, it's just the fact that Loreena got so mad when Edie said she'd asked me to come and take over rather than employing Loreena's nephew. Or so I've heard."

"Employ him? Loreena wanted Edie to sell to him."

"What?"

"You heard right. That was one of the things Loreena did best—meddled in others' affairs, and her nephew was not immune. Secretly, she thought he should do more with his life than sit on his trust fund." Matthew took a sip of his coffee and looked surprised that he'd already finished it.

Shelby's eyebrows shot up. "How would you know that?"

He grinned. "I'm not above eavesdropping, you know. I heard her reading him the riot act one afternoon right over there in the gardens. He, true to his upbringing, ignored her."

"Maybe he's got a motive, although I'd think overbearing aunt isn't the best excuse for murder."

"Nor is what you say about Edie. It should have been the other way around." He stood up and looked like he was ready to leave. "What else worries you about her?"

Shelby shrugged. "I guess I'm a bit worried that Chief Stone has it in for her. If that's truly the case, then she could manipulate the investigation to give Edie a hard time, at the very least."

"Sounds like you don't have much faith in the law, and I'd join you in that. But from what I've seen of Chief Stone, she's pretty much on the up-and-up. Although I wish she'd find another hobby."

"What do you mean? What's her hobby?"

"Me."

# Chapter Seventeen

When she woke the next morning, Shelby's brain scrambled to catch up to all that her subconscious had been working on while she slept. First and foremost was trying to find something that would get Matthew off the hook. For Edie's sake as well as his own, despite what he'd said.

She realized right away that the statement she had given the police was part of the problem. She'd seen his red shirt and he'd then admitted to being in the area. His explanation all sounded reasonable and true, but she knew that Chief Stone had taken it another way. Practically as proof of guilt.

Well, there was nothing Shelby could do about her statement now. She had told the truth. But the other thing she'd mentioned was hearing a small motored boat. What had it been doing in that area? Was it part of the smuggling ring? If there even was one, but somehow that boat had to tie in. Unless Loreena was killed by someone from town who'd managed to blend in on the island. That wouldn't be hard to do. Or maybe she'd been killed by Carter.

Okay, so she had two scenarios. One involved smugglers, and she knew she had no hope at all in following that line of inquiry. She'd have to believe Zack could do it and that he might share information at some point. Or maybe Cody had done some more reading on the subject and had some theories. She hadn't seen him since opening day at the castle. She'd have to check his schedule and make sure to stop by the main store to visit with him.

The second scenario, in which someone from town was the murderer, she could handle by asking more targeted questions. She would ask Edie and Trudy to come up with a list of people and the reasons why they might be guilty. As for Carter, she thought a face-to-face chat was in order. Relatives were always on the suspect list. She knew that from TV and from reading far too mysteries, and while she suspected there wasn't tons of money or the title to a different castle on a nearby island in the family, relationships could get awfully entangled and even, sometimes, messy.

She leapt out of bed energized and ready to put her plan into action. As she ate her cereal, she phoned Edie and asked for a list, then she asked if she had Carter's phone number.

"Be careful with that one," Edie warned. "I don't like him very much. He seems two-faced, if you ask me. Although he was the apple of Loreena's eye and her only living relative, or so I believe. Maybe that's something you could ask him about. Also, Chrissie Halstead may have her hand in this also, although I can't think of any reason offhand except for helping Carter. By the way, thanks for doing this, Shelby.

Just be careful and promise me you'll back off right away if something or someone seems a bit hinky."

"Hinky?" She stifled a chuckle.

"You know what I mean."

"I do. Now, you have a restful day and I'll let you know if I find out anything."

"And like I told you before, you should definitely try to have a chat with Mae-Beth Warner. She's in charge of the workshops. She's usually aware of most things happening in the castle."

"I almost forgot. Thanks, I will."

Shelby hurriedly showered and dressed, grabbed a latte at Chocomania, promising Erica they'd get together on the weekend, and just barely made it to the shuttle.

After going through the store's opening routine, Shelby excused herself, leaving Taylor in charge, and went in search of Mae-Beth Warner. She found her in the back office, off the pantry, going through a stack of notes at the desk. The only other furniture in the tiny room was a filing cabinet, a chair for a visitor, and an old-fashioned scuffed oak coat stand, the type that stood upright with large brass hooks near the top.

She knocked on the open door, hoping not to startle Mae-Beth, who looked like she would be more at home playing euchre at the seniors' center.

"Oh, come in, Shelby. It is Shelby, isn't it?" Mae-Beth wore her silver-blue hair in a pageboy that reached her shoulders. The coloring was obviously one of the favorites at local beauty shops, Shelby thought, because she'd seen so many retirees sporting it lately.

"It is. You have a good memory, since we only met once, and that was before the castle opened for the season."

"I don't have very good knees, which is why I'm grateful for the elevator in Blye, but I do pride myself on my memory."

"Great. That might be a big help, actually. I wondered if you might have a couple of minutes? There's something I'd like to talk to you about."

"Sure, dear. Have a seat. Just stick that pile of flyers on the floor. I must find some way to add some counter space in here, but I think it's a lost cause. Anyway, what would you like to know?"

Shelby did as she was directed, sitting on the only other chair in the room, and then leaned forward, trying to draw Mae-Beth into something conspiratorial. "Well, I'm sort of asking questions to try and find out what happened to Loreena. And I thought, with your position here and at the Heritage Society, you might be able to fill me in on some things. For instance, can you think of anyone who might have wanted to harm her? Maybe not kill her, because, who knows, there might have been an argument and, in the heat of it, Loreena was pushed and fell into the grotto." That thought had just come to her as she was talking, and it sounded right.

"So, you mean, it wasn't deliberate or, rather, premeditated?"

"Exactly. You know how, when you're angry, it's so easy

to just say or do something without really thinking about the consequences?" The minute she said it, she realized that calm, sweet, concerned Mae-Beth would never do anything like that.

Mae-Beth's reaction confirmed her suspicions. She shook her head. "Not really, dear, but I'm sure it can happen like that. And, keeping that in mind, I can't really think of anyone here at Blye who might get that angry at her."

*Except me. Or maybe, Matthew.*

"But maybe at the Heritage Society," Mae-Beth continued. "There's always a lot of politicking going on behind the scenes, and Loreena made sure she was in on all of it."

"Politicking about what?"

"Oh, this and that. Purchases, for example. Ticket prices. There's a lot of financials that go into keeping Blye Castle open to the public, you know, even though we have a benefactor."

"I know nothing about any of that. Can you tell me more?"

"Oh, I'm not the best person to talk to. I don't have a head for figures. Never did," she added with a chuckle. "But I just thought of something. Regan Jones—you've probably met her, too—she's a tour guide here. Well, she and Loreena have had several sharp conversations about Regan's appearance. It started last summer when she started getting tattoos, and they picked up right where they left off this year, too. Of course, when Regan showed up with a nose ring, that really set Loreena off."

"What can you tell me about Regan?"

Mae-Beth looked startled. "Tell you? Well, I probably shouldn't even have said that."

"I know. I'm feeling uncomfortable doing the asking. But it's what Aunt Edie wants."

"Edie? Oh well, that's that, then. She's such a wonderful, caring woman," Mae-Beth said, straightening her back. "I know you have the best intentions, dear. So, what can I tell you?

"Did the arguments get serious?"

Mae-Beth appeared deep in thought. When she answered, she looked relieved. "No, I don't think it was ever really serious. It was mainly about her appearance. And then, Regan had some suggestions about how things should be done, and Loreena had her own thoughts about it. Like with tours of school students. Loreena had it all laid out, what parts of the castle they should be allowed to go into, how long they could stay in the gift shop, even though I wasn't consulted about that, and even a time allotment in your store. That certainly got Edie's back up the odd time."

*Uh-oh.*

"Now, Regan, she thought they should just be allowed to roam. The volunteers know their duties and can keep an eye on things, and if something happens, they can call security."

"Why was Loreena against that?"

"Security could lead to a scene of some sort and that could end up on YouTube. You know how kids are these days. At least, that's what Loreena thought."

Shelby considered the information for a few moments. "So, how was it resolved?"

"It never was. It was ongoing, but as you can see, it wasn't anything earth-shattering. Regan, tattoos and all, would certainly never kill Loreena over it, if that's what you're thinking."

That was precisely what Shelby *was* thinking, but she wasn't about to admit it at this point. Mainly because it did sound like a fairly unlikely reason to commit murder. Bummer.

"Can you think of anyone else who might have had a rough time with Loreena?"

Mae-Beth looked like she was giving it serious thought. "I guess I have to admit we didn't really get along. But I certainly wouldn't do her any harm. I can't even kill a spider."

Shelby smiled at that admission. She couldn't claim that. "May I ask what upset you about her?"

"The volunteers, of course. These are our friends and neighbors in the community. We're all here because we love what we're doing. Blye Castle has such an amazing history, and we're all just so proud to be a part of this. But Loreena treated us like we were slave labor. She gave us no respect, and she thought our whole lives should revolve around this job; thus, we should be eager to obey her every command. That's not how family treats family."

Shelby noted the rise in Mae-Beth's voice. She was certainly passionate about Loreena's perceived mistreatment of the volunteers. Could that be a motive for murder? She looked a bit closer at Mae-Beth and decided that she was no killer. There was no way she could picture that.

"Thanks for talking to me, Mae-Beth. I hope I didn't ask

anything upsetting." She realized she truly meant that. She cared about Mae-Beth and her dedication to Blye and all those involved in sharing its wonders with the world.

Mae-Beth seemed to relax and smiled as she assured Shelby that was not the case. "I hope I helped a bit. By the way, you know you look a lot like your mother, don't you? She was such a pretty young thing."

"My mother?" Shelby was floored. Here she'd been wanting to find out more about her mom, and Mae-Beth might be able to help. "You knew her? What do you remember about her?"

"Oh, she was such a social butterfly. She took the village by storm, as they say. I didn't really know her, just to nod at in the grocery store. It was such a shame that she died so young."

Shelby wanted to ask her more, but the phone rang and Mae-Beth signaled goodbye. Shelby would have to make a point of visiting Mae-Beth again real soon. She tried to put that conversation out of her mind for now and focus on a day of bookselling.

Back at the bookstore, Shelby was pleased to see how crowded the space looked as she suggested some titles of nonfiction books set in the islands to a couple dressed in matching beige walking shorts and red polo shirts with logos for a Dallas golf course on the top left corner. She learned they were part of a bus tour from Texas and felt a particular thrill that her bookstore would be remembered when they got back home.

After the numbers thinned and before the next boat

pulled in, Shelby decided it was time to phone Carter Swan. She'd thought the best tactic with him might be meeting for coffee at the Coffee Café on her way home. She didn't want to meet him at Erica's just in case it didn't go well. Defeat was better handled alone. He agreed immediately, which took her totally by surprise.

As the rest of the day unfolded, she planned how to handle the meeting with Carter. She didn't have much time to dwell on it, as customers just seemed to keep appearing, much to her delight.

"What a busy day! A Saturday typical of summer, which is always good," Taylor said as they finally closed the store door behind them. "That's the fun thing about this business. You never know what the day will bring, although I would have thought that, with this fabulous weather, we would have had fewer customers."

"Why's that?" Shelby asked. "I'd think that's when they'd be wanting to take the boat cruises."

"Oh, for sure, but usually when they stop here, they tour the castle and then spend the rest of the time wandering outside. Blye has a reputation for its gardens that's equal to its interior."

Shelby nodded. That shouldn't have surprised her. Nothing about this marvelous castle and island should have been a surprise anymore. She realized that she, too, felt under its spell and understood totally the loyalty the staff had to the place. The splendor was apparent. What she wanted to know was more about its history, particularly in case the ghost of Joe Cabana had arisen to inspire smuggling once again. If that's what was going on. Sometimes it seemed so logical a conclusion, while at other times, she realized it might be completely fanciful. She was letting the allure of the castle and its history influence her thinking. But it still niggled her as to why Zack was involved in the investigation.

For all her faults, Loreena didn't seem to be an expected murder victim, nor was it likely she was involved in any smuggling scheme, so that might not have been why she was killed. Although Shelby could very well picture her taking a break and strolling to the grotto, only to stumble upon the smuggling operation and get murdered in the process. It could be as simple as that, being in the wrong place at the wrong time.

That probably meant the person she should be speaking to was Zack Griffin, but she knew he wasn't about to tell her much. She'd have to figure out a way of persuading him to do so. And she still had Carter to talk to. If it wasn't smuggling or something to do with someone at the castle, it could be family matters after all.

* * *

Carter sat at one of the tables for two at the far end of the Coffee Café, his attention focused on his smartphone. Shelby picked up an espresso at the counter and joined him, waiting a few moments until he acknowledged her. He looked like he owned the place, with that Roman nose and full lips. He looked like he belonged in the castle. Now where had that come from? But she mustn't romanticize him, not when the bookstore was under attack.

She tried not to let her irritation show. As much as she relied on her smartphone, she tried not to be absorbed in it when others were around, especially someone who'd come for a meeting. She took a sip of her espresso and tried to focus on the flavor. Nice crema. It was a good rival to Erica's, but she certainly wouldn't tell her that.

Carter finally looked up and then placed the phone on the table, not bothering to apologize. He didn't even greet her.

"I'll be right back," was all he said, and she watched as he went to order his own drink. He wore expensive-looking jeans that hugged him in all the right places, the kind that were also thread-worn, also in the right places. She knew the equivalent in the female section of the store cost more than she'd ever spend on a partial pair of jeans.

When Carter rejoined her, Shelby didn't feel the need to be polite. She knew she was being a bit childish, but she couldn't help it. *Hmm, childish and fanciful all in one day.* She'd have to do something about that. She waited until he'd placed his cup down and then asked him, "How well did you and your aunt get along?"

She took a bit of satisfaction at the look of incredulity on his face.

"What makes you think you can ask me that?"

She was ready for him. "Because I understand that Loreena wanted you to take over the running of my bookstore while my Aunt Edie was recuperating. For starters, that seems awfully overbearing to me, and I want to know if you were a part of coming up with that plan."

He sat back in his chair and barked out a small laugh. "You've got to be kidding. You're worried about that? Can you seriously think I was ever interested in a small-time operation like that? It was completely Loreena's plan, and I don't think she was thinking clearly. I think it had more to do with her wanting to take total control of everything to do with the castle. Since your store is in it, that's fair game to her. Or, rather, it was. I don't know about her master plan"—he waved his hands around in the air to emphasize his point—"but it wasn't mine. I have other plans."

"I also heard that her alternate plan was to buy the bookstore for you to run."

"Again, I have other plans. She never had to buy me anything. It's all gossip, you know. Everyone has to have a piece of what's going on, in this case, the sensationalism of Aunt Loreena's death. So, if I were you"—he pointed his cup at her—"I'd ignore it all and just get on with selling books. And that way you'll also stop prying into my life, which is absolutely no business of yours."

Shelby said nothing. She didn't want to stop this flow but realized he had no more to say. She tried desperately to come up with another plan of attack. It dawned on her that she knew how to handle him. She'd had to deal with a couple of authors with attitude over the years.

"If you think about it, anything to do with the bookstore has everything to do with me. My questions weren't meant to probe your personal life, though."

He looked surprised and didn't answer for a few seconds, then his shoulders relaxed and his glare softened. "You're right, I'm behaving badly. It's not you. I'm just really upset by all this, you know?" He reached out and almost touched her hand but stopped and pulled it back. "My aunt and I had an argument the day before she died, and I've just been wishing it hadn't happened or that I'd been able to apologize before all this. She was my only family and now she's gone."

Shelby couldn't think of a thing to say, she was so taken off guard. She hadn't expected Carter to open up like this, and she felt totally uncomfortable about it. There went the idea of the villain she'd painted in her mind. She had to say something; he was looking at her. "I'm sorry."

He nodded, seemingly satisfied, then finished his coffee. He glanced at his watch. "I've got to meet Chrissie." He nodded and walked off.

She sat for a few more minutes, even though her own coffee cup was empty. What had she learned before his emotional moment? Well, mainly that, as he said, the bookstore idea had been Loreena's plan. Could she believe him when he said it wasn't his plan also? Who might know more about it that she could ask? And more importantly, should she be concerned? Realistically, what would he get out of taking over the bookstore? She couldn't think of a thing. And therefore, it probably had nothing to do with the murder. Another dead end, so to speak.

Shelby decided she hadn't really gotten anywhere, except yet another coffee. Her phone rang just as she grabbed her purse to leave. She saw it was Edie and sat back down again.

"Hi, Edie. What's up?"

"It's Matthew. The police took him in for more

questioning a few hours ago, and I haven't heard from him since. He was supposed to join us for supper, and that was twenty minutes ago."

Shelby looked at her watch. It was that late? "Well, they might still be talking to him, and it could mean nothing more than that."

"I know that Tekla Stone, remember. If she can drag it out to inconvenience him, she'll do just that. But last time he called me was last night. I haven't heard a thing from him today."

"Then how do you know the police have him?"

"Buddy Hodgson saw them pull up to the main dock in their boat, and they had Matthew with them."

What to do? What to say? She didn't want Edie confronting Chief Stone again, but that's just what might happen. She heard herself asking, "Do you want me to stop over at the police station? I'm not very far away."

"Oh, yes please, Shelby." She could hear the relief in Edie's voice.

"Okay."

"I know you probably think I'm just being silly, but I have a terrible feeling about this."

"Well, you have to promise me you'll stop worrying if I agree to do this. How about it?"

"Fine."

"Just see that you stick to that," Shelby said, hoping to tease her aunt into a better mood. "I'll let you know what I find out."

She hoped Edie couldn't hear the worry in her voice. This certainly wasn't good news, but even more worrisome was the question of why they'd brought Matthew back in. She refused to believe he was the murderer. He couldn't be. Could he?

# Chapter Eighteen

Shelby hoped to find Chief Stone in her office, but if not, she decided she would next try the chief's house. She probably wouldn't be very welcome after the last visit with Edie, but she had to try. She headed home for her car.

As she figured, the CLOSED sign hung on the door of the police station. Even though it was the weekend, Shelby had learned that they kept regular hours thanks to the addition of several part-time officers for the summer months. She'd hoped someone, Chief Stone in particular, might be found behind a desk, but that obviously wasn't about to happen. She groaned getting back in her car and was about to leave when the police SUV turned into the lot. However, it was Lieutenant Chuck Fortune in the driver's seat. Shelby waited until he had parked, then jumped out of her car.

"Hi, Lieutenant Fortune. I'd been hoping to find the chief here."

"Nope. She had to go out of town on business." He leaned into the front seat and pulled out a laptop computer and his jacket.

"That's too bad. I wanted to talk to her. Do you know when she'll be back?"

"Sometime later tonight, she said." He straightened to his full six-foot-plus height and shut the door of the SUV, clicking it locked.

"Oh. I hope everything's all right." Surely she hadn't transported Matthew someplace out of reach?

He nodded. "As far as I know. She's not one for sharing much, you know. She's over in Clayton, so it won't take her long to get back once she's finished her business."

Shelby mulled over the fact that she wouldn't get any information until the next morning at the earliest. And also the news that Chief Stone had had to go to Clayton. About what? Something to do with the case? Wasn't that where Matthew was from?

She had already turned to walk back to her car when she looked back and asked, "Is Matthew Kessler still being held? I assume he's not here." Where would they keep him when the office closed?

Fortune looked a bit surprised. "Not with it locked up, he's not. Last I heard, the chief was going to drop him off at the State Police office on Route Twelve on her way out of town."

"Do you think I could talk to him? Would they let me?"

"Probably not. It's not as if he's under arrest, but since you're not a relative or otherwise involved, I doubt they'd agree. If he's still there, that is."

She thought about asking Fortune to make the call but then decided she'd drive there herself instead. It was probably less than ten minutes away.

"Now, if you'll excuse me, I have a pile of phone calls to make before leaving, and I know Taylor has something special planned for dinner tonight." A wide grin spread across his face at the thought.

Shelby smiled back. "Thanks. Enjoy your dinner."

She got back in her car, checked the GPS on her phone, then turned right on Walton Street. After about ten minutes, she pulled into the parking lot of the NY State Police. The building looked imposingly official and she had second thoughts about going inside, but only for an instant. She glanced around the room before walking over to the counter, where an older-looking uniformed officer sat. He watched her approach, and when she asked for Lieutenant Dwayne Guthrie, he told her he was off duty. So she tried asking if she could speak to someone being held there, namely Matthew. He motioned her to have a seat in the waiting area while he picked up the phone. After a short discussion, he waved her back over.

"He's no longer here," he told her, watching her reaction.

"Really? He's been released? Everything's okay then?"

The officer shrugged. "All I know is someone from the CGIS came and got him. I wasn't here, so I don't have all the details."

Shelby felt her jaw drop. Zack. Was it Zack? It had to be, although she probably shouldn't assume he'd be working on this all alone. She thanked the officer, and as she walked back to her car, her mind played with the reasons the Coast Guard would want Matthew. Obviously she'd been right about the smuggling. They couldn't still believe Matthew was involved. Or could they? And where were they keeping him? She tried calling Zack, but it went to voicemail, which made her even more agitated. She checked her watch. It was getting sort of late to head to his office, even if she'd known how to get there. She started the car and pointed it in the direction of Alex Bay. On a whim, she went straight down Church, turning left at the end, in search of Zack's house. How hard could it be to find with that red paint? He could at least give her an explanation and update.

She spotted his black Jeep Cherokee in the driveway and a light shining in his living room. Was he entertaining? And where was Matthew? She just had to know. She parked beside his Jeep and made her way around to the front steps, pausing a moment before ringing the doorbell.

Zack opened the door in an instant, leading her to believe he'd seen her pull up. She thought briefly and gratefully that she hadn't paused to put on lipstick or check her hair. No need for him to think she'd glammed up just for him. This wasn't a social call, after all.

He grinned. "Now, this is an unexpected pleasure. Come in."

"You may not feel like that for long."

"Uh-oh. I guess that means this has something to do with the case."

She'd followed him into the foyer and then waited for him to turn to face her. "Yes, it does. I'm wondering what you've done with Matthew Kessler."

Zack looked amused. "I haven't *done* anything with or to him. What makes you think I did?"

"I was just over at the State Police building, after checking at the local police office, looking for him. I was told the CGIS had taken him in. That's you."

"Well, thanks for thinking of me as the face of the Coast Guard, but I didn't 'take him in.' I gave him a lift home, or rather, to the shuttle."

"He's back on the island?"

"That he is. Now, can I interest you in some dinner? I just put together a pasta carbonara and I'm really a great cook, if not a modest one." He looked hopeful, but Shelby wasn't to be deterred.

"But why would you even do that unless you wanted some information from him? Maybe something to do with smuggling?"

Now Zack looked annoyed. "Is that a no to my invitation?"

Shelby felt a bit off balance. "I'm sorry, yes, it's a no. I'm having dinner with Edie, and she'd heard Matthew had been taken to the station yet again and was worried about him. So, here I am."

"Well, you can report to your aunt that he's home, has not been harmed, and although it's against my better judgement to tell you this, we asked him a few questions and that was the end of it. But, if I know Chief Stone, Matt Kessler will probably be questioned a few more times before this case is closed." He glanced back at the kitchen. "You know, this really is none of your business, and if you continue poking your nose in, one or the other of the enforcement agencies is eventually going to either make certain no one talks to you or even charge you for interfering. Take that as a friendly warning."

"Friendly? Friendly would be helping me understand what's going on."

"What do you think is going on?"

"I think that either Loreena's murder is tied to a smuggling operation or there could be two separate things happening at once. I mean, why else would you be involved if it's not smuggling?"

"I can name any number of reasons. The CGIS is not a single-issue agency, you know. And I am part of only one of its many facets. In fact, why don't you stop by one day when I'm in the station and I'll be happy to show you around. It will probably be an eye-opener. Now, I don't mean to be rude, but my dinner is getting cold."

She straightened her spine and bit back the urge to point out he *was* being rude. Sort of.

"Fine. I'm sorry to have just barged in. Enjoy your meal, and thanks for the invitation."

He nodded, and she left as quickly as she could manage without looking like she really wanted to run.

She felt his eyes on her even though he'd shut the door. She didn't look back as she made her way back to the car and drove off. She went straight to the Mango Lagoon, picked up the order Edie had phoned in, and then drove on to Edie's, trying not to think how foolish she'd acted at Zack's.

Edie had the table all set when Shelby arrived. While unpacking the food, she explained about tracking Matthew through the various agencies to finally find out he was back at his house.

Edie looked perplexed.

"I thought you'd be relieved that he's not being held," Shelby said.

"I am, believe me I am, and I'm grateful to you for finding out, but I wonder why he hasn't called to tell me. I think I'll give him a ring. You go ahead and eat, Shelby. I'll just go in the other room and call."

"No, I can wait. I'm not starving. You stay right where you are, and I'll go outdoors and enjoy what's left of the sunshine." She walked to the door before Edie could object.

It truly was a beautiful spot, and Shelby tried to picture her dad as a young boy playing in the yard. Somehow she couldn't get beyond the young boy part. She could imagine Edie climbing one of the many trees or lying on the grass looking up at the stars. Shelby wanted to try that one night. Maybe after she moved in with Edie.

When had she made that decision? She was struck by the sudden force of her conviction on the matter. She'd wanted to be on her own and Edie had finally conceded, but Shelby knew she'd have to find someplace for the winter. It did seem natural to move into the family home, aside from the fact that there'd be little privacy. Now, when had she decided to stay?

She heard Edie calling and went back inside. She tried to determine from Edie's face if it had been a gratifying conversation. She finally asked, as she removed the lids from the containers, "What happened?"

She heard Edie sigh. "He's done in, that's why he went home. In fact, he'd fallen asleep on the couch as soon as he sat down. I shouldn't have disturbed him. It's just that I worry about him. I was afraid he'd get depressed again. It was a long journey out of depression for him when his wife died."

Shelby wasn't sure what to say. She wasn't used to dealing with such intimate or dramatic details of someone's life. She'd always viewed others' lives from the outside.

Finally, Edie started dishing out some food onto her own plate. "I hope I've thanked you for doing all this, Shelby. I'm hoping the fact that they let him go means that's the end of it. Matthew seems to think there's nothing for them to go on and told me not to worry."

Shelby filled her own plate and nodded. "I guess that's good advice."

"I'm a Cox, Shelby. You must know by now that we're a worrying lot. That's why I'm hoping you'll stick with it, and maybe you'll be able to dig up something that will lead us, and the police, to the killer."

She looked so hopeful that Shelby nodded, although deep down in the pit of her stomach, the food suddenly wasn't sitting so well.

# Chapter Nineteen

Shelby slept fitfully that night. She knew it was all because of her talk with Edie. And then there'd been her encounter with Zack, of course. How could she stick her nose in any more than she already had? She wasn't a trained investigator, nor was Edie, and she was certain the police would not be pleased. In particular, what would Tekla do if she found out? What *could* she do? Shelby didn't want to find out. And besides, Zack had warned her, and for some reason, that seemed to have more of an impact on her than anything else.

She'd checked the work schedule for the main store before going to bed and knew that Cody was opening that morning. She wanted to talk to him a bit more about the smuggling theory, so she had made sure Taylor would be able to open the castle bookstore. Then she grabbed a latte on her way to Bayside Books, arriving twenty minutes before opening time, and let herself in. She wandered around checking the shelves, then turned on the computer to take a look at the pending orders. It seemed like a lot of books to be ordering, which would translate to a big invoice coming due soon, but if the books were selling, they needed to get them in.

Cody walked in as she was sitting there and looked totally surprised.

“I didn’t know you’d be in today, Shelby. I thought Trudy was coming in at noon.”

“I just dropped by and won’t be staying long. I’m curious after our talk the other day about the possibility of smuggling. Have you had any more thoughts about that?”

She watched as he tossed his backpack into the back room and came back with a cup of coffee in his hand. Today his bow tie was red with black horizontal stripes running through it, worn with a short-sleeved black cotton shirt. She looked down at her own black jeans, not even skinnies, and loose-fitting T-shirt. She definitely had to start upping her game. Couldn’t have the employees looking more professional than the boss. The thought made her smile.

“I have been doing some more reading and thinking,” he said. “And I’m glad you’re here, because I thought of something I should’ve told you before.” He looked so intense as he leaned toward her, and yet excited, too. His normally straight and thick hair had curled around his ears, still damp from the shower. She noticed he was wearing a small silver stud in his left earlobe, either something new or she’d never been this close before.

“What should you have told me?”

“Well, you know I took some books out of the library about the area and its history?” He didn’t wait for her response. “I wasn’t the only one. Loreena Swan was there, too, looking through the same stacks.”

"Did you talk to her?"

"No. She was focused, man, didn't even seem to notice that I was there."

"When was this?"

"A couple of days before she died."

"Do you think she was checking on the same kind of information? Did she have a hunch about some smuggling using the grotto? Do you think it's tied in to her murder?" Shelby knew these weren't questions she should really be asking Cody, but she was mainly thinking out loud.

He shrugged. "No idea, but it seems sort of strange that even though she's lived here all her life, or so I hear, she was looking through the section about the Bay and the castle, and on that particular day. Don't ya think? I mean, who knew more about the history of the area, so why would she bother looking it up unless something new had happened?"

"I agree. Now, if there was a way to know what it meant, I'd be thrilled."

He sat down on a pile of boxes, looking dejected. "Yeah. We'll never know."

Shelby roused herself. "Back to the smuggling. Do you think it's possible there's current-day smuggling going on?"

"I guess so. Anything's possible, right? You just have to have the means, method, and motive." He paused to grin. "I know, I've been reading Christie again. Why not ask that Coast Guard guy?"

Shelby chuckled. "I've tried. He thinks it's none of my business."

Cody smiled, showing off a perfect set of white teeth.

"He's probably right. But maybe we don't need him. Maybe we could stake out the grotto and see for ourselves."

Shelby almost choked when she heard that. "Uh, intriguing idea, but where would we start? We have no idea if it's happening, for starters. And if it is, we don't know their schedule. And even if we did, we'd have to figure out what to do about Matthew. I mean, do we tell him or go behind his back? And I know he's keeping an ear open for stray boats, so it would be awfully hard to get to the island without his knowing." Shelby had stuck her hand in the air and was counting off the reasons on her fingers as she went along. She now spread her hands wide and shrugged. "I can't even begin to figure out where to start."

Cody grinned. "You're probably right, but you do agree? There is a chance that someone is back in the smuggling biz? Otherwise, you wouldn't have asked me." He looked pleased with himself.

"You got me there. You're really into this. What are you planning on studying at college?" Something to do with law, she'd bet.

"Business, which I think sucks. It's mainly because that's what my dad wants me to do." He tugged at his left earlobe, not looking too happy.

"Gee, that would be great, having a business student working here in the summer. I might expand your duties." She raised her eyebrows. The question was out there.

He looked surprised. "Oh, yeah . . . I want to stay working part-time; it's just I don't think you should count on me doing anything great for you in the business end of things."

He leaned a bit closer to her and lowered his voice, even though they were alone. "What I'm really hoping is that once I'm on campus, I can switch into something real cool. Dad will blow a gasket, but it is my life, right?"

Shelby didn't want to get on the bad side of Mr. Tucker, although she'd never met him, but she could see that Cody needed some reassurance. She'd never been one for parents interfering in their kids' futures. But she was also his boss and felt it wasn't her place to get involved in this discussion.

"I hope you figure it out," was all she said. She glanced at the clock on the wall. "Yikes, I've got to get over to the castle. Thanks, Cody. It's been good talking this over with you. And if you come up with any theories, let me know, okay?"

"Will do. It's cool, you know?"

"What is?"

"Smuggling. Organized crime. Sleepy little Alexandria Bay."

*Spoken like a true teenager.*

"Makes an awesome mystery, don't you think?" he continued. "Maybe I should be a writer." He headed over to the mystery section and scanned the titles, softly whistling a tune Shelby didn't know.

* * *

The work day seemed to drag, especially for a Sunday. The cloudy skies and chilly wind of the morning had morphed into showers around noon, and although tourists were still coming ashore, the numbers were definitely down. Shelby admitted to being a bit uptight when it rained. She'd watch each customer, hoping they'd seen the sign and left any umbrellas in the stand she'd set up outside the door. Then she would watch to see who might be shedding water drops as they walked around. If any happened to land on books, Shelby was there in a flash with a cloth, trying to appear casual as she wiped up the offending water before stains could set in.

Around about early afternoon, Shelby wished she'd given Taylor the day off, business was so slow. She kept thinking about the salary that would have been saved and then would give herself a mental kick, reminding herself that Taylor probably needed the salary even more these days. They spent most of the time pouring over the catalogs that had been left by various publishers and gift company reps, tossing around ideas for new sections and playing the "what if" game—*what if we had all the money needed and could do whatever we wanted with the store?* Fun, but not useful.

At the end of the day, when Shelby exited the shuttle back on the mainland, she decided a truffle treat was needed, if only to cheer herself up. She had a dinner date at Edie's in an hour—plenty of time to start with dessert. The rain had disappeared, and even though it was late in the day, the sun was trying to poke through the low cloud cover.

Erica looked up from what she was reading when Shelby entered the shop.

"Caught you," Shelby joked. "I should report you to your boss."

"Consider me reported," Erica shot back. "I was just looking through some catalogs, wondering if I needed to change up some of the decor."

"That's what Taylor and I did this afternoon. Slow day." She let her gaze wander slowly around the shop, wondering what it would be like to work there. Of course, there'd be all that chocolate. Which would mean she'd have to come up with a whole lot of self-control. And then, she'd also have to know what she was doing and how to make the truffles. *Not going to happen.*

"I hear you. Now, I want you to try this new truffle I've been experimenting with. I think it might just be ready for public consumption." She led Shelby into the back room and pulled a small tray of truffles out of the cupboard. "See if you can figure out what flavors I used." Erica leaned against the counter, watching closely while Shelby bit into the truffle she'd chosen.

Shelby was aware of the scrutiny, realizing a reaction was called for. Fortunately, she felt the truffle was to die for, and broke into a smile, giving Erica a thumbs-up.

Erica let out the breath she'd been holding. "That's a relief. Take another one for good measure. Can you pick out the flavors?"

"Um, something spicy. Chili powder?"

"Close. It's chipotle. Now, anything else?"

"Something citrusy. Lemon, lime?"

"You got it. Lime. Do you like the mixture?"

Shelby nodded, and when she had finally swallowed, she answered, "So much so that if you don't hide that tray, it will be empty by the time I leave."

Erica pulled out a small carboard box and pieced it

together. She put five of the remaining truffles in it. "Here you go. Enjoy."

Shelby felt genuinely pleased. She liked Erica a lot and was pleased that the friendship had formed so fast. But she *loved* the truffles. She'd better get back to her morning walking routine or she'd soon be paying for all the extra calories.

* * *

She decided that fast-walking to Edie's would do her a lot of good after all those truffles, and she'd just turned onto High Street when she noticed Matthew going through the front gate at the house. By the time she reached it, he had disappeared inside. So she wasn't at all surprised when he opened the door for her.

"It seems I'm on door duty tonight," he said, "although that's a small price to pay for a delicious home-cooked meal." He took a long sniff of the air.

Shelby laughed and did the same as she handed him the bottle of wine she'd brought and then took off her jacket. She hung it in the closet and wandered into the kitchen, where she found Edie standing at the stove and Matthew opening the wine.

Edie walked slowly over to Shelby and gave her a hug. "You didn't need to bring anything, dear. But thank you."

"You're walking without any aids," Shelby commented, pleased that her aunt was healing so quickly.

"I give it a try every now and then, around the house, but

my body is quick to let me know when it's had enough of being adventurous. Would you mind setting the table? I think we'll eat in the dining room tonight. You can use the silverware that's in the top drawer of the sideboard."

That sounded special, Shelby thought as she did as she was told. Even though she now knew about their relationship, Shelby was still surprised that he was included in a Sunday meal. Family time. Could things be progressing? She hoped so. They made an interesting couple and neither was getting any younger. She'd just have to make sure never to mention that to Edie. Not if she valued her limbs.

She was also pleased to see that Matthew looked none the worse for wear after his questioning by the police.

They sat down about ten minutes later to a rib roast with all the trimmings, including Shelby's favorite—Yorkshire pudding. During the meal, the conversation flowed around the goings-on at Blye Castle. Edie loved gossip and clearly missed being in on the daily happenings. Shelby realized Edie might be returning to work full-time at the bookstore fairly soon at this rate. That was good news, wasn't it?

Over tea and a slice of the apple pie Edie had baked that afternoon, Shelby decided it was time to ask some questions. She couldn't pass up having them both in the same room.

"So, since you're both here, I want to run a theory past you. I know you'll both say it's preposterous, but just hear me out."

Edie looked over at Matthew, but Shelby wasn't sure what his reaction meant. She decided to plow ahead.

"I've been looking at some possible suspects and motives

for Loreena's murder. You both know that. What still stands out is the fact that Zack Griffin is involved in the investigation." She glanced at Matthew, but his face gave away nothing. "He keeps saying that the different agencies cooperate with each other, but I'd think, with the local police and State Police working on this, the Coast Guard isn't really needed. Besides, the murder happened on land, even though her body was found in the water. I mean, the grotto, cave, and water are all part of Blye Island, aren't they?"

This time Matthew nodded, but he didn't comment.

"I know where this is heading," Edie said. "Again."

"Please, Aunt Edie, just hear me out. I've been doing some reading about the Prohibition days and rum smuggling, and I know there was a lot of it happening in this area. What if it's happening again? I've also read that it didn't die out totally with the repeal of Prohibition."

Matthew shook his head. "While that's an intriguing theory, it's highly unlikely. For starters, in the twenties and thirties, it was much easier to smuggle. The authorities didn't have anywhere close to the types of electronic tracking they do these days. Their boats are more highly technologically fitted, and it would be incredibly hard for anyone to get by their patrols. And what would be smuggled? Not booze anymore. Drugs, I suppose. If we were farther downriver, I might agree that cigarettes were a possibility."

Shelby opened her mouth to answer, but Matthew held up his hand and continued talking, "Also, from the smugglers' side of it, there are certainly more foolproof ways to smuggle goods these days. Two or three hours in a small boat in open water with the risk of being pulled over by the Coast Guard seems downright foolish."

"But then why was Loreena murdered in the grotto?"

"What? Do you think Loreena was involved in a smuggling operation in some way? Do you hear what you're saying?" Matthew narrowed his eyes and tilted his head toward her. "I know you didn't know her well, but can you picture that?"

"I guess not," Shelby admitted with great reluctance.

"And besides, who's the brains behind this supposed smuggling? Not Loreena, and I can't think of anyone involved with Blye Castle who would fit that bill. Have you met the board yet? You'd quickly agree with me on that one."

Shelby had perked up at his question. "What about someone else in town?"

"Always possible, but highly improbable. No one appears to be unduly profiting or showing signs of a windfall. It just doesn't make any sense, Shelby. I wish you could see that and drop it. I don't want to see you get hurt."

"But how would I get hurt if nothing's happening?"

"There are always secrets, even if there's nothing illegal going on. Folks don't like having their lives looked into, especially by a newcomer. And then there's the police. I'm sure you've already been warned off, but I know for a fact, they don't like a civilian poking his or her nose into an investigation. They can get very uptight about it, believe me." Matthew shook his head and sat back.

Shelby took a deep breath, trying to release some of the tension she felt building inside her. "Okay, that all makes sense and you're probably right, but it could happen, couldn't it? Otherwise, why is the CGIS so interested? They even questioned you, Matthew."

His eyes darkened briefly, but his voice sounded unconcerned. "Just doing exactly what he said they were doing, Shelby. Helping out. I guess everyone wants a shot at the prime suspect."

She looked at him sharply. How could he joke about this? Because that's what it sounded like he was doing. She then turned her gaze on Edie, who looked as tense as Shelby felt. Well, this wasn't getting her anywhere. Shelby felt a shiver snake down her spine. It was all too weird. "Doesn't that mean something?"

Nobody seemed to have an answer for that.

"All right," Shelby finally said. "It probably is a dumb idea, and I know that I know nothing about police business. I was just trying to help."

Edie looked relieved as she answered in a choked-up voice, "And we appreciate it, Shelby. It's all my fault for asking you to do just that. But now I'm asking that you not get involved any further."

Shelby didn't bother to hide her surprise. That's what she'd been thinking, that she shouldn't do any more, but hearing Edie say it, she felt almost let down. She just stared, open-mouthed at Edie, unable to come up with a reply. Edie obviously took her silence as a sign of agreement, because she started stacking the pie plates and asked Shelby to carry them into the kitchen. After clearing the table and filling the dishwasher, Shelby joined her aunt and Matthew in the living room carrying a tray with a teapot and cups. She knew they'd been talking about her, because they went silent until she sat down. Then they began discussing Edie's garden as if it had been their original topic.

Shortly after, Matthew excused himself, saying he wanted to get back home before it got too dark. He said goodbye to Shelby, and Edie walked him to the front door. Once he'd left, Edie eased herself down onto the hard-backed chair in the living room that she'd been using since the surgery.

Shelby had refreshed their tea and handed the cup and saucer to Edie before taking the wingback chair across from her. "That was a delicious supper. I enjoyed it."

Edie smiled with delight. "And I enjoy cooking, so that works out nicely. Tomorrow, I'm thinking lasagna. Trudy picked up some groceries for me today, so I'm all set."

"Sounds equally delicious." Shelby took a sip of her tea, wondering how to frame what was on her mind. "I had an interesting customer the other day. Her name was Prissy Newmarket, and she said she knew my mom. In fact, she said I looked a lot like her. I didn't get a chance to really talk to her. She seemed all over the place, topic-wise. Her husband was with her. Do you know her?"

"Prissy? I'm not really sure. The name doesn't ring any bells," Edie said, although Shelby had a feeling she was stalling for time. She seemed to be having more trouble than usual getting comfortable. Of course, that could be legitimate.

"Do I really look like my mom?"

Edie's face softened. "Yes, you do, Shelby. She was a beautiful young woman."

Shelby blushed. "I've never thought of myself as being beautiful." And that was true. Passable, maybe. But this was her aunt speaking, and aunts were known to be biased. It was probably in the job description. "What was she like?"

Edie took a few moments before answering. She seemed to be giving it careful consideration. "She was full of life. She came from Greenville, Kentucky, you know, and was every bit the southern belle. Folks in Alex Bay didn't know what had hit them when your dad brought her home."

"Where did they meet?" Shelby wasn't sure for how long she'd be able to get her aunt to open up, so she chose her questions with care.

"Down in Lexington. Ralph had gone on holiday with a couple of friends one summer, and he ended up falling in love. It was a whirlwind romance, and they got married right away so that she could move here with him."

"Somehow I can't picture my dad doing something so impulsive."

"He was a different man in those days. And if you had known Merrily, you'd know why. Oops, I'm sorry, honey. That was insensitive of me."

"No, that's all right. That's life, isn't it? She died before I had a chance to really get to know her."

Edie stood abruptly, much faster than Shelby had seen her do in a long time. "I'm really feeling tired and sore, Shelby. I think I did too much today. I hope you don't mind if I just head to bed. I'll take care of the rest of the dishes tomorrow. If you could just turn on the dishwasher and then let yourself out, okay?"

Shelby looked at her aunt carefully. She did look exhausted, and something else. Jittery? Whatever it was, she knew there'd be no more shared information that night.

"You get yourself to bed and I'll wash up these cups before I go. I insist. Have a good sleep."

"Thank you, honey." Edie grabbed her walker that had been parked behind her chair and walked slowly out of the room. Shelby heard the bedroom door shut and then started gathering the dirty dishes, all the while thinking about secrets. Edie seemed to be keeping plenty of those about Shelby's mom.

And, somewhere, someone had a big secret about Loreena's death.

# Chapter Twenty

Shelby found herself looking at everyone in town with a new perspective for the next few days. How could any of these friendly folks who always smiled at her and said hi possibly be involved in murder? She felt welcome here, even though she had to admit she hadn't done very much in trying to fit into the community. That had been partly because, at first, she'd viewed this as a temporary change of address, just until her Aunt Edie had fully recovered and could get on with everything involved with the bookstore. She'd thought it might take up to a year. Of course, Edie would never admit it might take that long, and Shelby knew she'd be back into the swing of things as soon as humanly possible. Still, a year was what she'd been expecting. After that, she'd hoped to see what other possibilities were out there.

But now she realized how foolish it had been to make that assumption without knowing what Edie had in mind or, equally, what living and working in Alexandria Bay would be like. Now she knew, and she realized it was time to get to know the people and area better.

Matthew had pointed out an obvious omission on her part. She definitely needed to meet the board of directors for the Heritage Society. She really should have been at the last meeting, filling in for Edie in her role as director, but she'd felt being in the store was more important. As luck would have it, their next meeting was that afternoon at two PM in their offices at the Felix Heritage House down by the water.

She had arranged for Cody to help out at Blye, knowing that foot traffic in town on a Wednesday in early May would be minimal and Trudy could probably easily handle the main store on her own. To her surprise, Edie then decided to go in and help for a couple of hours, but Shelby had the last word and made Edie promise to spend most of the time sitting down.

They hadn't continued their discussion about her mom or even had a really good follow-up talk. Trudy seemed to be spending a lot more time at Edie's, even though the patient was nicely on the mend. A more suspicious mind might wonder if Edie had asked Trudy to do that, not wanting to be alone with Shelby. She scoffed at herself for even thinking it. Her aunt wasn't devious. She really must be getting on edge about everything.

Shelby had just arrived back in the village on the one PM shuttle and stopped in at the Mango Lagoon for a quick bite. As she checked over the menu, she realized someone was taking the seat across from her at the table for two. She was surprised when the stranger identified herself as Rose Denison, chief reporter, photographer, and editor at the *The Bay*

*Chronicle*, the weekly local newspaper. Shelby knew the byline.

After introducing herself, Rose added, "I'm surprised we haven't met yet. You've been in town, what, two months now?"

"Something like that," Shelby agreed. "Of course, I've been busy helping my aunt and getting up to speed with the bookstores. How long have you been with the newspaper?"

Shelby was leery about talking to the press and hoped she could put off any questions by asking her own first. Of course, maybe Rose was just being friendly. She was probably one of Edie's friends, judging by her appearance. She was approximately the same age, but although she dressed casually, there was none of the flair that surrounded Edie. Her long salt-and-pepper hair was held back by a sensible black barrette. Her blue eyes were inquisitive, which wasn't a surprise, given her profession, and her eyebrows added to the look with their high arch, like she was constantly questioning things. A good thing to remember.

"I was born into it, you know. My grandfather started it, and my dad took it over. Eventually, I fell into running it and doing almost every other job there. Typical Alexandria Bay. You don't mind if I join you, do you?"

Shelby nodded, though she was still apprehensive.

After they'd placed their orders, Rose leaned back in her chair and asked, "How are you liking it here?'

"I'm enjoying the village. Everyone seems friendly, Bayside Books is doing well, and I love working over at the castle. It's such an amazing place."

Rose chuckled. "It certainly is. I'm glad the village was able to get things going with the owner and have this added tourist attraction. It's not necessarily the best place to be right now, though, is it?"

"What do you mean?"

"You know, with the murder in the grotto. Shades of Joseph Cabana and all the illegal stuff happening in those days." She smiled. "I've been talking to Cody Tucker, and he's been doing a lot of research. I'm quite impressed. But I hear you've been asking around about it yourself."

*Uh-oh. Word does travel in a small town. Or maybe there are no secrets. But that's not true. Loreena had her secrets. She must have.*

That all ran through Shelby's mind in an instant. This was what she'd been afraid of. There went her privacy. Shelby shrugged, which she hoped showed she wasn't really concerned. "It just sounded like symmetry, although I know it's not true. Cody does tend to get caught up in things. You know teenagers and crime stories."

Their food arrived, and Shelby gratefully tucked into her grilled cheese sandwich. She'd been wondering how the slices of green apple listed in the menu description would work in the dish and decided they were a tasty addition. She was pleased that Rose also seemed engrossed in her meal and was reluctant to ask more questions at that point.

When she'd finished her coffee, Shelby looked at her watch. "I can't believe it's so late. You'll have to excuse me. I'm headed for the board meeting at the Heritage Society."

She stood quickly, grabbing her purse and her check at the same time. "It's been nice talking with you."

Rose smiled, a little too knowingly. "It has been. We'll talk again, I'm sure."

Shelby nodded and walked stiffly to the cashier to pay, leaving without glancing back at the table. The encounter had left her unsettled. She had nothing to say to the press and certainly nothing she wanted printed in the paper. But if Rose knew about her interest in smuggling, might the news reach the wrong ears? Had Matthew been right to warn her off asking more questions? Should she have a talk with Cody and ask him to do the same? She tried to put the thought out of her mind as she rushed down the street to the Heritage Society building.

Shelby made it to the board meeting with only a few minutes to spare. She had to walk the length of the room to take a seat at the far end of the dark oak table. So much for anonymity. She felt like all eyes were on her, but she tried not to meet any eyes until she sat down. Then she looked around the room. It appeared to double as a storage area, with file cabinets and bankers' boxes stashed along one wall. The table itself looked to be as old as the building, sporting gouges in the wood and discoloration from many spills and hot cups placed directly on it. The chairs were obviously where the budget had been concentrated. There were eight of them, the swivel kind with wheels, fully padded with navy nylon coverings. Shelby was not fond of meetings but knew the added value of a comfortable chair.

She was surprised to see Rose Denison take the chair across from her.

"I didn't realize you were on the board," Shelby said, hoping she didn't sound impertinent. She refrained from asking why Rose hadn't mentioned it at lunch.

Rose chuckled and leaned across the table. "I'm not on it. I'm working. These usually aren't the most scintillating meetings, but I do try to report on what happens in the Bay." She nodded at the woman who sat down to her left and said to Shelby, "If you haven't yet met Pat Drucker, she's our chief librarian and a font of information, particularly if there's a certain time period you're interested in researching, say Prohibition."

Shelby inwardly cringed. She'd probably hear a lot of references to this in the future. She smiled at Pat. "It's nice to meet you."

"And you. I've seen you around town but not had the pleasure before. This committee likes to talk a lot, but I'm sure you'll find it the ideal way to get caught up on what's going on both at the castle and in town. We've missed having Edie's input. How is she doing?"

"She's on the mend and anxious to get back into the store."

"Well, please give her my best wishes."

"I will." Shelby nodded and watched while Pat got up again and went over to talk to one of the men. She was wearing a long-sleeved multicolored tunic with black leggings, which gave her a decidedly un-librarian look. She must be a hit with the younger kids.

Of the remaining five people around the table, everyone seemed paired off except for an older man she'd passed on her way in, sitting at the end of the table, with a gavel in front of him. Obviously, the chairperson. She smiled when he looked at her, but it wasn't returned. Now she really felt uncomfortable, until the woman on her left introduced herself.

"I'm Felicity Foxworth. And you must be Shelby Cox, am I right?"

Shelby nodded. "I am, and I'm also surprised. How do you know my name?"

Felicity chuckled. Her black hair showed no signs of gray, though she had to have been at least in her fifties. It looked like she'd just walked out of the salon. In fact, Shelby was sure she could smell the hair spray. Her features were delicate, made even more obvious by her large oval red-framed glasses. She had a multicolored silk scarf draped under the collar of her white cotton blouse. *Very polished*, Shelby thought.

"Alex Bay is small, remember?" Felicity stated, not expecting an answer. "I'm so glad you're finally able to come and meet us all. Especially while Edie's laid up. How do you like having the store in the castle?"

"It's the perfect location. I'm really enjoying it." Shelby didn't get a chance to expound, as the sound of the gavel hitting the table captured everyone's attention.

"I'm calling this meeting to order. Did everyone get the email with the minutes and the agenda? Good," the man continued without even looking around the table. "Let's get all this fidgety stuff right out of the way. Anyone move for the agenda to be passed?"

Someone did, a young woman Shelby had never seen, at least not in her store. Hands rose around the table as everyone agreed. The same with the minutes. Then, as the chairperson was checking the agenda, Felicity put up her hand and cleared her throat. All eyes turned to her.

"I'd like to make mention of and welcome our guest today." She pointed, unnecessarily, to her right. "Shelby Cox is her Aunt Edie's business partner at Bayside Books and, as such, is filling in for her on the board."

She started clapping, and the others joined in for a few brief but unenthusiastic moments.

Shelby felt her face flame up and was glad when the attention shifted back to the chair. "Uh, yes. Welcome, Miss Cox. I'm Andrew Truelove, chairperson. I guess we'll go around the table. Everyone, say your name, please."

Even though there were only six names, Shelby knew she'd never remember them all. She was good with faces, bad with names. That might be part of the reason she had trouble making friends, she suddenly realized. Everyone wanted to be considered important enough to have their name remembered. Her musings were cut short as Duncan Caine, the man sitting to Felicity's left, interrupted the chairperson.

"I'd like to cut right to the chase. This is our first meeting since the tragic demise of Loreena. I'd first like us to take a moment of silence in her memory." He bowed his head, displaying a large shiny bald spot unsuccessfully covered by strands of limp, light-brown hair. He looked visibly shaken and had even removed his glasses to wipe his eyes.

Everyone followed his lead, and Shelby took advantage of the time to take a closer look around the table. Felicity hadn't closed her eyes either, but the others looked respectful, even a bit distressed. Shelby wondered what she'd been hoping to see and managed to close her eyes just in time to open then again.

The rest of the meeting seemed to drag on. There wasn't much on the agenda of interest to Shelby, although she supposed she should be keener to know the ins and outs of her hometown. And there didn't seem to be anything that directly concerned Bayside Books, either. When they came to a report on the volunteers, a woman whom Shelby recognized from the castle, though she didn't know her name, read a statement from Chrissie Halstead, who'd sent her regrets.

"So, in summary, everything seems to be going quite nicely at Blye Castle." Then she turned to Shelby. "Ms. Cox, would you have anything to add to that?"

Shelby was momentarily thrown off guard. She hadn't planned to say anything other than hello and hadn't thought to ask Edie if there was anything she'd wanted brought up. Shelby certainly didn't feel she knew enough about the volunteers and the running of the castle to chime in on that. But all eyes were on her, so she felt she had to oblige.

"As I said earlier to Felicity, I feel that everything's going really well at the bookstore and the castle in general. The volunteers seem well trained and keep everything in order, and the grounds are so well cared for, it's really a pleasure to go over each day." Might as well put in a plug for Matthew while she was at it. By the look on the volunteer's face, she seemed to have said the right thing. That was a relief.

"Thank you for that, Miss Cox," Truelove said, his voice and face emotionless.

It made Shelby want to shake things up a bit. "I'd also like to add that, although I barely knew Loreena Swan, it was such a tragedy, losing her like that. My condolences to you all."

Felicity sniffed, and Shelby hoped she wouldn't burst into tears. Truelove nodded while clearing his throat. "I hope the police resolve it soon."

Caine's head shot up from the paper he'd been so interested in just a few seconds before. "I think they already have their man, which means we will need to look for a new caretaker soon."

"That's not true," Shelby answered, seeing as all the others looked like they'd been thunderstruck. "Matthew Kessler was questioned, just as we all were. He hasn't been charged or anything."

"As yet."

"Nor will he be," Shelby continued a bit more forcefully, "because he's innocent."

"Oh, now you're an expert in police investigations?" Caine threw back.

That stung. Shelby hadn't expected the question nor the caustic tone of voice. Before she could think of anything to say, Felicity came to her rescue.

"That's very rude of you, Duncan. Shelby is our guest, and she and Edie have done us the honor of opening their bookstore in our castle. As you know, that brings us much-needed funds, besides being a wonderful addition for the tourists." She sat straight up and turned her glare at Caine.

He opened his mouth, then quickly closed it. To Shelby, it looked like he might have been kicked under the table. Interesting.

Truelove quickly took back control of the meeting, and when no one raised any further business, he adjourned them.

Felicity took hold of Shelby's arm as they stood. "We usually go next door to Jody's Tea Room for something to drink after the meeting. We used to have it here, but no one wanted to be in charge of making tea and coffee and cleaning up, and we couldn't ask our executive director to do something so menial. Won't you join us?"

Shelby glanced at Duncan, and Felicity noticed. "Oh, don't let him get to you. He's been really out of sorts these past couple of weeks. Besides, he doesn't often go out with us after."

Shelby thanked her, but she was desperate to escape them all. She'd never liked meetings when she'd been working for the publishing house, and apparently, that hadn't changed. She wondered how soon Edie would be able to get back to attending. Felicity gave Shelby a quick hug, then straightened a lightweight pink-and-mauve pashmina she'd pulled around her shoulders.

"If you have any questions about us, anytime, please feel free to get in touch with me." She left quickly, trying to catch up to the others, before Shelby could ask any more questions.

Of course, Shelby admitted to herself, she didn't have any real reason to suspect a board member of the murder. But she also didn't have any reason *not* to.

# Chapter Twenty-One

After a quick supper of cold chicken and a green salad, she checked a map, grabbed her book, and walked over to Trudy's.

Shelby was as curious about Trudy's house as she was about the Bayside Book Babes Plus One, she realized as she climbed the wooden stairs to the two-story clapboard house with the inviting wraparound porch. She paused to admire the already colorful flower gardens, knowing that this was another interest Trudy and Edie had in common. She was about to knock when she heard the laughter from inside. It sounded like this group knew how to have fun. Shelby took a deep breath, shoving aside the jitters she usually felt when meeting new people, and knocked.

Trudy opened the door almost immediately and ushered her inside. They went into the living room, which opened to the right of the small foyer. It was a burst of color, from the yellow walls to the numerous bouquets of flowers in various spots around the room. And the people occupying most of the chairs seemed to be right in keeping with the setting.

"Babes," Trudy said with a smile at the one male in the room, "I'd like you to meet Shelby Cox, Edie's niece and co-owner of Bayside Books."

Shelby smiled and responded with small waves to the six book club members. They sure seemed friendly. She began to relax as Trudy started the introductions.

"Now, I know you won't remember all the names tonight. I should have made name tags. Oh well, too late now. But the twins sitting on the love seat are Mimi and her sister, Dolly. I'll dispense with last names to make it easier for you. To Dolly's left is Juliette, wearing the awesome fascinator. Patricia was just telling us about her choice of new hair highlights, purple and green. And, last but not least, our Plus One, Leonard."

Leonard gave a slight bow of his head, but it was enough to dislodge the flap of dark hair that had been draped across his forehead.

"We're so happy to finally meet you," Mimi said, her white curls not moving despite the bobbing of her head. "Aren't we, Dolly?" She nudged her sister in the side.

"Yes, yes we are."

Shelby felt overwhelmed by the introductions and hoped not much would be required of her other than listening to the discussion. She'd tried to get the book, the latest by mystery author Louise Penny, read in time but hadn't been able to finish it. Although she'd normally have read it when it first came out—she was a big fan and always got the latest—she'd been doing less reading since moving to the Bay, she realized. That had to change, and soon.

She wondered if she should own up right away or try to fake it. Before she could do anything, Trudy indicated a chair for her, between Juliette and Patricia, and Leonard leaped up to fetch her a glass of what turned out to be fruit punch.

She'd been so hoping for wine.

Juliette tapped her on the arm and asked, "How are you liking Alex Bay? Are you having any problems settling in? Where are you living? With your aunt?"

Shelby had just taken a sip of the punch and nodded, then answered, "It's a very unique town and I love the bookstores. I'm actually renting a houseboat for now."

Patricia leaned across her, saying to anyone who'd listen, "I'll bet Shelby is as enchanted with the castle as we all are. I'd love to work there."

"Why don't you volunteer, then?" Dolly asked pleasantly.

"Oh, I'm far too busy. Isn't that right, Leonard?"

He nodded. "Far too busy."

"But I do admire those who donate their time. Although, I don't really think I'd want to be there now, what with the murder and all. How do you cope, Shelby? I'd think it would be eerie."

Shelby gave it a moment's thought before answering. "I try not to think about it." *Not true.* "The bookstore is a busy place, so it's not hard to just go in and work, then go home. I guess most of you knew Loreena."

"Oh, my, yes we did," Mimi said, fanning herself with her napkin. "Her family has been in the area for years, even longer than ours. It's a real blow to such a tightly knit community when someone like that passes, and such a horrid death." She leaned forward, a small glint in her eyes. "They say it was Joe Cabana's ghost who caught up with her in the grotto."

"Oh, pooh-pooh, Mimi," scoffed Dolly. "You're the only one in this room who believes in ghosts, you know."

Mimi's face fell. "No, I don't know that, Dolly, and neither do you."

"Well," Leonard jumped in, "I'd heard it had to do with smuggling."

Shelby's ears perked up. "Where did you hear that?"

"Um, I'm not sure. Somewhere in town. Maybe at the barbershop. Or the marina."

Juliette shook her head so hard her fascinator looked like it might go flying. "No, that's nonsense, Leonard. I heard that she died at the hands of her secret lover, in a fit of jealousy."

Shelby looked at her. Now this sounded interesting.

"In fact," Juliette went on, "she was found floating in the grotto, her hands folded on her chest, with a single white rose in them." She sighed. "Isn't that romantic?"

"Aside from the dying part, yes," Patricia said, a deadpan expression on her face.

*Hmm, gossip is alive and well*, Shelby mused.

"I've heard your aunt has herself a beau," Mimi said, a look of delight on her face.

Shelby couldn't think of what to say. She didn't want to discuss Edie's business, but at the same time, she was interested in what was being said.

"Yes, she has," Mimi continued. "She hasn't said a word about who he is though. Not to any of us, anyway, and we share a lot here in book club. But she has a special glow about her. At least she did when I saw her last. I haven't seen her since her operation." She looked a bit confused.

Trudy chuckled. "And we do all so like sharing, don't we? Now, how about we share some of our thoughts about our book tonight. I, for one, am amazed that after writing so many books in the series, Ms. Penny is still able to keep each new one fresh and challenging to the reader."

After a half hour of lively conversation, Shelby's attention started to wander. She liked the group and thought she might make the effort to attend it on a regular basis. That surprised her. She usually wasn't a joiner. And here she'd had two meetings in one day. She wondered what would be next. The Chamber of Commerce? She smiled at the absurdity of that.

Juliette leaned closer to her. "What are you thinking about, Shelby? Have you found a handsome young man here in the Bay?"

Shelby felt her cheeks turning red and wished she could control it. She didn't want to be the subject of any of the town gossip. "I was just thinking about how much I'm enjoying the bookstore and everything associated with it," she answered smoothly.

She was pleased with Juliette's response. "That's delightful. I love it here, having grown up and lived in the same house all these years. It's always so gratifying to find others who love the town too. But now, what have you heard about the murder?"

Shelby looked from one Babe to the other before answering. They all looked expectant, even Leonard. She had her theory, of course, but that was about all.

"I know Loreena drowned in the grotto, but I don't have any other facts, just suppositions and questions. Have any of you heard anything else?" That might be a more productive question.

Mimi cleared her throat. "We all know that Loreena Swan was a very, how should I put it, formal person."

"You mean she was uppity, Mimi," Dolly interrupted. "Just say what you mean."

Mimi looked embarrassed but then nodded. "If the Bay had royalty, Loreena would think she was part of it. She was very concerned with the impression she made and what people thought of her. So, I'd venture to say, she was involved in something mighty scandalous, like maybe a love triangle, you know, with someone from the wrong side of the tracks, who was already married. The wife did it."

Mimi looked pleased with herself. Dolly shook her head, while Shelby hid a smile. Why not? It was as viable a theory as anything she'd come up with.

"I agree that it was probably because of either love or hate," Juliette said, leaning forward in her seat. "They're polar opposites, although love can turn into hate, given the right circumstances."

As Shelby looked around the room, she saw all the women nodding while Leonard looked distinctly uncomfortable.

# Chapter Twenty-Two

Shelby was still thinking about the book club the next morning as she unlocked the door to the bookstore. It had been an entertaining evening, especially when they'd gotten back onto the topic of Loreena's death. Obviously, the book club liked to discuss a lot of different topics. Although there had been some theories, it didn't really seem like any of the members had been close to Loreena. So, bottom line, it was probably all gossip.

Shelby looked at the clock as she got the coffee started. Taylor was coming over on the next shuttle, and she just hoped she would arrive before the eager shoppers descended. They'd been warned that two school tours had been booked to visit the castle, part of the *what-to-do-with-the-students* the last few weeks before summer vacation. Apparently, Blye Castle was a favorite year-end field trip, and schools from miles around found their way there. The kids ranged from grade school to high school, and while many were interested in what the castle had to offer, more were just happy to have the day off and away from their desks. As Shelby had already found with one such group, those who made it to the bookstore were prone to shoving, trying to get inside, only to do the same thing on the way out once they found out there were no comic books, coloring books, or graphic novels on the shelves. Their short visits could be totally exhausting, though.

One such group had just left when Shelby looked up to see Leonard, the Plus One, walking through the door. He spotted her and waved as he made his way around an older couple that had squeezed in before him.

"Hi again," he said. "Uh, I'm Leonard Hopkins, from last night, you know?"

Shelby smiled. "I do know. Although I didn't know your last name. It's nice to see you again. Are you playing tourist today?"

He chuckled. "I've been through this castle so many times, I could give the spiel with my eyes closed. Every time a relative, especially one with children, visits, it's a must-see. And I have a lot of out-of-town relatives." He winked in a conspiratorial manner.

Shelby warmed to him immediately. "That's very nice for you."

"Oh, it is. But the reason I came here today, besides always enjoying the boat ride, and because I had nothing else going on, was to suggest that you talk to my daughter. About Loreena, I mean. I own Goldy Locks, you know. Or maybe you don't know. That's the hair salon on James Street. I own it, but Amanda, it's her baby. I bankrolled it for her. All of which is neither here nor there. But she did happen to mention, right after the murder, that Loreena was a client. And you know what they say about beauty parlors. A hotbed of gossip. I just thought she might have heard something that might be interesting and useful."

"I'll bet she has, but I'm curious, why would you think I need this information?"

"Because it's all around town that you're doing some investigating, much to Chief Stone's dislike, I'd imagine. Anyway, more power to you. Now, I think I'll just snatch up a bag of Erica's truffles, take a stroll around the lovely gardens, and head home to do some of my own yard work."

"Thanks for stopping in, Leonard. And I appreciate the tip." Shelby smiled.

He winked and headed to the truffle display.

Shelby didn't notice when he left; she'd been recommending something from the local-authors shelf for another customer. She thought about him later, though, and decided it wouldn't be a bad idea to talk to his daughter.

By the end of the day, both Shelby and Taylor were more than ready to close up shop and drag themselves to the shuttle. Although Shelby often enjoyed talking about books to teens, she found that the level of noise with these groups usually increased to such a high level that she could hardly hear herself think. To top it off, Taylor had felt ill and spent some of the time either huddled in the back room or sitting in the castle foyer beside the tranquility of the water feature. Shelby had suggested she leave early, but Taylor had been adamant that she'd be fine.

Shelby hadn't heard back from Chief Stone, even though

she'd left a highly detailed phone message saying she had some questions to ask about her mother. Shelby had ended her message by saying she'd stop by the police station after work. She spent the short ride from Blye Island back to Alex Bay trying to decide if not hearing from the chief meant anything or if she should just go ahead and show up. Of course, there was no guarantee the chief would be there. Maybe the station wasn't such a good place for a personal talk anyway. She did, after all, have the chief's home address.

But first, she wanted to stop by Edie's and fill her in on a plan to introduce a magazine section to the castle bookstore. Shelby had been putting the proposal together for a few days now, and she wanted to get Edie's take on it. But if Trudy was already there for supper, she would just drop off the details and then leave. She didn't want to look like she was angling for an invitation.

She walked faster than usual, wanting to get some exercise after being cooped up most of the day, and had just turned onto Edie's street when she spotted the local police SUV parked at the curb outside Edie's house. She hoped nothing was wrong and quickened her pace.

She paused to catch her breath, then knocked on the front door before pulling it open. She found Edie and the chief sitting at the kitchen table, coffee mugs in front of them. It looked like some baked goodies had also been shared. Were they friends again now?

"Oh, Shelby," Edie said, "this is a surprise." She glanced at Chief Stone, who immediately stood and grabbed her hat from the table.

"I need to be getting along." She nodded at Edie and also at Shelby and put her hand on the back door.

"Chief Stone," Shelby said. "I left you a message."

"Oh, yes. So you did. I'll get back to you on that." She put her hat on her head and left.

Shelby just stared at the door for a moment, feeling supremely brushed off. Then she turned to Edie. "What was that all about? Why was she here? She didn't come to harass you?" *Or arrest you?*

Edie started clearing the table, answering but not looking at Shelby. "She just stopped by to update me." Shelby couldn't have been more surprised.

"After practically kicking us off her property the other week?" Shelby remained standing, focused on the door the chief had just exited, trying to let the pieces fall into place. "Did this have anything to do with the message I left the chief? All I want is to know more about my mother. I want to see pictures of her. I want to find her grave site."

"What?"

"That's right. I've been wandering through the cemetery, and although I've found lots of Cox tombstones, I haven't found one for my mom. What's with all the secrecy?"

Edie groaned and sat down hard on a kitchen chair. "It's complicated, Shelby. And I made a promise to your father, my brother. This is all very hard on me." She shook her head and then slowly pushed herself off the chair with the help of the tabletop. "I'm sorry, dear, I think I have to go lie down a bit until Trudy gets here. It's all just too much while I'm still recovering."

Shelby held her tongue. She wanted to scream, but she could see that Edie was indeed tired and upset. But what was it about the topic of her mother that brought on that reaction? Or maybe it was something about Matthew. Had Chief Stone indeed been telling her something about the investigation? That seemed highly unlikely. One thing she did know, she wasn't going to get any more answers that night, out of either of them.

She left the large manila envelope she'd brought on the kitchen table and let herself out. Her walk back home was a slower one as she went over everything in her head, not really coming up with any answers. Or questions. She almost stepped on the cat when she got back to the houseboat. It had been sitting on the deck but whisked out of her way just in time.

"Oh, cat. You almost gave me a heart attack," she said, leaning against the door. "Are you hungry? I seem to have lost my appetite, but a glass of wine would hit the spot."

She opened the door and waited for the cat to precede her. She turned the radio on and hummed along with Justin Timberlake singing "Summer Love" while she poured her wine and filled the cat's food dishes. "That's it. Justin Timberlake. That's what I'll call you. You can be very vocal sometimes, and I can't be calling you 'cat' all the time."

The cat sat next to the food for a few seconds, giving Shelby a long stare before finally turning his back and starting to munch on the dry food.

"I'll take that as a sign of approval. But maybe it needs to be shortened, especially when we're outside. Otherwise, the neighbors might talk. Yes, I'm sure they will. J.T. it is, then."

Shelby sat on a stool at the counter and watched J.T. finish off both sides of his food dish in record time. She wasn't sure if his eating habits matched those of his namesake, but he certainly was a handsome cat.

"Why can't you also be a mystery-solving cat, like the one in the 'Cat Who' series?"

# Chapter Twenty-Three

After over a month of working in the main bookstore and now, with the days of preparation included, just over two weeks at Blye Castle, Shelby foolishly thought she'd experienced almost everything the bookstore business could throw at her. So she wasn't really prepared when the book sales representatives started calling to make appointments for her to view and buy their winter stock.

She realized it would be better if she left Taylor on her own at the castle location one morning and spent that time with Trudy, going through catalogs with the reps at the home base. The entire database was in that computer, and she'd have Trudy's knowledge to help make the decisions. She toyed with the idea of asking Edie if she wanted to be a part of it but thought better of it. Shelby wanted to impress Edie with how well she now fit into the Bayside Books scheme of things, and she could only do that if she wasn't constantly leaning on Edie for help.

She felt excited but also a bit anxious, not sure of what would be involved in the process. On the walk to the bookstore, she kept telling herself she was a competent and savvy bookseller and retailer. This business wouldn't get the better of her or her self-confidence. When she arrived, she found Trudy already there with the lights and computer turned on and the drip coffee maker ready to brew.

"What time did you get in, Trudy? I thought I was early."

Trudy laughed. Her copper pendant earrings shimmered as she brushed a stray hair off her forehead. "I'm an early riser. You tend to be as you age. Your body clock adjusts to early bedtimes and rising. So, I fixed Edie her breakfast, helped her get ready for the day, and here I am. Besides, I love walking through the near-empty streets in the morning."

"Yeah, I guess once the summer tourist season really gets in full swing, there aren't many times when it's like that."

"That's right, especially when the sports fishermen take to the water, some at the crack of dawn. I hope it will be okay for you in your houseboat. Are there many smaller boats moored there?"

Shelby hung up her lightweight sweater and finished her coffee before answering. "I haven't seen many. There are four houseboats along the dock I'm on, and the other two docks have a variety of different boats tied up, usually the bigger cruisers. Their owners are actually sleeping on them."

"I'll bet. There's a lot of money afloat in these waters in the summer. Now, before the book rep arrives, take a look through the entries in the computer. Here, I've already grouped them according to distributor so that you can see the types of books we order from there and in what sort of numbers."

Trudy moved aside and Shelby sat at the desk. She took a minute to glance around. Although it was the larger of the two stores, over twice the size of the castle store, it managed to look just as cozy. That was probably because Edie had used the same color scheme at both locations. Smart woman. The two comfortable chairs at the back of the store were placed in front of a large window—not a bay one, unfortunately—overlooking a small stone patio. By late afternoon, it would be completely bathed in sun and usually sported a small bistro table and two matching chairs. Unfortunately, they'd been stolen one night in the fall, and Edie was reluctant to replace them until she could be on the spot to keep an eye peeled for anyone casing them, as she liked to say. Everyone in the village was shocked that this had happened, but no one had any leads. Edie's solution, as she liked to tell everyone, was to bolt down the next set. Even so, she would be watching them closely.

This location also had a small love seat tucked between two small bookcases. A low wicker table sat within reach and doubled as a catchall for magazines and some advance reading copies that the publishers sent on a regular basis. If customers looked interested in one of the copies, they would usually be loaned the item with the hope that they would become hooked on the series.

Shelby turned her attention back to the list in front of her and had almost finished with it when the front door swung open and a stocky middle-aged man, about five foot six, entered. He wore a sports coat that even from a distance looked a bit frayed over a plaid shirt, and jeans, also frayed, along with a big smile on his face. His hair was graying around the temples, which gave him a dignified although mischievous look.

Trudy looked pleased to see him. "Kent, so good to see you again."

He set his two cases on the ground and gave Trudy a big hug. Then he turned to Shelby. "I'm assuming you're the Shelby I've been hearing so much about. Kent Thompson. Great to meet you, and I hope we sell many books together."

Shelby shook his extended hand. "I do too, Kent. Can we get you a cup of coffee?"

"Sure, sure. Black, please. And I brought the goodies." He reached into one of the briefcases and pulled out a small paper bag, which he placed on the desk. In went his hand again and out came a paper plate, plastic forks, and napkins. He pulled three lemon-cream Danishes out of the bag and displayed them on the plate.

"Hope you like these. I got them in Clayton, fresh this morning before I left."

Shelby eyed them with delight, even though she'd just finished her breakfast. "I didn't know that's where you lived."

"I do, although I'm originally from Syracuse. I'm on the road a lot visiting my bookstores. You'll get used to my comings and goings, at least two times a year in person. And then, if we have special offers or hot titles we're inserting into the next season, I'll call first and then email you all the info. Please, eat," he added, holding the plate toward her.

Shelby chose the smallest pastry and placed it on a napkin while she went to get Kent's coffee and a fresh one for herself. Trudy declined for the moment.

"How are you liking Alexandria Bay, Shelby?" Kent asked between bites.

"A lot of it's still new, but I'm sure I'll enjoy living here."

"That's good. And how is Edie doing?"

Trudy answered that question. "Her doctor is pleased with her progress. Hopefully, she'll start physiotherapy in the next couple of weeks. She's sure getting restless. But the surgery went well."

Kent chuckled. "I can't imagine Edie taking well to being confined." He took another sip of his coffee. "Well, then, I think we should get started. The way this works is you can either look through these catalogs or go on our website and follow along there. I wasn't sure what you'd prefer, so I'm ready for anything. I'll point out the books I think will work for you and give my little sales pitches as we go along. Okay?"

Shelby nodded. "I'm a little old school and like to flip through pages, so maybe I'll use the catalogs, this time anyway."

"Right." Kent pulled the briefcases over to the chair Trudy had pointed out for him and unloaded a stack of catalogs. He set his laptop computer on the edge of the counter and opened it. "Now, I'll fill in the order form on my computer as we go along, and then I'll email you the final copy later so that you can enter it in your system."

"By the way, that was a terrible thing that happened on the island. I find it hard to imagine a murder at such an idyllic spot. Has it made any difference to traffic at the bookstore?"

"Not from what we can tell. The sales patterns seem to be

similar to last year at this time. It was horrible, though. Did you know Loreena Swan, by any chance?"

"Sure, who didn't? I've lived in Clayton for around twenty years now, and she was a well-known figure there, too. She had a lot to do with our local community theatre, helping to bring the troupe to the Bay for performances. In fact, I ran into her a few weeks ago. She seemed in too much of a hurry to stop and talk."

"That sounds like Loreena," Trudy said. "Where was she headed?"

"Well, she was in the parking lot at the wharves and seemed to be looking for someone. I didn't stick around to see if she had any success. Now, let's have a look at what I've got here. The winter season will be a good one this year."

Trudy seated herself on a stool she'd pulled over beside Shelby so they could share the catalogs. Kent had pulled up another stool and leaned toward them at the counter, ready to do his sales pitch.

"So, what I usually do," Trudy explained, "is look at the write-up of the book, and if it's of interest, I check the author on our database. If he or she has a track record with us, it makes for an easier decision whether to order it. That will also help me decide the quantity."

"Sounds good," Shelby replied, eager to get started.

After about an hour, Kent stood to stretch and Trudy went to put on some fresh coffee.

"So, what are your thoughts on being a bookseller, Shelby?" Kent looked genuinely interested in her answer.

"I was in publishing before, so I was already interested in

books. But this is such a different part of the industry. I guess my biggest concern is in getting comfortable and trusting myself to make the right decisions about the books. Like today, what to buy and then how to display everything."

Kent chuckled. "That'll fall in place soon enough. It just takes doing it over and over. You'll soon find you develop an instinct for it. At least, the successful booksellers do, and I have a notion that you'll be one of them."

Shelby raised her eyebrows.

"You ask the right questions, and what you've been choosing seems on track. Trust me."

"Are all sales reps as helpful and congenial as you?"

Kent's smile filled his face. "I hope not. I want you to make most of your choices from me, of course. But seriously, it's a friendly group you'll be dealing with. We're not out to do any backstabbing or pull any tricks. We all love books and want them out there for the readers." He handed over another catalog as Trudy put their coffee cups down on the counter.

They finished the appointment just before noon. "So, what do you think?" Kent asked.

"It's really interesting," Shelby admitted. "I wasn't quite sure what to expect, but I love the chance to see what's new, even if it doesn't fit in our store."

Kent grinned. "Spoken like a true bookseller. I'll leave the catalogs with you in case you're tempted to take a second look." He packed away his computer, stood and stretched again, then said his goodbyes. "I'll make an appointment in late January to go over the spring list."

"I'm having a hard enough time coming to grips with seeing Christmas books. Now you're talking about spring?" Shelby said.

"Get used to living simultaneously in two time periods. Have a good selling season. Thanks for the coffee. Trudy, you take care."

When the door closed behind him, Shelby did her own stretching. "I can't believe how exhausting that was."

"It's the concentration and also just sitting still for so long. As much as I like Kent, sometimes it's a whole lot easier and quicker if he can't make it and just mails the catalogs and order forms." She smiled. "But then we'd miss out on his treats. He always has baked goods with him."

"Do all of the sales reps do this?"

"The ones from the big publishing houses or distributors do; the others, mainly regional ones, just mail everything. You'll get used to it."

"I'm looking forward to it. Thanks for your help. I could never have made all those decisions on my own."

"My pleasure. Now, are you working here for the rest of the day?"

"No, I'll take the next shuttle over to the island. I'll also take the box of stock that needs to go over."

Trudy pointed to a cardboard box stashed on the floor in the corner behind the counter. "It's on the heavy side. Do you think you can manage? I can always get Cody to bring it over later."

Shelby tested the weight of the box. "I should be able to

handle this. Isn't there a wheelie-thingy hanging around somewhere?" She glanced toward the back room.

Trudy nodded. "Not always a reliable tool, but probably better than nothing." She had already headed to the back and returned quickly with the small luggage cart—really just a stand on wheels—set it up, and strapped the box to it. "There you go; that should work."

Shelby smiled as she gathered up her things. "Thanks, Trudy, and thanks again for helping me get through all this ordering business. I realize I still have a lot to learn."

"You'll get it soon enough. I really don't think there's much you haven't covered. Now it's just a matter of repeating it so that it all becomes second nature. By the way, you're doing a fine job, Shelby."

Shelby felt her cheeks turning red. She wasn't used to a lot of praise. She glanced at the clock. Just going on noon. "I'd better get going. Thanks again, Trudy."

Trudy gave Shelby a brief hug, which took her by surprise.

"Enjoy the afternoon," Trudy said, already shifting the catalogs to the back room. "Oh, by the way, Edie is coming in to work for a couple of hours. Just thought you should know."

That sounded good. "One second, Trudy. Can I ask you something?"

Trudy stuck her head around the corner. "Sure."

"Did you know my mom?"

The phone rang, and Trudy held up a finger to Shelby

while she ducked back into the room and grabbed the receiver. Shelby thought it sounded like the call might be a longer one, so she left wondering about the surprised look on Trudy's face. This was getting silly. Someone had to answer her questions, and soon.

# Chapter Twenty-Four

Shelby took her time walking home to the houseboat after work later that day. She lingered along James Street to do some window shopping but didn't allow herself to give in to temptation. Nor did she stop by Chocomania either. It felt good just walking along with nothing pressing on her mind for a change. She did sometimes miss the quietness of her previous life, the days she'd be ensconced at her desk behind the baffles, absorbed in reading the manuscript of a hopeful new author. A time when she would spend her evenings in much the same way, not bothered by suspicions or murder. The good old days.

She found herself in front of Goldy Locks and guessed her subconscious sleuthing mind had been at work. There was only one person in the shop, and her name tag said AMANDA. Shelby introduced herself and got right down to the reason for her visit.

"I met your dad at the book club the other night, and he suggested I talk to you about Loreena Swan. Apparently she was a customer?"

Amanda put away the broom she'd been using to sweep behind the counter and poured herself a cup of coffee from a carafe on the counter.

"Would you like some?" she asked, holding it out to Shelby.

"No, thanks. I hit my limit a while ago."

Amanda grimaced. "Probably a good idea. I can't even remember when I made this, it's been so busy."

Shelby glanced around. There were four styling stations, and she suspected the washbasins were behind a partial wall she glimpsed at the back. Two walls were painted in mauve, and the other two sported floral wallpaper. It looked bright and clean. Maybe she'd give it a try. So far, she hadn't really bonded with the stylist she'd been seeing at a salon at the other end of the street.

"Well," Amanda began, "Loreena was a longtime customer. She wasn't a gossiper, though. Nor was she a good tipper. Sorry, I shouldn't speak ill of the dead. Anyway, *she* didn't talk much, but everyone else did after she'd leave an appointment. She was a source of envy, maybe some pride, and a whole lot of speculation."

"How so?"

"Well, she did have a position of esteem. Maybe that's not the right word for it. But she liked to come across as being someone who should be admired. So, of course, she was fair game behind her back." Amanda shrugged as if saying, *That's just how it is.*

"Did you ever hear anything that might provide a clue as to any enemies she had?"

Amanda took a sip of her coffee, made a face, and poured it back into the carafe. She appeared to be giving the question serious thought. "I don't think *enemies* is the right word either. Just some women who envied her. She was a very stylish person, you know. I did hear a rumor at one point that she had her eyes set on Duncan Caine. He's a local realtor. But we all know that Felicity Foxworth, who runs the art store, thinks she and Duncan are an item, even though she'll likely deny it."

"Everyone knows that?"

Amanda nodded. "Small town, you know."

Shelby thought she should take that to heart. Small towns meant lots of gossip, and since Amanda couldn't come up with any other information she thought might be useful, Shelby thanked her and walked home.

She quickly fed J.T., who'd been waiting for her, or so she liked to think, on shore at the end of the dock. He'd followed her into the houseboat and started meowing the instant she opened the fridge door. After watching him get started, she rooted through the fridge but couldn't find anything that enticed her. She obviously needed to do some grocery shopping in the next couple of days. She didn't have a dinner invitation from Edie that night, and although logically she could just pick something up and drop by to find out how the afternoon had gone, Shelby was reluctant. She wanted some sign from Edie, some recognition of her feelings of needing to know more about her mom, before she got back to the dropping-in stage. She still felt weird about her last visit to her aunt's.

Shelby did, however, have a standing invitation from Drew Bryant to dine at his restaurant, Absinthe & Aurum. He'd seemed interested in her the first time they met and had also mentioned his restaurant along with the invitation. She hadn't seen him since a couple of weeks before when he'd stopped in at the chocolate shop just as she had gone in for her weekly fix. That wasn't surprising, given the news that he was back with his old girlfriend.

*Oh well*, Shelby thought as she headed along James Street to Market. She had to eat, and she enjoyed trying new places, even if she didn't have any extra motivation to check it out. She found the old house that had been renovated and now sported a vintage-inspired sign announcing that she'd indeed found Absinthe & Aurum. She smiled, enjoying the whimsical name. She knew that absinthe was a liqueur but wondered about aurum. A conversation starter for when she saw Drew.

Shelby realized that she'd walked past the restaurant before but hadn't taken the time to pay much attention to the aged building. She took a closer look now and guessed it dated from around the 1920s. She liked what she saw. The moss-green paint popped next to the white trim, and it had a wraparound porch, something Shelby had always wanted when, and if, she had her own house. The one she'd shared with her dad in Boston had been a small bungalow, but there was a small front porch where she'd been able to sit and watch the world go by.

She gave her head a small shake. It wasn't the time nor place to be thinking back to her childhood. Every time she thought she'd stored it tightly away, to be brought out only when the circumstances were right, something snuck back and caught her off guard.

She heard someone singing to the right of the front door. As she climbed the stairs, she saw a young man setting a table, then standing back for a view of his handiwork.

"That looks romantic," Shelby called out as she reached the porch.

He spun around, and a smile broke out across his face. She took him to be in his late teens, but the black tie and dress shirt made him look older. "Believe me, it is. With the lanterns turned on at night and the great food, along with some wine . . ." He left the rest to her imagination.

"I can see why you were hired," she said, smiling.

He grinned and gave her a small bow. "Table for one, two, or more?"

"For one, inside, please."

"You've got it. Follow me, please."

Shelby stepped into a small entry that opened into a lopsided room. To her right were three tables for two spaced in a row alongside a large bay window with a padded window bench. To the left looked to be the main eating area, with tables of all sizes filling the space. A large stone fireplace claimed one wall, and a wide, dark oak staircase stood beside it. The colors were an earthy mixture, making the room feel warm and inviting.

"As you can see, we're not full up for tonight yet, so you can have your choice of seats. Unless there's a reserved sign on it, that is," he added hastily, sounding a bit embarrassed.

Shelby tried to keep a straight face. She could see how hard he was trying to sound professional about it all.

"How about over in the far corner, the table for two facing the front verandah and with a side window?"

"Excellent choice. I'll just grab a menu." He walked over to an obviously antique desk and took a menu from the top of the pile. "Right this way, please."

"Shelby. It's great to see you." She heard the voice and turned to face Drew Bryant, surprised that she hadn't heard him enter the room. "Thanks. It's good to see you, too."

"I was worried you didn't like Italian food and had decided not to give my place a try."

"I don't know where the month has gone," she admitted. "In some ways it seems like I just got here and in others like I'd never left. But no excuses, I'm really looking forward to treating myself to a delicious meal."

"Then you've definitely come to the right place. I see that Blake is taking good care of you. I'll let him seat you while I check out something in the back, then I'll be right with you. In case you have any questions. About the food, that is." He smiled the charming sincere smile she remembered.

He also looked just as tantalizing as the image ingrained in her memory. She took a quick breath to calm her breathing and hoped she didn't look too eager. She watched his retreating back, amazed at the impact he'd just had on her, and then switched her attention to Blake, who held out a chair for her.

"This looks perfect," she said as Blake then unfolded her napkin and placed it on her lap.

She smiled, enjoying the attention, happy to imagine she was dining in a five-star restaurant.

When Drew returned, he was carrying a glass of red wine. "I hope you don't mind that I went ahead and chose something. If you're not a wine person, that's quite all right. I'll replace it with whatever you want. But it's a Sangiovese, recently added to my wine list," he explained. "I'd be interested in your opinion."

*Mine*? She nodded and took a sip after swishing the wine around in the glass and taking a sniff. Not that she really knew what she was looking for; she just knew that's what was done.

"It's very smooth, and I like the deep texture," she finally told him after struggling to come up with a description.

He smiled. "Just what I thought, too. It's good to know we have something in common. Now our specials tonight are Seafood Moilee, and Avocado Gnocchi with herb pesto and a creamy tomato sauce. You might prefer a Sauvignon Blanc with that. Now, sorry, but I have to get back to the kitchen. You enjoy your wine, and Blake will be back to take your order in a bit."

"You're the main chef here?" she asked in surprise. Trudy had mentioned he was a chef, but she had thought that since it was his place, he'd abandoned the cooking duties.

"When I finally got my own place, I said I'd only be in the kitchen for the odd special dish, not that I don't like being in there, but I also enjoy talking about the food to guests. But my head chef quit yesterday, and it's not easy to replace someone like him, with a lot of experience, so I'm back at it until that happens. So, you know who to complain to if you don't enjoy the food."

*As if.* Instead, she said, "I'll remember that. I do have another question though."

His smile broadened.

"I'm embarrassed to show my culinary ignorance, but what is a moilee?"

He chuckled. "That's a perfectly allowable question, Shelby. It's a South Asian dish featuring shrimp and chunks of white fish, I choose to use halibut, sautéed in a coconut milk mixture and served over Basmati rice. Delicious, if I do say so myself."

"It does sound tempting, though unusual for an Italian restaurant."

"I like to surprise my guests, and myself also. I try to switch up some of the menu choices to keep them coming back."

He gave her a dazzling smile again and then left her to peruse the menu. After making her choice, she sat wondering why there was no one else dining in this room, though it did sound like some diners might be toward the back of the house. Maybe the late diners all came here. She gave her order to Blake when he returned, deciding not to have a second glass of wine, and then watched the pedestrians passing by on Market Street while she waited.

To her surprise, Felicity Foxworth was climbing the front stairs, on the arm of a well-dressed, well-groomed man. He looked to be in his midfifties, although Shelby couldn't see much of his face since he was hunched over, talking intently to Felicity, who seemed to be thoroughly engrossed in what he was saying. Shelby couldn't see where they'd been seated but did wonder if that was Felicity's husband. But that couldn't be, since Amanda had said Felicity was interested in Duncan. Or was that a bit of malicious gossip? She didn't know anything about the woman, she realized, other than that she owned a store.

By the time her Seafood Moilee arrived, Shelby had almost finished her glass of wine, but a small basket of warm sourdough bread that had come with a dipping sauce was empty. She probably shouldn't have finished it all, but it tasted so good. She eyed her meal with delight and eased a forkful of the fish into her mouth. Absolutely delicious.

She took her time, enjoying the delightful mixture of flavors along with the setting. The night felt truly special, even if it was a dinner for one. After dinner, she finished the last sip of her espresso, then sat back feeling relaxed and content. She should have come here sooner; in fact, she'd gladly make this her go-to spot, except that Drew might get the wrong idea. That wouldn't do.

She seemed to have conjured him up, because the next thing she knew he was sitting across from her.

"I really enjoyed that, Drew. You're a terrific chef."

He grinned and did a quick bow of his head. "Music to my ears, Shelby. I thought I'd take a quick break. We have a large birthday party coming in later, so this might be my only chance tonight. I'm glad I can take it with you."

She felt flustered. Flirting wasn't her strongest skill, if that's what they were doing. What about his girlfriend? Was she reading too much into this? She had to admit, she was flattered by the attention. But she wouldn't let it go to her head. Or at least she'd try not to.

"I should probably get going and let you get prepared for the onslaught."

He nodded. "Okay. Thanks for coming and for being so appreciative. A chef loves it when the food is praised, you know. This is on the house, by the way."

"No, I couldn't accept that."

He put out his hand to stop her from opening her purse. "If this were a date, I'd insist on paying, and since I really would like to take you out, please let me at least treat you tonight."

She couldn't think of a thing to say, so she simply nodded. "Thank you."

He followed her to the door. "I really mean it about a date; it's just that things can get crazy here. I do manage to sometimes get a personal life, though, so if you don't mind a last-minute phone call sometime . . ." He left the question hanging.

"I'd enjoy that," she answered with a smile, and realized she meant it. *But what about his girlfriend?*

# Chapter Twenty-Five

Duncan Caine was on Shelby's mind the next morning as she got ready for work. She'd meant to find out more about him the day after the board meeting, but somehow the week had gotten away from her. What she most wanted to know was why he had been so snippy with her at the board meeting. He didn't even know her. And why had he been "out of sorts," as Felicity had said, for a couple of weeks? About the same amount of time that Loreena had been dead. Was it important? Shelby wondered as she filled J.T.'s dish and put it on the floor for him.

The cat had been sitting just a foot away from the mat she'd recently bought to put his food on and sauntered over to give her offering a sniff. It looked like he couldn't decide where to start—with the dry or the canned. Shelby sympathized. She often had trouble deciding about her food, also.

She picked up the phone and gave Edie a quick call. Even though Edie seemed to be avoiding her, Shelby needed information and if that meant phoning her, so be it. "Hi, Edie, how did it go at the store yesterday? I tried calling last night."

"Oh, I guess Trudy told you. It went fine, though. I really enjoyed being with the customers again. How did you find meeting with a sales rep and doing the ordering? Exciting, isn't it?"

"Yes, but also tiring. I'm finding I still have a lot to learn about the book business."

Edie chuckled, which Shelby took to be a good sign. It was almost as if there hadn't been any tension between them. Perhaps Shelby had blown it all out of proportion in her own mind.

"I've also been wondering," Edie continued, "how did you find the board meeting?"

Shelby filled her in. "I want to talk to Duncan Caine a bit more. Where can I find him?"

"Duncan? He's a funny bird, or at least he thinks *I'm* a funny bird and doesn't really have that much time for me. But he owns the real estate office on Market Street, Caine Realty. It's at the fork in the road before you get to the Cornwall Brothers Store Museum. Don't mention my name and you should be fine."

Shelby couldn't tell if Edie was kidding or not, so she let it pass.

"Do you think he'd be there today? It is a Saturday, after all."

"I think he lives there. Not really, of course. But it seems to be his home away from home."

They hung up shortly after that, and Shelby glanced at the clock, deciding she'd stop by Duncan's office on her way in to work. It would be just a short detour.

She quickly got dressed and went in search of J.T. He was stretched out in the window in her living room, soaking in some serious sunlight. She decided to leave him in for the day even though it would be good wandering weather. She just hated to move him when he seemed so pampered and happy. If J.T. was unhappy with the situation, she was willing to listen to his complaints later. After work.

She walked quickly over to James Street and then along Market until she found Caine Realty. The office looked small from the outside, although the building itself was a large two-storied old stone structure. It had to have been around for decades, she mused as she checked for traffic before crossing the street. The building looked to be divided in two, each side mirroring the other. Caine Realty took up the right-hand side, while Modern Pine Interiors occupied the adjacent space. As she approached the front door, she could see Duncan through the window, sitting at a desk, talking on the phone. She hoped he was in a good mood this morning.

She opened the door, and he looked up, then back down, but not before she'd noticed the scowl. *Hmm, maybe not such a good idea after all.* She wandered to the wall and checked out the many photographs of current listings, amazed at the prices on some of the vacation homes. She knew her budget would never stretch that far.

When Duncan finally hung up, she approached his desk, a smile on her face. "I'm sorry to just drop in like this, but I wanted to see you before I went in to work."

"You looking to buy?" He sounded hopeful.

"Uh, no. I'm renting right now and probably will be for some time."

He stood up. "You know, I've offered your aunt a good price for that house she's living in. I don't have a buyer, but I'm willing to take a risk. You know what she did? She turned me down flat." His scowl had returned.

"Well, it is the family home, and she's lived there a long time. Where would she go?"

"A condo? Apartment? Old folks' home?"

Shelby swallowed her retort. *Old folks*? That would get Edie's blood boiling for sure. Time to change the topic.

"I found the board meeting the other day very interesting." She turned to look at the numerous listings again. "Have you been a member for a long time?"

"Why do you want to know?"

She willed herself not to throw her hands up in the air in total exasperation. When she looked at him, she noted the suspicion in his eyes. "Just curious. The group seems to work so well together, like you've all known each other a long time."

"That's because we have." He looked like he'd won a point, although she hadn't known they were competing. "We all grew up here. You really do need to know what this town is all about before you take on the challenges of such a board." He sat back down and eyed his phone.

Oh boy, was that directed at her? She knew she'd better make this quick. "I could see how upset you were when Loreena's passing was mentioned. I'm sorry for your loss."

His head jerked up. "What are you talking about? We

are all upset, equally. I'm no more upset than anyone else on the board. Why would you say that? What are you getting at?"

*That you're protesting way too much, for starters.* "Oh, I'm sorry. I didn't realize this would be such a big issue, or is it a nonissue? I'm confused."

He stood abruptly. "I had known Loreena since we were kids, so of course, I was upset. When you live in a town the size of Alexandria Bay, you know everyone you grew up with. Those relationships are important. It gives a sense of history. And, as you know, we served on the board together. Now, I don't know what you're trying to infer, because that's what it sounds like you're doing, but that was the extent of it. Now, if you'll excuse me, I have important work to do."

He walked over to the door and held it open for her.

"Thanks for your time," she said as she slipped past him. He didn't answer, but she felt his eyes on her as she crossed the street. That's when she finally let out the breath she'd been holding.

* * *

Her conversation with Duncan kept creeping back into her mind throughout the day, no matter how hard she tried to stay focused. After a particularly noisy set of customers had left the bookstore, all of them seniors, Shelby noted, she found herself thinking that she really needed to talk to someone who knew more about Duncan Caine and Loreena. If there was anything to know, that is. But who?

*Felicity Foxworth, that's who.* She had been very pleasant at the board meeting, after all. Besides, Shelby didn't have a clue where else to start. Another call to Edie got her Felicity's contact information. Edie hadn't even asked what it was about, Shelby noted, hanging up. She must have guessed, or else she was avoiding a longer conversation that might end up with more questions about Merrily Cox.

By the time Shelby had locked up the store at the end of a busy afternoon, she had formulated some questions in her mind. Her next stop, once she got back to the Bay, was at the Gallery on the Bay, Felicity's shop, which was, surprisingly, right next door to home base, Bayside Books. Shelby guessed that they had probably just missed running into each other on several occasions, seeing that their stores shared the same main entrance. She realized, once again, that she hadn't really gone about integrating herself into the community very well since arriving.

On the shuttle back to the Bay, she asked Taylor, who seemed to be fitting in just fine with the locals, for any background information about Felicity and her gallery.

"You mean, you haven't even met her yet?"

"I met her at the Heritage Society board meeting, but I do feel odd about not yet having dropped into the gallery. Or shop. I love looking at artwork."

"Well, it works both ways. She could have come in to see you. It's not as if you just moved to town or started working in the bookstore. I'm sort of surprised she didn't, because she's a great gossip. Oh well, I guess she's had a lot on her plate with her dog and all."

"What about her dog? Is this something I should ask her about?"

"She'd be delighted. She has a bichon that she treats like her baby and shows him, so she's often running around the state appearing at the different dog shows."

"That must be quite a commitment. Who takes care of the gallery when she's not there?"

"Chrissie Halstead."

"You mean the Chrissie who's also taking Loreena's place?"

Taylor shrugged and pushed her reading glasses onto the top of her head. With the white cotton blouse she'd buttoned to the collar and the spring-toned multicolored scarf casually wrapped around her shoulders, she looked very professional. Shelby avoided glancing at her own green tunic top and casual cream pants. She felt so dowdy sometimes.

"What can I say?" Taylor continued. "It's a small place; people and jobs often overlap. There are a couple of part-timers on staff, just like at the bookstore."

"Hm. I gather Felicity never had children, the usual source of cheap labor."

"She never married, much like Loreena. They used to chum around a lot until Loreena suddenly got a serious boyfriend."

Shelby turned her head and looked at Taylor. A font of information. She wondered who that man was that she'd seen Felicity dining with. "Why haven't you told me any of this before?"

"You never asked me. You've been more interested in what Chuck knows or says," she said with a "got you" smile.

Shelby nodded. "I guess that's true. Is there anything else?"

Taylor looked like she was giving it some thought. "Nothing important, I guess. Anything else would be gossip. It's better that Felicity fill you in on all of that and the love triangle."

Shelby looked sharply at Taylor again, who gave her a quick smile and wiggled her eyebrows. Shelby remained deep in thought until they reached shore, then they walked together toward the bookstore. Taylor turned right on Church, headed toward home.

Shelby opened the front door of Bayside Books and stuck her head into the bookstore to say hi. She thought it might look strange to Trudy if she happened to see Shelby going into the gallery next door without stopping by. Trudy looked up from the computer and gave her a small wave. "Just finishing up, then I'm heading to Edie's."

"Of course," Shelby said under her breath. No invitation for her. She was definitely feeling a cold shoulder from Edie. In a normal voice, she added, "Have a nice evening. I'm going to take a look at Felicity's shop next door."

The sign at the Gallery on the Bay said it was open for another twenty minutes. Shelby pushed the door open, hoping she'd find Felicity, not Chrissie, at the store. The fates were with her. Felicity looked up from a letter she was reading and smiled.

"Why, Shelby. So nice to see you again. Welcome to my little shop." Felicity wore her almost-shoulder-length hair tucked behind her ears. It looked like she'd recently come from a salon, with maybe a touch-up to remove any errant signs of gray in her coal-black hair. She was obviously proud of her appearance, and that included the mint-green pantsuit she wore.

Shelby could hear a small dog barking behind a closed door toward the back of the shop.

"That's my Wainright Walton the Third. He's such a friendly lad, but I find it difficult to do my day-end tally when he's poking around, so I give him a nice liver treat and encourage him to have a rest. Would you like to meet him?"

"For sure," Shelby said, hoping the fact that she was gritting her teeth wasn't apparent. Shelby was even less a dog person than she was a cat one. Her dad had never even allowed neighbors' dogs in their yard. She had always supposed he'd had a bad experience with one, and over time, she had come to adopt the same resistance to them.

Felicity walked quickly across the floor in her ballet flats. Shelby thought they were probably ideal for the finish on the hardwood floor, then looked at her own shoes, covered in who knows what from the island. She hoped the floor would survive her visit.

Felicity opened the door and knelt down, shoving her face into the furry back of a white curly coat. When she stood up, the dog waddled over to Shelby and gave her a thorough sniffing. Shelby wasn't sure if she was allowed to touch the dog, being a show dog and all, but Felicity looked encouraging, so she leaned over and gave him a quick pat on his head. His nose snapped up, and she felt the cold sensation on her wrist before snatching back her hand. "He's so, um, cute."

Felicity nodded her head vigorously. "Isn't he just! He's a three-time winner in his class at the dog shows. I guess he can stay out with us now that he has a visitor."

Shelby forced a smile and sidled over to the counter. Felicity followed, as did Wainright.

"I hope you don't mind my dropping in like this. I wanted to have a little talk with you, but I realize this is probably not a good time of day. You must be busy closing."

"I've just finished," Felicity said. "If you'd like to just take a look around, I'll finish putting things away, and then we can go across the street for a coffee, if you'd like. I often like to end my day with a treat."

Shelby nodded. "That would be nice."

She glanced around and noted that the artwork ran the gamut from oil to watercolors and charcoal sketches. The gallery seemed to go in strictly for traditional artwork, or maybe anything mixed-media or experimental was in the back room. A variety of small sculptures decorated the various tables, along with ceramic dishes and figurines. Hanging from a few small tree branches were about a dozen Christmas ornaments. Two glass balls attracted her attention. A closer look showed they were scenes from around the Bay, and a small sign attached to one branch gave the artist's name and stated that they were hand-painted. Shelby would definitely be back for a selection to add to her Christmas tree.

There was also a round table with a selection of silk scarves and pashminas hanging from an elegant metal rack. Shelby noticed a scarf very similar to the one Felicity had worn the day they'd met at the council meeting. Obviously, Felicity liked to wear what she sold. That was an excellent recommendation if ever there was one.

Shelby assumed the layout of the rooms was similar to that of the bookstore, which meant there was also a large space off to the right. She started wandering, enjoying the variety of works, all by local artists, according to the sign, and had made her way around the walls and movable displays in the center of the room when Felicity signaled she was ready.

"Just let me tuck Wainright back into the office with another treat. He'll settle down as soon as he realizes we've left the shop. I'll be back for him on my way home."

Shelby waited by the front door until Felicity rejoined her and locked the door behind them. Felicity, much to Shelby's surprise, linked their arms as they walked across the street. The coffee shop was almost empty, not unusual given the late hour, and Shelby was actually surprised Felicity would want to go for a coffee now. Then she realized that, like her, Felicity was another single person with no one except her pet to get home to.

Shelby bought the coffee, feeling it was the least she could do in order to get the answers she wanted. She added two Danishes after checking with Felicity. The strawberry ones. After Felicity had her first bite of the Danish and a sip of coffee and had a look of delight on her face, Shelby started talking.

"I'm embarrassed to admit that I didn't know who you

were when we met at the board meeting, even though we're store neighbors. I'm also surprised you didn't mention it."

Felicity looked flustered. "Oh, dear, didn't I? I guess I assumed you knew. I've had so much on my mind lately with Wainright, who hasn't really been feeling too well lately, and there's another show coming up. And then, of course, what happened to Loreena. It threw me for a loop. I still can't believe all that's happened."

Aha. The opening Shelby had been hoping for.

"It was a shock. Did you know I'm the one who found her body?"

Felicity looked surprised. "No, I don't think I did. Or maybe I did but I forgot. Oh, I'm not sure."

"It doesn't matter. But what does matter is that I think the police have it all wrong. You heard what Mr. Truelove said at the board meeting? Well, I'm certain Matthew Kessler is not a killer."

"Oh, I don't know anything about that. I haven't really talked to the man, although I had heard that your Aunt Edie is a good friend of his."

"You've heard that?"

"Oh, yes. Small town, you know."

Shelby was getting a bit tired of hearing that but was starting to get used to it. "Well, neither of us believes it, so I'm just asking a few questions since I'm new to town and don't really know anyone."

Felicity nodded and finished off the Danish. Shelby looked at her own, surprised it was still untouched. She left it like that.

"I understand that you and Loreena were good friends, is that right?"

Felicity kept nodding but looked a bit cautious. "We grew up together and were best friends throughout school. We hadn't seen as much of each other as we aged and got involved in our own lives. Running a business is so time-consuming, you know, and Loreena gave her all to the Heritage Society."

"But knowing each other for so long, you would know all about her relationship with Duncan Caine."

Felicity started coughing and quickly reached for her coffee. She finished it before answering. "You know, there wasn't really what I'd call a *relationship*. Nothing romantic or anything. We're all, at least we *were*, all very good friends and would often do things as a threesome."

Shelby nodded. "All right, so you're saying he wasn't her boyfriend or anything then?"

Felicity also nodded. "No, no. In no way. She was seeing someone else, you know."

"She was? Who?"

Felicity looked around as if wanting to make sure no one could overhear. "Barry Pellen. He's a big developer from Buffalo who's working on buying some property to build a hotel and casino."

*A new name in the mix.* "Wow. That would be a big project. Where would it be?"

"Oh, I'm not sure. It's all very hush-hush. Duncan is the realtor, but he hadn't told either of us anything about it. I know it's a big-bucks deal. Loreena liked to let on that she had some inside information. That was Loreena. She said she got all her information from Barry, you know. I'm sure I shouldn't be telling you any of this, so please, don't spread it around."

"Was her relationship with him a secret?"

"Well, let's just say there are some townspeople not too pleased with the idea of another resort in the area. If it became common knowledge that Loreena was going out with the developer, it might have gotten her a few enemies."

*Was a murderer on that list, perhaps?* "Do you think Duncan might have been upset about her going out with Barry?"

Felicity's eyes opened wide. A glint of anger flashed across them but disappeared so quickly, Shelby wondered if she'd really seen it. She did have the distinct feeling it had been the wrong question to ask, though.

"Of course he wasn't upset," Felicity finally answered. "I already told you, they were just friends."

Shelby knew she had to repair whatever damage she had just done, but she wasn't sure how to do it. She watched as Felicity grabbed her purse and stood up.

"Thanks for the coffee and Danish. I'd better see to Wainright. He doesn't like being left alone very long."

Shelby kicked herself for driving away a promising lead. What had gone wrong? Duncan Caine was obviously a touchy subject with Felicity. Just what was his game?

# Chapter Twenty-Six

Shelby's conversation with Felicity hadn't done much to explain Loreena's relationship with Duncan Caine. In fact, Shelby thought it sounded like Felicity might have been a bit jealous even though she claimed they were all just friends. That would fit in with what Amanda had said. Did that bring Felicity into the suspect pool? Could she have been jealous enough to kill her childhood best friend Loreena? Well, that certainly sounded far-fetched. Felicity seemed to be a sweet but slightly muddled older woman. Which, when Shelby gave it some thought, didn't jive with the business woman who owned the successful art gallery next door. Why would she want to come across as the former? Was it some sort of game or part of a larger plan?

Of course, Barry Pellen deserved his own visit, Shelby decided. Even though he wasn't an Alex Bay resident, he did have an interest in the community, and he seemed to be a possible love interest of Loreena's. But he did seem like an unlikely suspect also, mainly because he wasn't living in the community. Of course, it could have been a long-distance relationship. Those were common. She needed to know how often he came to the area, for starters. Was there a love triangle of another sort and Duncan was the one feeling himself pushed out? Was that a possible motive?

Or maybe it had something to do with the proposed development. If it was such a big secret, that might mean they were worried about the reaction from people in town. Or maybe even the reaction of the town council. There were all sorts of possibilities, but Shelby was the first to acknowledge that she knew little to nothing about real estate schemes and dreams. There must be someone she could ask, aside from Duncan Caine, that is.

She obviously wouldn't get much more information out of Felicity. Maybe Edie knew something more about Loreena's romantic possibilities, but Shelby figured her aunt would have already mentioned it if that were the case. Who could she talk to? When in doubt, go for the chocolate. She needed a truffle to be able to cope, and maybe Erica could give her some suggestions.

Shelby reached Chocomania right before closing, though despite the lateness of the hour, the chocolate lovers were still out in force. Shelby waved at Erica and sidled close to the large display case, noting with a sigh that there was an empty plate where the spicy dark chocolate truffles should have been. She concentrated on what other flavor called out to her and still stood in place when the final two giggling teenagers left.

Erica let out an exaggerated sigh of relief, then quickly said, "Don't worry, I put aside some of your favorite hotties just in case you stopped in."

Shelby clapped her hands. "Yay for you. I so need a lift."

Erica disappeared into the back room and returned almost immediately with a small box. "There are four in there. Didn't want you to overdose."

Shelby pulled out her wallet, and when Erica waved it off, Shelby insisted. "I can't always be the freeloader around here. But instead, you can throw in some information, if you have it."

Erica looked interested. She tucked a curl back in place that had escaped the scarf she'd twisted into a headband and then leaned her arms across the top of the glass display case. "About what?"

"I just learned about the possibility that a new hotel and casino might be built in the area. What do you know about it?"

"Only what I've heard at any of the council meetings I've attended or read online. You should plan on going to the next monthly meeting, you know. Our little community might grow on you." She said it smiling, although Shelby had a feeling there was a message included there.

"It *is* growing on me, believe me. So, what about the hotel?"

"There's a developer who's been leading the negotiations, and from what I hear, it's moving ahead smoothly. Of course, there's a lot of pushback from the owners of the present hotels in the area, and there are several residents who are also against bringing more tourists—read, more traffic—into the area."

"But it's still going ahead?"

"Well, according to Duncan Caine, it is. He's handling the deal on behalf of the current property owner, which means he's dealing with the town and its concerns and the developer."

"Barry Pellen?"

"I think that's his name. He lives in Buffalo or someplace not all that far away, but Duncan rented him a house in the village."

"That's interesting. So he must be in town a lot then?"

Erica shrugged. "I'm really not sure. Like I said, I only know what I read. Why?"

"Felicity Foxworth just told me that Loreena Swan was involved with him."

"As in an affair?" Erica's eyes widened.

"So it seems."

"Loreena? I can't picture her like that, but that may be because I've known her, sort of, all my life. Just like I can't imagine my mom in a relationship."

"What about my Aunt Edie?"

Erica smiled. "Uh, you mean as in Edie and Matthew."

"That's exactly what I mean. It would have been nice to hear about their relationship sooner, from a friend perhaps."

"It wasn't any of my business. She must have had a reason to keep it a secret from you. Or, you know, she just might not have thought of mentioning it. I doubt a lot of village people know either."

"Huh. She seems to have a lot of secrets."

"What do you mean by that?"

Shelby debated about sharing her woes with Erica and

then decided she needed a sounding board. "I keep trying to get information from her about my mother, and she always changes the subject or pretends not to hear. It's driving me crazy." She watched Erica's face closely to see if there was any change in her expression.

"That sounds weird. Maybe you're misinterpreting it. Or else, once again, she must have her reasons."

"If she does, I want to know what they are. It is my mother, after all. Do you think your mom would know anything about it?"

Erica shrugged. "We've never discussed your family, now that you mention it. But Mom seems to know everyone in town, so it's possible they met."

The bell over the front door in the shop jingled, and Erica led the way out front, giving Shelby an apologetic smile. The customer, a woman Shelby recognized but didn't know, made her purchase and left.

"I have another question, Erica, if you don't mind."

"Shoot."

"What about your brother and his girlfriend? What's going on there?" She knew she'd need to explain it all when she saw the look on Erica's face. "I had dinner at his restaurant the other night, which he comped for me. It was really very nice of him, but I thought you'd said he was back with his girlfriend."

Erica helped herself to a truffle before taking a seat on the nearby stool. "Huh. That's our Drew. I don't know if he'll ever settle down, although he does like being in relationships. Serena, his ex-now-new girlfriend, is a high-maintenance model from a wealthy family who lives in Buffalo. It's a long-distance affair at best, although she used to come to the Bay frequently for long weekends. She's gorgeous, and she knows it, but in spite of that, I kind of like her. She keeps Drew on his toes so that he doesn't take things for granted. When she dumped him, he was in a real slump. I hadn't seen him that bad off in a long time. She came back to him, by the way."

She held out another tray to Shelby, who all of a sudden felt like she needed another treat. This wasn't quite what she'd hoped to hear.

Erica resumed her story. "But I think he's a much wiser man these days and he won't be committing his heart too soon. So, if you'd like an enjoyable evening with a really nice guy—and remember, I'm a little bit prejudiced—I think you should go out with him. Just don't get too emotionally involved until you see how things are going. Okay? I don't want to see you get hurt." Erica ended with a lopsided smile, and Shelby couldn't help but laugh.

She shook her head. "I promise, I won't get hurt. I'm kind of leery about relationships myself."

"And why is that?"

"That is a story for another time and place. Wine must be involved." Shelby sat on the stool behind the cash register. "But thanks for being so forthright. He certainly is handsome and a terrific cook too. So, I'll keep your advice in mind."

"He is a great cook. Remember the adage about food being the way to someone's heart."

The bell jangled as the front door opened again. Shelby

was surprised to see Zack Griffin saunter in, his eyes fixed on the display of truffles to the right of the door. When he looked at the counter, he seemed surprised.

"Are you moonlighting, Shelby?"

"What? Oh, no." She looked down at the stool she was sitting on. "Just being lazy. Although I can recommend some great truffles."

Erica laughed. "Zack is my second-best customer after you, Shelby."

"Oh." Shelby wasn't sure what to say next. It was nice to know they had something in common, but the last time she'd seen him, she'd been decidedly rude. "Well, I should be getting home anyway. Thanks, Erica." She held up the box.

"I just stopped by for a small mixed box of the dark chili truffles and the butter cream, Erica," Zack said. "Were either of those what you would have recommended?"

His question was addressed to Shelby, who wondered for a moment if he was being sarcastic. Deciding he wasn't, she answered, "The dark chili is my first choice, followed very closely by the butter cream."

He grinned. "Awesome. Can I give you a lift home?"

Shelby almost answered that it wasn't far, then noticed the look on his face. He was obviously joking, knowing what a short walk it was to the houseboat. "I'll take a rain check, thanks. For when it's raining again."

He laughed. It sounded genuine and pleasant. Shelby wasn't sure why she was surprised. She grabbed her bags.

"In that case, I'll walk you home, if you don't mind. I have a couple of questions."

*Figures.* "Sure." She kept her voice neutral and gave Erica a small wave.

Erica walked them both to the door and gave Shelby a hug followed by a wink. "See you later."

# Chapter Twenty-Seven

Zack held the door open for Shelby and then walked beside her, waiting until a U-Haul cube truck passed by before crossing the street.

"Busy day at the store?" he asked, falling in step beside her.

"Not really. But I have made an observation about being in retail, the ordering-books part anyway. I've decided it doesn't matter how much I assume about tourists and weather patterns, it's all a matter of chance."

"Sounds about right."

They walked to the end of the block without Zack saying anything else. She glanced at him, and he seemed to be enjoying just looking at the store windows. She had to admit to herself that he did kind of take her breath away.

And then, when she couldn't stand his silence any longer, nor the direction her thoughts were headed, she asked, "What did you want to ask me?"

"It can wait."

"So, have you decided to share the lowdown on the

smuggling ring?" Shelby asked, keeping her eyes straight ahead.

"You don't quit, do you?" He sounded more amused than annoyed.

"Not when I have my Aunt Edie as my conscience. And since the police chief isn't letting us in on anything, you just might be my only source. Unless you can put in a good word with the chief for me."

Zack snorted. "That's not going to happen. Let's just say the chief and I don't always see eye to eye. Haven't since one summer when me and my folks were staying here. She caught a bunch of us repainting the goal lines on the football field at the school."

"I'm almost afraid to ask. What color?"

"Pink."

She started laughing. "You didn't!" This gave her a totally new opinion of Zack Griffin.

"We did, and I'd do it again."

Shelby mulled that over, smiling at the image. "That's sort of cool."

She heard Zack chuckle. Then he added, "I thought so, at the time. But my dad didn't agree, and if it wasn't for the fact that he'd inherited the family vacation house when my grandfather died, we wouldn't have set foot in the Bay again. I'm certain of it. He had a reputation to uphold."

"So, you didn't grow up here?"

"No. I'm from Seattle originally, but we came here every summer when I was growing up. You couldn't find a spot more different from our house. Besides, I love being close to the water. That's why I rented the house from Dad when I was transferred here."

"But transferred means you move around. What will you do with the house when that happens?'

He smiled. "It will be my vacation destination." He looked at his watch. "No wonder I'm so hungry. Would you like to grab a bite to eat?"

Such a casual question. Was it a date or just a matter of convenience? Either way, she wasn't really hungry, but it sounded like the ideal way to get some more information. "Food sounds good."

He pointed at Riley's by the River, a two-story brick pub restaurant overlooking the dock. Shelby had eaten there several times and had always enjoyed the food. She hoped they could get a table by the window, as she never tired of looking at the water.

"That sounds good. Sure."

She felt the pressure of his hand on the small of her back as they crossed the street. He held the door open, and she followed him up a few stairs to where the hostess stood. After they were seated, he asked if she'd like something to drink.

Why not? He obviously wanted information from her. He could reward her with a glass of wine. He ordered a Corona Extra for himself, and they perused the menus until their drinks arrived, at which time they placed their orders.

"Cheers," he said, tipping his glass toward her.

"Cheers. Okay, I'm really curious what you want to know," she said, all out of patience.

He crossed his arms on the tabletop and leaned on them. "I know you've been asking some questions around town about all this, and I'd like to know what, if anything, you've found out."

"How about we do a trade?"

He raised his eyebrows. Those eyes again. Even though this was serious talk, his eyes looked like they were laughing. Such an enticing look.

"I'll tell you what I've found out if you tell me why the Coast Guard is interested. Is it because of smuggling?"

He shook his head. "Why do you keep bringing up the subject of smuggling?"

"Because that's what you do, isn't it? Of course, I know you do a lot more, too. But since this murder didn't take place in the middle of the river, and, if there were any smuggling going on in the area, the Coast Guard would be on it, right?"

He sat back and let out a deep breath. "You've obviously been doing your research, but why does that matter to you?"

"Why? Because Blye Island, the grotto in particular, has a history of smuggling."

"So?"

"So that's where my store is located."

"And?"

"And I did find the body, after all."

"So this is just curiosity, is it? You're being nosy." He crossed his arms on the table and leaned forward on them.

He had a point, sort of, but she wasn't about to admit it. She also couldn't read him. Was he teasing her, or did she detect a hint of annoyance? "Well, not really. My Aunt Edie is really worried about Matthew."

"Which in itself is not a good enough reason for you to get involved in all this. However, I will tell you that I don't think Kessler is involved in any smuggling, if there is any going on, that is."

It was Shelby's turn to sigh. "You're not very helpful."

"And here I thought I was. Ah, saved by the meal," Zack said as the server brought their orders. The waiter took great care in placing the dishes on the table, then asked if they needed anything else. They both shook their heads.

They spent a few minutes in silent appreciation of their choices until Zack finally said, "Look, I know this is important to you and your aunt both, but I don't know a whole lot about what's happening with the local and state police. I have a specific avenue to investigate"—he paused and held up his hand—"and I'm not sharing what that is with you. Now, tell me what you've learned. Please."

"Nothing."

"Really?"

"Well, nothing relevant. I know about the politics of the castle, the store in particular, and how Loreena wanted her nephew to take over the store in Edie's absence. I'm just not sure of the why. It doesn't make a lot of sense to me. And I know that Loreena was a tyrant at work. As for her personal life, she's been romantically linked with Barry Pellen."

"The hotel developer?"

"The same. And I kind of think Duncan Caine, the realtor, was also interested in her."

"Busy woman."

Shelby shrugged. "Maybe none of which has anything to do with her murder, but it could make for an interesting and possibly deadly triangle, don't you think? And then there's the fact that she was a bully in her domain at the castle, from what I can gather and from what I knew personally, so there might be a better motive somewhere there." She took a bite of her crab cake, and when she'd swallowed, she added casually, "Of course, if there is smuggling going on at the grotto, maybe she was involved in some way and that's why she was killed. I mean, she was well placed to oversee anything that was happening. Maybe she was the mastermind of the operation. Or maybe love is blind."

"You're now suggesting that either Pellen or Caine is a smuggler?"

She shrugged, then looked around her, suddenly hoping nobody else in the restaurant could hear their conversation. No one seemed interested even if they had heard.

"Okay, maybe I'm way off base. If it's not that, I'm going with the love triangle." She watched him for a reaction, hoping to discover if she was on the right track.

Zack shook his head, a wry twist to his lips. "How are your crab cakes?"

"Very tasty." Shelby feigned excessive delight, knowing a change in topic when she saw one. "And your meal?"

"The same."

*Of course it is.*

Zack smiled, appearing to Shelby like he thought he'd won that one.

*We'll see about that.*

Shelby turned her attention to what was happening on the wharf. Two couples were wandering along its length, one on the older side seemingly in deep reflection about the stunning scenery, the other much younger and stopping frequently to peer into the water. A group of young children several feet in front of harried-looking parents ran onto the dock and knelt down, excited about what lay under the water. Shelby would have loved to join them and take a look. She turned her attention back to her tablemate.

"So, tell me some more about Zack Griffin from Seattle."

She could tell by the look on his face that she'd caught him off guard. She was pleased. Then came the calculating look. She felt like he was weighing the pros and cons of telling her so much, or maybe nothing at all.

"Hmm. Okay, since you asked. Zachary Griffin the Third, that would be. Father, an attorney with a high-powered law firm, as was the original ZG the First. Of course, I was expected to carry on the family tradition, and when I dug my heels in, choosing a career that offered more adventure and less prestige, I was no longer the family favorite. So, here I am, on my own, in Alexandria Bay, a proud member of the Coast Guard Investigative Service. That, in a nutshell, is that, as they say."

So not what Shelby had expected to hear, but then again, she wasn't really sure what she had assumed, not since she'd found out he wasn't born and raised in the Bay. And not since she'd realized she actually was really interested.

"That must have been hard for you," she finally said.

He shrugged. "At times, but my dad and I have been at loggerheads most of my life. It's a good thing I have siblings who fit more into the mold. I miss my mom, though. If I could figure out a way to avoid an argument with Dad, I'd visit them more often."

He turned to gaze out the window. "There you have it."

Shelby didn't have a clue what to say, and she resisted the urge to reach out to touch his hand. He probably wasn't telling her all this to garner sympathy. It was just a fact of life for him. She turned and spent a few minutes watching scenery.

Finally, after she declined dessert, Zack suggested they leave. He walked her back to the houseboat, and she debated about whether to invite him in for a drink, deciding that since this wasn't a date, it wouldn't be a good idea. She felt less anxious after making the decision and dared to ask him some more direct questions.

"If it turns out Loreena's murder is related to smuggling, what would they be smuggling?"

She felt the hesitation in Zack's steps. "That's not information I can share, Shelby. And, if there is anything going on, it has nothing to do with you."

"Is that just another way of saying it's none of my business?"

"Yes."

"But you know, if there's smuggling, it adds to the legend of the castle and the island itself."

"You're a romantic."

"I never thought of myself as one." That was the truth. She'd never been one to believe in heart-thumping, breathless reactions. Probably because she'd never met a man who'd ever caused one. "Would that make a difference? What if I wanted to further the legend in order to increase the traffic to the castle and thus the store?"

"I hadn't taken you for the calculating type."

She felt her spine stiffen. "I'm not. It's just that everything isn't always as it seems."

"Don't I know it. I'm in law enforcement, after all."

"Ha. Well, I hope this seemingly enjoyable dinner has provided you with some information relevant to your enforcing."

He glanced at her. "Best check I ever paid."

She hadn't expected that answer. "Good." She quickened her pace and turned to face him at the dock. "I enjoyed the meal. Thanks."

"My pleasure." He smiled and she hastily retreated along the wharf and to her houseboat, unsettled by the talk.

And that smile.

# Chapter Twenty-Eight

Shelby's cell phone rang as she was struggling to unlock the door to the houseboat. She should have just put her purse down on the deck before inserting the key. Instead she pushed the door open and almost tripped over T.J., who made a mad dash outdoors. Finally she managed to pull her cell out of her purse. She answered, trying not to sound too breathless.

"It's Drew. I was just wondering if you're free for dinner on Monday, as in tomorrow night."

His voice sounded warm and inviting. "Monday?"

*How uncool.* She could have slapped herself.

He chuckled. "Yes, short notice, I know, and also an odd night for a date, I know, but the restaurant is closed on Mondays, so I actually have a day and evening to myself. I was thinking we could drive to Clayton. There are a couple of newer restaurants I've been wanting to try. How about it?"

She tried to corral her thoughts. They were all over the place. She remembered Erica's warning, and she thought about Zack. Plenty of good reasons to say no, except for the

Zack part. He had no interest in her as someone other than a pesky citizen poking her nose in police business. And since when had she been concerned about that, anyway? Drew was the question at the moment.

"Sure, that would be nice." She couldn't believe she'd just said that. But what did she have to lose? Nothing, and like tonight, she'd at least have some tasty food.

"Great. What time works best for you? I know you'll probably be back on the last shuttle, right?"

"Oh, right. Tomorrow is Monday and usually my day off too, but I'm covering for someone. How about five forty-five? Would that make it too late?"

"Not at all. I'll make the reservation and pick you up at five forty-five."

"Uh, no need to come up to the houseboat. I'll wait on shore in the park."

"Sure. Whatever you say. I'll see you then. I'm looking forward to it."

"Me, too." She hung up feeling a bit dreamy, followed quickly by a deep sinking feeling. What had she just done?

* * *

Shelby awoke Monday morning with Zack Griffin on her mind. She sure hoped she hadn't been dreaming about him. Surely she was too old for that silly schoolgirl romantic stuff. She hadn't even gone through that stage at the right age. Maybe she was making up for lost time. *Ugh!* And then there was Drew Bryant. Two dates, sort of, with two different men all within a few days. What was going on in her life?

Of course, Zack hadn't really set up a date with her; it was just a chance meal. And Drew, although it *was* a date, had a girlfriend, sort of, so it probably wouldn't be overly romantic.

Besides, she wasn't interested in a romance. *Right?*

She did notice that she'd awoken without the help of the alarm and in plenty of time for a run or jog, or at least a power walk. An omen, at the very least.

Shelby was kept hopping at the castle bookstore all day long, not even taking a lunch break. It was exactly what she needed. She was so pleased she'd decided to go in to work to cover for Taylor, who had wanted the day off, since her husband had it also and they needed to pick up something in Watertown. Shelby could have asked Cody to cover but thought a day of work was better than sitting at home thinking about murder.

*Oh, well.* She'd wished for a busy day to keep her mind busy. And now it felt like someone had heard her wishes. Not only were the school tours noisy and crowded, but there seemed to be boatload after boatload of tourists stopping by at regular intervals. She tried to re-stock the empty spaces on the shelves but eventually gave up. By five PM, Shelby was more than ready to leave. She debated about just taking the cash and counting it later, maybe getting away a bit early herself. But then she wondered why. She'd just have to wait for Drew. So she eventually locked the door and settled in to do the counting. All in all, a very good day.

She realized, however, that she was excited about the date, as she should be. She admired the colorful short-sleeved tunic top she'd recently bought as she took a quick glance in the mirror in the back room. She ran her fingers through her hair and tried to make herself as presentable as possible.

The shuttle ride was smooth and not too crowded. She spotted Drew waiting in the parking lot as she walked up the dock. He waved, and she gave him a small one in return.

"This is great, Shelby. I'm glad you were able to fit me into your busy schedule," he said as he kissed her on the cheek.

She glanced at him sharply. Was he being sarcastic? No, he looked to be a combination of serious and pleased. It was nice to think he thought she might be in demand or, at least, have a lot on her plate.

He led her to his car in the parking lot, a fairly new black Mustang convertible, its top down. Of course. It so totally fit the image. She couldn't resist a smile and a quick look around. What if Zack were to see her now?

They said little during the twenty-minute drive to Clayton, finding it hard to compete with the noise of the wind. However, Drew would often tap her on the arm, drawing her attention to, among other things, a couple of frisky Shetland ponies in a paddock off to the right of the road. She enjoyed glimpses of the river also as it sped by. She'd driven this road a couple of times but had not been able to enjoy the view. That was one nice part about having someone else behind the wheel. She really needed to make time to drive out again soon though, to visit Prissy Newmarket and find out what she remembered about her mom.

The restaurant Drew had chosen was right downtown

and on the water's edge in a tall and narrow heritage-looking red house. She admired the outside as they walked up the steps.

"You have an affinity for older houses, I'd say," she suggested.

"Got me there. This house has been in a few hands over the years. The location is great and the menu has been varied, but for some reason . . . well, I said there were several owners. I'm not quite sure why. Anyway, I've been anxious to try it in this newest iteration. I hope you like Italian food."

He held the front door open for her, and she didn't get a chance to answer. They were seated fairly quickly at a table with a view of the river.

Shelby looked around and spotted the sign for the restrooms. "I don't mean to abandon you right away, but I think I need to make use of a brush." She smoothed her hair and smiled a bit hesitantly.

"You look great, but I do have a sister, so I know how that works." He patted the top of his head. "Maybe I should do the same?"

Shelby realized he was kidding and laughed. "I'll be right back."

When she returned, Shelby took a few minutes to admire the view of the river before turning her attention back to Drew.

"First impressions?" he asked.

"Full marks for the view, that's for certain." She swiveled in her chair for a better look around the interior. "And more good marks for the decor. I like this combination of blue and green. It blends well with the outdoors. What about you?"

He propped his elbows on the table and leaned his chin on his hands. "I totally agree. If they weren't competition—and I know that's stretching it—I'd probably want to dine here fairly often. Good thing it's a bit of a drive. Of course, if we lived in a big city, twenty or thirty minutes would be nothing to get to an evening's entertainment. You were raised in Boston, right?"

"I was. We moved there when I was three. I love the city, but there wasn't a lot to hold me there after my dad died."

"That's rough. I was twenty when my dad died, from throat cancer. I still miss him, but I'm glad I had some time with him as an adult. What about your mom?"

"That's why we moved, after she died." Suddenly, it was a topic Shelby didn't want to dwell on. Here she'd been spending so much time trying to find out details about her mom, but tonight, she wanted to let it go.

The server arrived to take their orders, and they sat in comfortable silence until he returned with their bottle of wine, a California red chosen by Drew. He'd also recommended the Spaghetti Carbonara, which she'd chosen.

"So, tell me, what got you interested in the restaurant business?" she asked after taking a sip of the wine.

Drew chuckled. "Food, basically. You can probably tell, what with Erica into the chocolate business and me a chef, that food was important in our family. My mom wasn't much of a cook, but she encouraged me to play around in the kitchen and experiment. I appreciate that. I don't think I'd be doing this today if it wasn't for her support."

"That's nice. I was very impressed with both your cooking and your restaurant, you know."

He reached across the table and took her hand in his. "I know. You did tell me that. But I can't hear it enough. So, tell me what Shelby Cox likes to do in her spare time."

"Spare time? What's that? Seriously, I haven't had much of it since I got here. In between learning the book business and trying to help Aunt Edie with errands and things, I've spent what time I had left enjoying living on a houseboat."

"Do you cook?"

"Not so you'd notice," she admitted after a moment's hesitation.

Drew laughed. "Good. I don't like to be upstaged. It must be unique living on a houseboat."

"I love it, and I'm really not looking forward to the late fall, when it will be dry-docked for winter and I'll be living elsewhere, probably with my aunt."

"I can imagine it would be hard to go from being on one's own to living with an older relative."

"I've thought about that; hence, no firm decision as yet."

Their meals arrived, and Drew spent several minutes sampling each item on his plate. "Very good," he finally remarked. "I'm impressed."

"I'd say that's a major compliment for them."

He smiled at that. "So, tell me what's happening with the murder investigation on the island."

The abrupt change in topic surprised Shelby, but she

guessed they'd really exhausted the personal stuff anyway. That said something right there.

"I don't really know. Chief Stone isn't one to share information."

"But you must have some theories. Erica said something about smuggling?"

"That's my theory, but no one else seems interested in it."

"Why's that? It sounds plausible to me, although I seriously doubt it's happening."

"Why do you say that?" Shelby was getting tired of people dismissing her theory.

Drew smiled, a "Come on, now" look. "That belongs to the old Joe Cabana days. It makes an exciting tale for the castle to tell, that their grotto was once part of the operation, but that time has long passed. No, I think it's something more personal." He leaned closer to her and lowered his voice. "Like a jilted lover. Isn't that usually the prime motive?"

So, back to Duncan Caine as the main suspect? She'd have to give that more thought, but certainly not at the moment. She wanted to enjoy the rest of the evening.

She finished her meal and decided to skip dessert, settling for a cappuccino instead. Drew joined her and they sipped in comfortable silence.

After Drew dropped her at home, with a kiss that didn't send sparks down her spine, saying he'd call soon, she went inside. She poured herself a glass of water and went up on deck to enjoy the mild evening. Thoughts of the evening raced through her mind. The main one turned out to be that, while it had been a pleasant evening, she didn't see any romance in their future. It would be good to be friends. But what if he was the smuggler?

Where had that thought come from?

He had been the one to bring up the topic of the murder, certainly not a romantic topic. And he'd been quick to discount her theory about the smuggling.

She sat for several more minutes trying to clear her mind and then went back inside. As she got ready for bed, she wondered how she could possibly even momentarily have considered that Drew might be involved in a smuggling scheme. He was Erica's brother, after all. And when she thought back on the evening, he was handsome and charming but also a good listener and interested in what she had to say. All very positive attributes. But from the crime novels she read, she knew that the point men in the smuggling rings were often able to charm their way out of sticky situations. *No, not Drew.*

She was just being silly or desperate. Why was she so determined to go down the smuggling path? What if she was totally wrong? There were the other possible motives, and although she was a bit reluctant to admit it, the police might have gone down a totally different path with suspects she'd never even considered. Which would mean that Matthew was off the hook, right? So she could back off and put an end to all her investigating.

She shook her head but decided to stop by and have a talk with Erica after work the next day. She still had questions about Drew's love life, and she'd probably need more chocolates anyway.

* * *

In the morning, she changed that plan to stopping by for a coffee and to pick up the chocolates on the way to work. She didn't think this could wait.

Erica greeted her with the usual big smile. "The usual?"

"Please." *How to bring it up?* "By the way, guess who I had dinner with last night."

"My dear brother."

"How did you know?"

"Why else would you ask me? On second thought, it could have been someone who has something to do with guarding our coast. Again. Now, that date I'd really want to know all about. You can spare me the Drew details." She made a face but leaned over the counter, looking eager to hear all.

"You can put together a variety of two dozen truffles while we're talking, if you don't mind. So, tell me a bit more about this girlfriend of his. What's the secret of her charm?"

Erica straightened and grabbed a small white box. "Uh-oh. Don't even go there. It's money." She opened the door to the display of truffles and began choosing some.

"What?"

"Yes, money, and lots of it. Daddy's in the auto business and making lots of money, and Serena is in the business of spending it. Although I think she must also make tons as a model. Drew lucked in as one of her interests, and she's been investing in his restaurant right from day one. He was very worried she'd withdraw her money when they broke up. You know, it's really hard to get a restaurant going these days and keep it viable. But she said it was an investment and the money would stay put. He was very relieved, I can tell you."

Erica placed the box of truffles on the counter. "But that leads to my asking why you want to know about Drew. Don't tell me you've fallen for my charming bro after only one date?" She reached across the counter and grabbed Shelby's hand. Her voice was pleading as she said, "Please don't tell me that."

Shelby laughed. "Not to worry. You're right, he is a charming guy and I had a great time, but there weren't any sparks. I don't think for either of us."

"Whew. Consider yourself lucky. But I have to warn you, that could make you seem like a challenge to Drew, so don't let down your guard. Your total will be one girls' gossip night, for the advice, and twenty bucks for the truffles, or shall I add it to the bookstore tab?"

"Bookstore, please. And, thanks again for the advice. I'd better run now. Hope you have a busy day."

As she walked to the shuttle, Shelby mused on the news about the source of investment in Drew's restaurant. Maybe when they'd broken up, he'd been so worried about losing the money he'd gotten involved in the smuggling. On the other hand, maybe it was because he needed even more money. Then she spent the ride over to the island wondering why she was determined to make him the bad guy in this, since she'd already eliminated him from her suspect list. She liked him, he was a terrific cook, and he had a girlfriend.

None of that added up to a motive. Besides, there were plenty of others still on that list.

So why couldn't she figure it out? Because she wasn't a trained investigator, that's why. And she didn't have the same type of access to the suspects. So she'd better try a different approach. And she'd better do it quick.

# Chapter Twenty-Nine

When she finally arrived home after work, Shelby kicked off her shoes and sat with a *thunk* on the nearest tub chair. The cat had followed her indoors, much to her delight, and jumped on her lap immediately. He did seem happy to see her, what with all the rubbing of his head and purring. Shelby indulged him, and herself, for several minutes just stroking his soft coat, and then, because her stomach was growling, stood up and placed him on the warm spot where she'd been sitting.

She noticed the message light on the phone flashing as she walked around the kitchen counter. She couldn't imagine who it could be. Most people called her cell. She picked it up and listened to the message, stunned to hear that Felicity wanted her to call her back. What now? Had she thought of something belittling to say? Shelby did a mental head slap. That wasn't likely; after all, Felicity was the one who had felt offended at their meeting.

She dialed, and the call was answered almost immediately.

Felicity was still at her store and sounded mildly cheerful and not in the least upset.

"I'm so glad you called tonight rather than leaving it for tomorrow. I wanted to let you know that Barry Pellen is back in town. If you want to talk to him, now's as good a time as any. He's staying at the Inn on the Bay, apparently, because his place is being repainted."

Felicity obviously had a good pipeline. That was a lot of information. "Do you know how long he's in town?"

"I'm not sure; that's why I thought tonight would be best. He'll tell you how it was between him and Loreena. You'll see that Duncan had no place in her life." It sounded like her voice caught on that last bit, and Shelby felt sorry for her.

"Thanks, Felicity. I'll go over right now and hope I'm not interrupting his dinner."

"Good," Felicity said, and hung up without saying goodbye.

Shelby looked at the receiver and made a face. Nothing subtle or muddled there. She was onto Felicity's personal agenda here, but she did want to talk to Barry Pellen.

She took a few minutes to feed J.T. and then grabbed a banana for herself. She decided to drive, one of the few times she took her car these days, since there was no direct road across Otter Creek. And although the walk would have done her good, she didn't want to take the time.

She checked at the main desk at the Inn and asked if there was a house phone to call Barry Pellen's room.

"I could, but that wouldn't do you any good."

Shelby stared at the desk clerk, who looked to be a few years younger than her. Her name tag read WANDA. "He is staying here, isn't he?"

"Oh, yeah. He's a guest, but he just went into the bar, over to your left."

"You're sure that's where he went?"

"Definitely. He invited me to join him there when I get off shift." She looked at her watch. "Which is in about twenty minutes. Short shift today, ya know."

Shelby thought the girl's smile said she'd be joining Pellen and was definitely looking forward to it. It seemed he certainly wasn't pining for Loreena. Did that mean something? Was that another theory shot down? Wanda looked as different from the older, more conservatively dressing Loreena as was possible. Hmm.

Shelby thanked her for the information and followed the directions. She took a minute to enjoy the bay and view of the river, then she walked into the bar and straight over to the bartender, waiting until he turned around to face her.

"What can I get you?" he asked, leaning an arm on the bar and flashing a smile.

Shelby returned the smile. "I'm looking for someone. Do you know Barry Pellen?"

"That's me," she heard a male voice boom to her left, and she leaned forward, looking past a young couple sitting at the bar, to see a hulk of a man, at least six feet and broad at the shoulders, like a football player, or maybe a wrestler, tip his drink toward her. His light, sandy-colored hair was tied back in a ponytail, and a small gold hoop pierced his left earlobe. Both looked out of place with his black suit, mauve shirt, and dark-purple striped tie. She was truly at a loss for words. Especially since it was the same man she'd seen having dinner with Felicity Foxworth.

"What can I do for you?" he prompted. His smile spread across his face and put her at ease.

Shelby quickly marshaled her thoughts and walked over to him. "I hope I'm not interrupting your evening plans. Do you have a couple of minutes to talk? I'm Shelby Cox, co-owner of Bayside Books." She held out her hand.

He grasped it and gave a firm shake. "Nice to meet you, Shelby Cox, and I'm intrigued. It so happens that I do have a few minutes. Would you care to join me for a drink?" He pointed to the empty chair next to him.

She almost felt like she was taking advantage of him. Almost. "That would be nice, but I want you to know, I'm here about Loreena Swan."

He looked surprised and then chuckled. "Well, that requires a drink for sure," he said. "I'm having a whiskey on the rocks. What about you?"

After she'd ordered a glass of red wine, he asked, "What are your questions about Loreena? And why are you asking them?"

"I'll start by answering your second one. I'm asking questions because I'm the one who found Loreena's body." She watched him closely because she'd been surprised that he'd seemed rather jovial when she first mentioned Loreena's name. Not exactly the suitor in mourning.

"Fair enough. And why did you want to talk to me about Loreena?"

Her drink was placed in front of her, and she took a sip before answering. "I'm just trying to get a feel for who Loreena was. I didn't know her well. I'm fairly new to town. But we were both working at Blye Castle. I'm asking people who knew her, and I'd heard that you two were dating. Is that true?"

He shrugged. "Yes, I suppose it is. That's a rather outmoded word though, isn't it? And besides, I don't see what this can add to your profile about her except that she had a bit of a life outside that damned castle."

Shelby caught his tone and wondered what his problem was with the castle. "She was fairly involved in the day-to-day running of the castle."

"You can say that again. And she was always trying to drag me over to see how things were going as they were getting it ready for the grand opening." His voice added quotation marks around the last two words. "I have a limited amount of time to spend in Alexandria Bay, and when I'm not involved in business meetings, I wanted to spend it with Loreena, not at her job."

That was pretty straightforward, Shelby thought. "May I ask what your dealings are in Alex Bay?"

He raised one eyebrow in a quizzical gesture. "You mean you haven't heard? Are you really that new to the area?"

She nodded. "I've only been here for a couple of months."

"Okay. Fair enough. Well, I'm negotiating to buy a tract of land to build a hotel and casino. It should be quite straightforward, but I hadn't counted on some of the local citizenry getting so involved in the decision. I expected the usual concerns about increased traffic in the town and the strain on the environment, but the bottom line is, it's a good deal for the economy in the area. The businesspeople know that, but it's the others, the do-gooders and the retirees, who are causing delays. Loreena was also stubborn about it, towing the line of the Heritage Society, saying the casino would distract tourists from the castle."

"I would have thought more tourists in the area would automatically mean more touring the islands."

"Exactly my point." He leaned toward her, his enthusiasm showing. "But the real problem for some of the locals, I'm sure, is the casino. They don't think that gamblers are sightseers."

"And are they?"

He shrugged.

"That must be a bother, if that's holding up the project."

He made a face and finished off his whiskey, ordering another. "It's more than a bother. It's costing me money, each day this drags out. I was hoping Loreena could use some of her influence in the town, being from such a longtime well-known family, to help persuade her neighbors."

"Is that why you were dating her?" Shelby knew it was cheeky to ask, but she wanted to see his reaction.

He burst out laughing, a deep, belly-shaking roar. "To someone as young and attractive as you, she must have looked old and possibly a bit past her prime. But let me tell you, she was *very* good company." He finished off his drink and winked at her.

"So, you mustn't have been too happy to have some competition on that front."

He cocked his head to the right. "What do you mean?"

"Duncan Caine. You must know who he is, given that he's one of the major realtors in the area. And I'd heard that he and Loreena were also an item. That must have been a bit hard to swallow."

Barry looked taken aback and took his time answering. "I suppose it would have if I'd been serious about Loreena. It was just fun, you know? We'd said nothing about not seeing anyone else. I certainly played around, and I assumed she did also. It was all quite civilized." He sighed. "I will miss her, you know."

Feeling a bit unsettled, Shelby finished her wine and looked at her watch. "Oh, look at the time. I've really taken up too much of yours, but I thank you for the wine and the chat. I really appreciate it, but I must get going, and you'll be late for dinner."

She grabbed her purse and slid off the stool. He stood and nodded. "Anytime. I'm always happy to have a drink with a beautiful young woman."

Shelby gave him a small smile in return for his almost too-subtle one, then left at what she felt was a respectable pace. When she reached the door, she stopped herself from looking back at him and left quickly.

As she drove home, she went over the conversation in her mind. What had she proven?

*A—He was seeing Loreena, which doesn't necessarily mean Duncan was off her list of male friends;*
*B—He is trying to build a hotel and casino, which is meeting resistance;*
*C—He'd hoped Loreena would help him with that; and*
*D—He is a flirt by nature.*

None of which necessarily made him a killer. Or gave him a reasonable motive.

# Chapter Thirty

What if he'd lied? Shelby bolted upright in her bed. She glanced at the clock on her bedside table and realized she'd been trying to get to sleep for two hours with no luck. Possibly because she kept going over in her head what she knew about Loreena. And now that Barry Pellen had inserted himself into her thoughts, who knew when sleep would come.

So, where had that thought come from? What if Pellen had lied about . . . what? Well, his interest in Loreena, for one thing. If he had actually fallen in love with her, and if he knew about Duncan, if there really was anything to know about Duncan and Loreena, then maybe he'd murdered her. That would give him a sound, if not clichéd, motive—jealousy.

Or maybe he had lied about Blye Castle and his supposed disdain for Loreena's attachment to it. What if he was the one involved in smuggling? He could easily have the connections, being a businessman and big land developer. Maybe he'd used Loreena to gain knowledge about and access to the grotto. And what if she had figured it out, and so he'd had to kill her before she turned him in? Not that Shelby had any proof or even reasonable doubt that any of it was true.

But it could be true, and the two events might not be connected. There might well be a smuggling ring in the area, but it still might have nothing to do with Loreena's death. There were far too many questions for such a late hour. Especially when she didn't have any proof, just suppositions. She wished she could talk it all over with Zack, but she knew he'd just get upset with her. Maybe Matthew was a better sounding board, even though he had also suggested she drop the whole thing. But he had written true crime books, after all, so if she could just appeal to his inner inquisitiveness, maybe his writer's mind could work this all into some semblance of a plot.

Right now, she needed something to help her sleep. Hot chocolate was out of the question, but maybe some hot milk might do the trick. She'd never tried it before, thinking it an old wives' tale. But she was desperate. She slipped out of bed and pulled her robe on without turning on the overhead. The light from the full moon shone through the windows as she made her way downstairs. She thought she heard the dock creaking and wondered if there was a deer or some other wild animal making its way along. She almost tripped over J.T., and even though he rushed to the door, she refused to let him out. Not with late-night creatures on their very doorstep.

She looked longingly at the fridge, then thought maybe she'd see just what nighttime visitors were making use of the dock. She hoped it wasn't a drunk trying to get to one of the boats or maybe some late-night two-legged party animals, although it was far too quiet for that.

She pulled aside the curtain at the front of the houseboat and almost screamed out loud. That wasn't a four-legged creature but rather someone dressed in black, with a hoodie pulled up over his head. And he was doing something to the ropes that moored the houseboat to the dock. She slowly dropped the curtain back in place and tiptoed to the phone. She'd left her cell upstairs. She grabbed the landline receiver and hid behind the fridge, dialing 911. She wasn't sure who would answer. Certainly not Chief Stone. The call would be forwarded to the State Police. Sure enough, in a few seconds, a female voice asked Shelby what the problem was.

She filled her in as quietly as she could and was told to stay on the line and that the State Police were on their way. Shelby felt the houseboat rock slightly and hoped the intruder hadn't stepped onto it or, just as bad, pushed her away from the dock. It felt like hours passed, but when she glanced at the clock above the fridge, it had only been ten minutes of waiting when she heard the siren approaching.

That sent her intruder flying back along the dock toward shore. His footsteps pounded against the wood, and the motion rocked the houseboat again. *That's right, scare him away.* She could hear male voices in the distance and then the heavy-footed steps of someone walking purposefully toward the houseboat. He knocked on her door, then identified himself as a State Patrol officer. She demanded that he show his badge through the window before she let him in.

"I'm Officer Target. You phoned about an intruder?"

Shelby realized she was shaking. "Yes, he was bent down doing something to the lines at the front of the houseboat but then ran away when he heard the sirens."

"We spotted someone running and my partner gave chase. The lines, you say? Stay here while I take a look."

He returned several minutes later, his flashlight still in his right hand. "The lines aft are secure, but someone was definitely tampering with the forward ones. It looked like he gave up trying to untie them and had started to cut through them."

"Cut them? Are they strong? I'm not going to drift away, am I?"

He shook his head, and she could see the trace of a smile. "Not tonight, you aren't. We'll make sure everything is secure before we leave, and then maybe you should have them looked at in the morning. Are you the owner?"

She shook her head. "No, I'm renting it, but I'll contact the owner. Why would anyone do that?"

He looked at her closely. "You have no idea?"

"No."

"It could have been some drunk kid on a dare, I suppose. It happens." They heard more footsteps, and a second officer appeared at the door.

"I lost him."

"He was trying to cut the houseboat loose," explained Officer Target.

The second officer nodded, closed the door, and went to check it out.

"Maybe you'd feel better staying with someone tonight?" Target asked.

Shelby thought about it. "No, I don't think whoever it was will try it again now that the police are aware."

"It's not like we do regular patrols around here, and he probably knows it, but you may be right. He might be content with just scaring you, if you're the target. We'll let Chief Stone know in the morning, and if it's kids, I'm sure she'll track them down. We'll take a final look around before we leave. Be sure to lock your door and windows." He touched the brim of his hat and stepped outside.

"Thank you, I will," Shelby said, and proceeded to do just that. When she felt safe and heard their footsteps leaving the dock, she realized she was exhausted. She went back to bed, and soon after J.T. jumped up, then snuggled at her side.

His purrs and the reassurance of his presence finally lulled her to sleep.

* * *

The next morning, Shelby had just turned on the coffee machine at the bookstore when the door opened. She looked up as Zack strode across the room to her, a stormy look on his face.

"What have you gotten yourself into?" he asked, with none of the demeanor of their friendly dinner date of a couple of nights earlier.

"What do you mean?"

"I got a call from the State Police this morning. Something about vandals or an attacker at your place?"

"Well, someone tried to cut the houseboat loose, but it might have just been a prank."

A shiver snaked down her back, and she knew as she was saying it just how much she didn't believe it to be true. In fact, she'd spent a restless night followed by a morning being spooked by everything from J.T. jumping off the bed while she was downstairs to a distant boat horn being sounded. Even the usual creaking of the dock, usually a reassuring sound, came across as sinister, and she made frequent checks at the window to make sure no one was trying to pull off a surprise visit. She pushed it all out of her head and gave Zack a friendly but noncommittal smile.

He snorted. "Not bloody likely. You did admit you've been asking questions around town about Loreena Swan. So, I'm wondering, whose feathers did you manage to ruffle?" He threw out the question and planted his fists on his waist.

"I don't know. I certainly haven't found anything out, so it seems unlikely as a reason for what happened last night." Again, she felt a shiver. Was that going to happen every time the topic came up? She sure hoped not.

"Unlikely to you, but whoever tampered with your ropes had a reason."

The phone rang before he had a chance to go on. With relief, Shelby grabbed it, but found herself answering the same questions from Chief Stone.

Shelby looked over at Zack as she replied and found him smiling, although it wasn't a smile filled with pleasure.

When she eventually hung up, he merely said, "You see? We're all taking note of it. So, what haven't you told me?"

The door to the store was pushed open by a noisy gang of teenagers. Shelby silently groaned. They usually did a lot of talking and looking but not much buying. At least they would make sure her conversation with Zack couldn't continue. *Small mercies.*

He had obviously reached the same conclusion. "I'll be back," he said abruptly, and left.

Shelby tried to get her brain back into gear. She focused on two girls who had stopped at the local-authors stand. One looked to be around fifteen or so, but then again, Shelby was the first to admit she was a poor judge of age. The blonde had her long straight hair pulled back behind her ears, twisted and anchored Princess Leia style.

The girl beside her tittered, and the bun girl, as Shelby dubbed her, turned back and whispered something. They both laughed and moved over to where a revolving stand held a variety of bookmarks for sale. They took turns spinning the stand.

A male teacher, who looked to have just recently graduated school himself, entered and blew a whistle. That got everyone's attention. After he herded the group out, the store became almost spookily quiet.

When Zack hadn't returned by noon, Shelby felt a bit let down, but she was also relieved. She hadn't told him about her visit to Barry Pellen, nor had she told Chief Stone. It wasn't that she'd intended to hide the details; she just honestly hadn't thought about him, not when Zack had confronted her so suddenly. She knew she'd need to do so, and relatively soon, to avoid any future confrontations with the oh-so-touchy Zack Griffin. Maybe his case wasn't going so well.

She also realized just how slow business had been after the teens all left. She wondered why she'd bothered coming in that day, but it was always hard to know what a day would turn out like, as she'd noted to herself many times. And, she had to admit, she had little desire to be alone on the houseboat. But this was the middle of the day. Not a time when anyone was likely to try anything. What would she do about tonight? Surprisingly, Edie hadn't called, so she must not have heard the news. If Shelby were to suddenly beg a room, she knew she'd have to tell all and Edie would be worried. Not something Shelby wanted to add to her recovery process.

"Do you want to take the first lunch break?" Shelby asked Taylor, who shook her head. She'd spent the past twenty minutes doing some intense reading. Shelby wasn't sure what book she had in her hands, but since it had been so quiet, she had no objections.

She grabbed her tuna-salad sandwich and walked until she found one of the more secluded picnic tables on the back side of the island. She'd taken the long way around, hoping to bump into Matthew, but hadn't spotted him anywhere. She bit into her sandwich and wished she'd also brought along a book, although looking out at the water and the odd passing boat seemed to be the perfect thing to do over lunch.

"I was hoping to find you off on your own, since you weren't at the bookstore," Zack said as he sat down beside her. He crossed his arms on the table and leaned forward. "This really is the perfect place to relax or eat," he added, eyeing her sandwich.

"You didn't bring a lunch?" She looked at his hands and then back to his face.

"I never could get into the habit of making something that early in the morning. I usually grab a bite on the go."

She gave it some thought, debating whether to suggest he grab something at the Sugar Shack, before saying, "Well, you could grab this other half of my sandwich if you'd like." She held it out to him.

"Tuna. My favorite." He took it from her and bit into it. "Delicious."

She laughed. "Hardly, but it works. I guess this is our time to talk, is it?" Might as well meet it head on.

"You sound like I'm about to make you walk the plank or something. I just want to make sure you realize how dangerous it is to be messing around in a murder investigation."

She straightened her shoulders. "I'm not messing; I'm just talking, getting to know people. It is about time. I've been here two months now."

"Interesting time to take note of your fellow citizens. So, let's go over this again just in case this incident has refreshed your memory and there may be someone or something you need to add to your original list. Who have you questioned and what did you ask?"

He kept his eyes straight ahead, watching the scenery, as

though what she had to say was of no consequence. She relaxed a little.

"Okay, I'll start all over, again. But this might not be the right chronological order. I've talked to Carter Swan about his what now appears to be *supposed* interest in taking over the bookstore in the castle. And his fiancée, who then talked to me about how upset Carter was after our talk."

She glanced at Zack, who raised his eyebrows. "And just what was it that upset him?"

"I got the impression he didn't like my poking around in his life."

"Understandable."

"But he did say that it was totally Loreena's idea to have him in the bookstore. Something to do with her desire to be in charge of everything to do with the castle. He assured me, it wasn't his idea. And, I believed him."

"I also talked to Felicity Foxworth at the Gallery on the Bay about the Heritage Society board. She got a bit upset with me when I suggested that, from what I'd heard, Duncan Caine and Loreena were an item. I think she wants Duncan for herself, although I could be reading her all wrong. She told me about the planned development for a new hotel and casino, which seems to be a touchy subject in town, and that the developer, Barry Pellen, was actually the man in Loreena's life."

She took another bite of her sandwich and chewed slowly, organizing her thoughts. She had nothing to hide. She would tell him everything.

"And then I went to see Pellen at his hotel last night."

"You did what?" He groaned. "Let me get this straight, you just invited yourself over to his room and started asking questions? About the murder?"

"Not exactly," she hedged. At least Zack seemed outwardly calm. "We had a drink in the hotel bar, and I asked about the proposed development, and then I went on to talk about his relationship with Loreena. And let me tell you, he was quite forthcoming about it. A bit too much so, actually. However, I didn't ask any questions about her murder, nor did I imply he could be the killer."

"Small wonders. And, I hate to ask this, but *do* you think he could be the murderer?"

Shelby eyed Zack a little more closely. "You don't look like you're taking this seriously. You're not, are you?"

"That's a look I often get when talking to a meddling member of the public. Now, go on. What did Pellen say to you?"

"He confirmed his relationship with Loreena and also said that he knew about her seeing Duncan Caine, although he told me they weren't exclusive. Then he told me exactly what I already knew about the proposed development."

"Did he mention any other enterprises planned for around here?"

"Like what?" She looked at his face closely. "Like smuggling? Do you think he's the smuggler?"

Zack shook his head. "I don't know where you get this smuggling thing."

"Why did you ask about any other enterprises?"

"Because I live here, too. I have an opinion about whether or not we need more expansion and, in particular, a casino."

"Oh. Of course."

After a couple of minutes, he prompted, "And? That can't have been everyone. I mean, it's been over two weeks since the murder."

She turned to him. "But I didn't start asking questions until Aunt Edie got so upset about Matthew Kessler being arrested."

"He wasn't arrested, just questioned."

"Whatever. That reminds me, I can't remember if I mentioned it earlier, but Edie suggested I talk to Mae-Beth Warner, one of the main volunteers at Blye because she knew Loreena fairly well. And Mae-Beth told me that there'd been an argument between Loreena and Regan Jones, one of the volunteers, over something that certainly didn't sound like it would end in murder."

"Let me be the judge of that. What was it about?"

"Apparently, Regan had some suggestions to do with all the groups of high school tours coming through. She thought it should be a less-structured time, and Loreena thought the opposite. At least, that's how Mae-Beth explained it to me."

She looked at him with raised eyebrows. He nodded and jotted some notes on the small pad he'd pulled out of his pocket, then said, "Is there anyone else who has gotten to know you better because of your inquiries?" She could hear the sarcasm in his voice but also a hint of humor.

"Not that I can think of." Although she briefly flashed on Drew Bryant. Not the kind of "getting to know better" that Zack meant, she thought.

"You see, I was right, you've been busy, and any one of

those people could be upset with you or spoken to someone else who got upset and tried to make you disappear."

She shuddered. He noticed and put his arm gently around her shoulders.

"I'm getting to feel comfortable in the community, and I really like the people here. Well, most of them," she finally said. "I'd hate to think any of them is a murderer. Or even a smuggler."

Zack removed his arm, and she realized she felt a little sad about that. She didn't know what to say, so she finished her sandwich in silence. When he'd finished his own portion, he stood up and faced her. "Thanks for sharing your lunch. One of the better tuna sandwiches I've eaten."

She smiled with a tilt of her head in acknowledgment.

"You do realize you were in danger last night, right?"

She nodded. "Although I was just as worried about what might have happened to the houseboat."

"Well, if it had drifted out into the main channel, which was highly likely, you could have grounded on a rock or an island or been hit by a freighter."

"But my houseboat has lights. I'd have been seen, wouldn't I?"

"The police report stated that the lights were off. Do you remember turning them off before going to bed?"

"No, I always keep the ones at the corners of the top deck on. How could that have happened?"

"Well, you'd better have them checked. And you'd better stop questioning people and keep your eyes open when you're on your houseboat. Are you staying there tonight?"

She nodded. Yes, she would, she decided on the spot.

"Do you want any company?"

She looked at him to see if he was joking, but it was hard to tell.

"No, thanks. I'm sure I'll be fine. I'm assuming the State Police will keep up extra patrols. And who would be foolish enough to try something a second time, knowing that?" She hoped she was right.

"Well, call any of us if you're at all worried. You have my home number." He stood, then paused. "Look, if I told you that I think you might be onto something with your theory, would you back off and leave the investigating to me?"

Did he really want an answer? She thought about it and nodded. At least she'd *try* to back off.

"I don't want anything to happen to you." He touched her shoulder briefly and then sauntered in the direction of the dock.

Shelby sighed. Things were certainly getting complicated around here.

# Chapter Thirty-One

Thursday morning, Shelby groaned as she woke to the sound of a boat motor close by. She felt the gentle action of a wave washing against and under the houseboat. She opened one eye and glanced at the clock. Six AM. Who was out on the water at this hour? A fisherman, that's who, she reminded herself. Or someone with menacing plans.

She leapt out of bed, sending J.T. flying to the floor. She'd forgotten he'd spent the night inside again. She looked out the windows and saw a large black cabin cruiser slowly navigating the channel. She knew that boat. It was moored on the next dock over. Certainly no one who was planning to do her or her houseboat any damage. She felt the stress in her shoulders and did some stretches, trying to find some relief.

The tension continued to bother her as she got ready for work. She guessed the trauma and loss of sleep the night before had been all she'd needed to ensure she didn't lay awake listening for noises the next night. She'd slept deeply and, clearly, awkwardly, if the knots in her shoulders were any indication. Sleep was good, but she could sure use a massage.

She stopped in at the main bookstore before heading for the shuttle. Trudy had left a message late the afternoon before that there was a box of new books that needed to go over to the castle. If it wasn't too cumbersome, Shelby would take the box with her. If it needed more muscle, she'd leave it for Cody. He was doing a half-day shift that day. She tried lifting it. She could manage.

"How's Edie doing?" she asked Trudy once she'd tried lifting the box and decided to leave it.

"What do you mean?" Trudy looked up sharply, concern in her eyes. "What's going on, Shelby?" She straightened the collar of the pale-blue blouse she was wearing, the color a perfect match for her eyes.

Shelby shrugged. "I haven't seen very much of her these past few days. She seems to prefer short telephone conversations that she can control rather than longer chats where I could possibly ask questions. About my mom in particular."

There, she'd said it. Would Trudy take Edie's side? Would she tell her what Shelby had said? Did she know anything about her mom?

Trudy sat down behind the desk and looked thoughtful. "Do you think you might be feeling a bit sensitive?"

"No, I'm not. I've gone over it all in my mind several times. Ever since I asked Edie a bunch of questions about my mom the other night, she's always busy when I try to talk to her. Even too busy to have supper with me, it seems."

Trudy smiled. "We know why that is. She does have a certain male distraction in her life these days. But about the other, maybe you need to let Edie be in charge of when to have such a discussion."

"Did you know my mom?"

"No, I didn't. When I married Robert, he got a job in Phoenix right away, so we moved there. Your dad got married after I left. Then my husband died fourteen years later, so I brought the kids back here and tried to get my life in order. You and your dad had moved by that point."

Shelby reached out to touch Trudy's arm. "Oh, I'm sorry. I had no idea. I didn't mean to bring up painful memories."

Trudy patted Shelby's hand. "You haven't. It's been quite a while now, and I don't mind talking about Robert at all. In fact, it's nice to have him pop up in a conversation every now and then."

"You talk about him to your kids, also, I'll bet. My dad never talked about my mom. I always thought it was because he missed her so much that it hurt to talk about her. But that can't be Edie's excuse too. I was hoping to get some answers now that I'm back." Shelby felt the frustration returning but was determined not to get whiny when talking to Trudy.

"As I said, let Edie drive that conversation. By the way, she's coming in shortly to work for a couple of hours. Now"—she glanced at her watch—"you'd better put your running shoes on if you want to catch the shuttle."

Shelby gasped. "Oh, wow. I didn't realize what time it was. Thanks, Trudy. Hope it's a busy day."

"The same to you. Will you please flip over the OPEN sign on your way out?"

Shelby waved and did as asked, then practically ran all the way to the dock. She'd just stepped on the shuttle when it started pulling away. She did a mental dance of relief and pulled her jacket closed. The wind had turned cooler overnight.

She stayed inside the boat for the entire ride over and then walked quickly up the path to the castle. By the time she'd opened the store and put the coffee on, Cody had appeared.

"Sorry, but I missed the shuttle," he said.

"So how did you get here so quickly?"

He grinned. "My secret. Okay, maybe not. I saw Matthew Kessler at the dock, getting into his boat, and bummed a lift."

Shelby wondered briefly what Matthew had been doing on shore but decided it probably wasn't any of her business. But she did wonder if he had been at Edie's house. She smiled at the thought.

"So, guess what we talked about," Cody said, pulling up one of the stools behind the counter.

Shelby looked pointedly at the stool and Cody said, "Oops." He grinned and disappeared into the back room, reappearing a few seconds later, Swiffer duster in hand. He began dusting the countertop, all the while sneaking glances at Shelby. Finally, she gave in.

"Okay, I give. What did you talk about?"

"Smuggling." Cody looked pleased with himself.

Shelby hid a smile. She admired his enthusiasm and dogged determination. "I'd imagine his response hasn't changed much. He thinks it's totally impossible and silly for us to be thinking about it."

"Well, sort of. But, he didn't say totally impossible. Get this. It was more like 'improbable.' So I came back with all these dynamite possibilities, and he sure changed the topic quickly." Cody folded his arms and leaned back against the counter.

"What sort of things?" He had Shelby's attention.

Cody glanced around the still-empty store and leaned a bit closer to Shelby. "What if there's a smuggling ring from farther along the coast and the grotto is a safe point on the route? Like, supposing a Coast Guard ship appears in the distance. Head for the grotto. Or what if the grotto is an exchange point? Like, the smuggler drops his shipment of illicit goods inside there, and another boat comes by to pick it up. If it's done in the dead of night with no long gaps in between, it seems totally over the top but cool."

Shelby considered what he'd said. "I think you might have a future in organized crime," she admitted with a smile. "Never tell your dad I said that, though."

Cody chuckled, but before he could continue, a young couple dressed in heavy jackets, the man carrying a toddler, entered the store. Shelby nodded at them and offered them some coffee to help them warm up. They accepted with relief, and Cody went off to get their drinks.

Shelby kept meaning to get back to their earlier conversation, but when Cody wasn't busy chatting up customers, he was busy shifting boxes in the back room, or finding things to do that kept him close to the door. The fact that he kept looking out into the hallway every hour on the hour led Shelby to believe he might have a crush on one of the volunteer tour guides. Possibly the very attractive but nerdy-looking high schooler with the shiny braces. *Good choice*, Shelby thought.

When she got home that evening, Shelby tried doing housework. She even sat down with J.T. on her lap and flipped through a couple of magazines she'd picked up earlier in the week at the pharmacy, but she couldn't concentrate. Edie was on her mind. Although they hadn't been close before Shelby had arrived in town, in just a short period of time she'd come to rely on Edie and felt she'd finally found home. But she hadn't been prepared for the way Edie had been treating her lately. There was an elephant in the room, of that Shelby was certain. She needed to confront her aunt and try to get things back on track, not only for her own peace of mind but also for the store.

Shelby quickly got changed and did a fast walk up the hill to the family house. She knocked on Edie's front door and went over in her mind everything she meant to say. When the door opened, she could tell by the look of hesitation on Edie's face that her aunt probably realized what this visit was all about.

After they'd settled at the kitchen table, each with a mug of coffee and a fresh cheese scone that Edie had baked earlier in the day in front of them, Shelby began.

"I know you've been avoiding talking about my mom,

but I have questions, Aunt Edie, and I need answers." She eased her grip on her mug and told herself to relax.

Edie sighed. "I know. And I can tell you I'm flaming mad at your dad. It's not my place or responsibility to be having this conversation with you. He should have done it himself a long time ago."

"Well, he didn't, and I'm sorry, but I need to know. Mainly I need to know why it's such a big deal. All I want is to know what she was like. I haven't heard anything about her, what she liked doing, who her friends were, even what she looked like. There were no photos of her on display in the house. I know Dad was blown away when she died, and I guess I can understand that he didn't want reminders of her around because it was too painful, but that's not fair to me."

She knew she sounded like she was pleading; in fact, that's exactly what she was doing. She stared at Edie, willing her to answer all her questions.

Edie held her look and Shelby felt encouraged.

"No, it's not fair," Edie answered after a few moments. "I totally agree. I always believed he'd taken the wrong track in handling this, but you know your dad; he was stubborn and could not be told what to do."

"And he's gone now. It's time for me to know."

"Yes, it is, and I'm so sorry to be the one to tell you."

"That's okay. I mean, I know she's dead. Nothing could be worse than that."

Edie took a long drink of coffee and slowly put her mug down. "It's much worse than that. Your mom isn't dead, honey. She left when you were three years old. She ran off with a wealthy banker from Georgia and never looked back."

Shelby sat, stunned. She couldn't process what she'd just heard. It didn't make sense. "That's not true. Dad said she was dead."

"He couldn't accept what she'd done. He'd fallen head over heels in love with her and was still in love with her when she left. And even more than that, he didn't want you to know she'd just left you both."

Shelby felt like she'd had the air sucked out of her. Her mind went blank for a few seconds and she felt herself gasp for air. *I won't cry.* "She hasn't tried to get in touch and find out anything about me? Not once?"

Edie shook her head. "No, Shelby. I'm so sorry. A few weeks after she left, she sent me the papers for the store, signing over her share to you. We had started it together, you know. It was my dream, but I needed some help. Merrily wanted something to do, and your dad wanted to keep her happy. So, she invested her own money in it. She came from a fairly well-off family but was disinherited when she married your dad, you know. She started out all eager and thought of the store as an adventure, but she soon tired of it and I ran it by myself. I guess it was on her mind, though, as were you, because she signed it over, but that's the last we ever heard from her."

Shelby stood and walked to the window, staring at nothing. "My mother didn't want me?"

Edie got up and went to put her arms around Shelby. "I'm sorry, Shelby. I know how it must hurt. And you've got to understand that your dad was only doing what he thought was best for you. He thought a three-year-old should not know those particular facts. I wanted him to tell you once you'd gotten older, but he wouldn't budge, and I couldn't go against his wishes."

Shelby couldn't stop the tears, nor could she bite back the words. "But what you're saying is that my mom didn't want me. And my dad didn't tell me. I can't believe he'd do that." She pushed Edie away. "I can't believe you'd do that. I trusted you. Both of you. You betrayed me, and now I have no one."

She grabbed her purse and ran out of the house, doing a quick march to the end of the street. She stopped and leaned against a white picket fence once she'd rounded the corner. Her tears were flowing fast and furious. Pretty soon she was gulping for air, but eventually she felt herself calming down. No wonder Edie had avoided any questions Shelby had tried to ask all this time.

What now?

# Chapter Thirty-Two

Shelby didn't sleep much that night, not after learning the upsetting truth about her mom. But it was better that she knew what had *really* happened, although she had no idea what to do with that knowledge. She'd felt devastated when she'd gotten home, and after a large glass of red wine, she'd tried putting it all out of her mind. But it wouldn't go, and she knew she had to deal with it. Her mom hadn't wanted her. Still didn't, apparently, or she would have tried to contact her over the years.

Well, that was just fine with Shelby. She was tough. She was independent. She'd been brought up by her dad to think for herself and not rely on anyone else. But how could she rely on anything her dad had said over the years? He'd lied to her about one of the most important things in her life.

She stood up, displacing a contented T.J., and started pacing. What if she tried to contact her mom? Maybe Merrily Cox, or whatever her name was now, had tried but her dad had blocked her attempts? Maybe he'd even told Merrily that Shelby was dead, just like his other lie?

No, that was just too far-fetched. She could imagine him cutting off all ties with his former life. That would be the extent of it.

But what about her mom? What to do?

She finally crawled into bed just before dawn and stole a couple of hours of sleep. She tried not to think about any of it while she got ready for work. It took two cups of strong coffee before she could even think about what to wear.

When Shelby arrived at the castle bookstore, she was surprised to find Barry Pellen waiting outside the door. No, this was not what she needed this morning. However, she did wonder how he'd arrived. She figured he must have his own boat. Somebody else with special docking privileges?

"Good morning. You're here early. Are you in need of a book?" Shelby asked, signaling to Taylor to start the coffee once they were all inside.

Barry stood just inside the door and looked around the shop. When Taylor had disappeared into the back room, he said, "This is very charming. I'm sure you do a good business over here."

Shelby glanced around, trying to see it through a land developer's eyes. What did a small room, crowded with shelves and books galore, mean to a land developer? There was certainly no land to develop. The fact that the large bay windows looked onto the verandah meant there was usually activity to look out at. But there was definitely no potential for expanding the space or even opening a door to the outside. She knew. Edie had already explored that possibility.

She eventually nodded. "Good enough to continue on

each season. What can I do for you?" She was beginning to feel a bit uneasy. He obviously wasn't in need of a book.

He approached her and said in a softer voice, "We need to talk." He glanced toward the back room. "Perhaps we can take a walk around the gardens? It's a pleasant enough morning."

"That would be fine, but I need to grab my coffee first. Would you like some?"

He shook his head. "No, I've had more than enough already."

Shelby nodded. She probably had too, but she walked to the back room and quickly explained everything to Taylor, hoping Barry didn't have super-hearing.

"Are you worried?" Taylor whispered.

"Not really, but I am curious." She filled her mug when the coffee had finished dripping, then said in a louder voice as she headed for the front, "I'm going out for a short while, Taylor. I shouldn't be long." *Or if I am, send reinforcements.*

She forced a smile for Pellen and indicated the front door. He walked through and kept going until he was outside on the castle verandah, knowing she would follow. They walked down the stairs and Shelby pointed to the right, away from the grotto and toward the flower beds that might be receiving some care from Matthew that morning. She hoped. She wasn't quite sure why she felt uneasy around this man. Their last talk had been pleasant enough, but whatever he had to say must be important if he would come to the island to see her.

She'd taken a couple of sips of coffee when he finally stopped walking and turned to face her.

"I understand your aunt is recovering from a knee operation. I hope she'd doing well?"

Shelby felt puzzled but supposed he was making chit-chat. "Uh, yes. She's actually starting to get slowly back to work in the main store. Do you know her?"

"Only in passing, but she's got a way about her that attracts attention. I was hoping maybe you could introduce us." He glanced at her with an easy smile.

*What?* "Uh, sure, I guess. Is this business or pleasure?" *Are you looking to replace Loreena so soon?*

He laughed his deep-belly roar. "You come right to the point, don't you? I'd say it's a bit of both. She seems to be an astute businesswoman and I'm a businessman. And I think she'll be interested in what I have to propose. But I also think she'll be more open-minded about it if you put in a good word for me first or even come with me when I meet her."

Shelby hesitated, not really sure how to answer. She didn't like being put in that position, but she guessed that Edie could make up her own mind about talking to him.

"After all," he continued when she didn't answer, "I was willing to help you the other night and answer all those questions."

She bristled at that, but she guessed it shouldn't have surprised her. "I'll talk it over with her," she finally answered.

He touched a nonexistent hat brim and made his way down the path toward the dock.

Had he come all the way to the island just to ask her that? What a strange man. What was he planning? One thing was for sure, she knew she couldn't trust him.

* * *

She needed to talk to Edie about Pellen. And a great many other things, too, but she wasn't ready to do that just yet. But she couldn't avoid her forever, and she hoped that if she dropped in unannounced after work, she'd find Edie alone. She rang the doorbell and then knocked on Edie's front door. It was opened fairly quickly.

Edie looked hesitant but welcomed Shelby inside. Shelby realized how much she'd been both dreading and looking forward to seeing Edie again.

"I need to talk to you." She said it without emotion, and she could see that Edie picked up on that. Hesitation flickered back into Edie's eyes before she turned and walked to the kitchen. Shelby followed, wondering where to begin. The facts. Just the facts.

"I just wanted to tell you that I had a visit from that developer Barry Pellen today. Do you know him?"

Edie turned to her. "I know who he is, but we've never met. What did he want?"

"To meet you. He wants me to introduce him to you."

Edie's jaw dropped. "Why on earth would he want to meet me, and why would he ask you?"

"Well, according to him, it's because I went to see him to ask a few questions." Shelby decided she'd better tell her aunt everything. There had been too much secrecy in the past, and look where it had gotten everyone.

"Why did you do that?" Edie pulled out one of the

wooden chairs and sat at the kitchen table, indicating that Shelby should join her.

"Because I'd heard he'd been romantically involved with Loreena."

"And?"

"Well, I'm trying to find the murderer, and he could be a possibility, but I think I'm all over the place."

Edie sat completely still for a few seconds and then grabbed the napkin holder and ran her finger along the top. She seemed totally absorbed. Finally, she said, "It worries me that you're still looking into this. It could be dangerous."

"But you were the one who asked me to help. You were worried about Matthew."

Edie nodded and looked up at Shelby. "I know, and it's because I was so frightened about Matthew not having a fair chance. But I'm much calmer and more settled about that now. And, as you well know, I did ask you to stop."

"I know, and I tried. But it's really bothering me, and I feel like if I just keep going a bit longer, I can figure it out."

Edie shook her head. "Well, tell me about Barry Pellen. What does he want to see me about?"

"He wouldn't say, only that it had to do with business and would be something that could help you both. Or something like that."

"I wonder what that could be. I suppose it wouldn't hurt to talk to him. But how did you connect him to the murder?"

Shelby realized she hadn't shared much about what she'd

found out, other than her theories about smuggling. Now was obviously the time.

"Felicity Foxworth told me that he was dating Loreena. So I wondered if they might have had an argument, like a really heated argument that had turned violent. And I'd also heard that Duncan Caine had dated Loreena, so maybe there was a triangle that one of the guys found out about and that led to her murder."

"It's all so hard to imagine. These are just normal everyday folks. Nothing like murder is supposed to happen, especially around here."

"I don't think Alexandria Bay is immune to murder, and from what I've read and seen on TV, it's often ordinary folk that get involved in bad things happening."

Edie was silent for a few minutes, then said, "Now that I think about it, I'd heard that Pat Drucker—she's the chief librarian—had been seen having dinner with Barry Pellen. I wonder if he was dating two women at the same time?"

"For someone who doesn't get out much these days, you sure know a lot about what's happening," Shelby teased. "By the way, I saw him having dinner with Felicity Foxworth, too."

"It helps to have good connections in the community, although I hadn't heard that part," Edie said with a small laugh. "It's very unsettling, though, that's what it is. Who do you trust?"

"Well, I guess you trust that justice will be done, even if it needs a helping hand at times. And speaking of justice, I was wondering what had brought about the change of heart with Chief Stone. She seemed determined not to be friends."

"There's a lot more than an old boyfriend that we have to deal with right now."

Shelby stood and started pacing. "Does it have anything to do with the fact that I left her a message saying I wanted to talk to her about my mom? It does, doesn't it? I can see it on your face."

Edie looked at her a few seconds, then looked like she'd reached a decision. "She came to ask me what to do. She knows the whole story because she remained good friends with your dad. Can we put that aside for now, though, and you stay for some supper? Please. I just made some lasagna."

Shelby thought she might as well, particularly since the aroma had her mouth watering. She sat at the table while Edie pulled the dish out of the oven, served some pieces onto dinner plates, and set them on the table. She then opened the fridge and pulled out some tomatoes, cucumbers, and green peppers and sliced them, arranging them on a plate of field greens. She added some lemon-garlic vinaigrette to the salad, grabbed a baguette and the blue butter dish, and placed everything on the table.

After a few bites, Shelby felt her tension disappearing. The glass of white wine Edie had poured for her also helped.

"I know everyone's been telling me to forget about the possibility of smuggling taking place, but Zack Griffin as good as admitted it to me."

"He did? I find that surprising."

"Well, it was sort of tied in to my agreeing not to look into it anymore. I guess I may have gotten a little carried away."

"You're just now coming to that conclusion? I'm happy to hear you say that, though. I hate to think of you being in any danger from looking in the wrong places."

She debated whether to tell Edie about the shadowy figure at her houseboat the other night. It might make her see that Shelby wasn't merely gadding about with a dumb theory, but on the other hand, Edie might insist she move into the house. Which would not be good. Not now. Besides, Shelby liked living on her own, and she wasn't about to be bullied into moving by some unknown visitor in the middle of the night. However, if that same person was a killer . . .

She sighed.

Edie reached out and patted her arm. "Maybe you should concentrate more on the business and get your mind off the murder."

Shelby felt like she'd been punched in the stomach. "Why? Am I doing something wrong with the store? You have to tell me if something isn't right. I wouldn't want to mess it up." She loved the store.

"No, I'm sorry, I didn't mean to make you feel that things were going wrong. You're doing an excellent job, from what I see and what I hear. It's just that I thought you could come up with a project like your magazine idea or a way of doing things differently. I'm grasping at straws here. I just want you to stop all this poking around. I really do worry about you. Matthew worries about you too."

"Matthew does? While that's sweet, why would he worry about me?"

"Well, maybe it's because of me."

Shelby looked at her aunt and smiled. Now, that really was sweet. And it took care of Edie, but it didn't move her any closer to solving the murder, and no matter how much she was warned off, Shelby knew that she couldn't let it go.

Her late-night visitor had made it personal.

# Chapter Thirty-Three

Shelby got a surprise the next morning when she stopped in the main bookstore on her way to the island. Edie was sitting behind the counter, inputting the details of a small stack of books into the computer.

"I didn't know you'd be here today," Shelby said as Edie looked up. "And you're early."

"I couldn't sleep, so I thought I'd get a jump on things. And I didn't get a chance to tell you last night, not with all the smuggling talk going on." Edie smiled, and Shelby decided there was no hidden message there. "What are you doing here?"

"I thought I'd bring over some more books for the local-authors bookshelf, if we have them." Shelby walked over to the section and pulled five books, three different titles, off the shelves. She put them in front of Edie. "Would you mind checking to see if this would leave you in low stock here?"

Edie checked the computer. "No, we're fine. There are more in the back room."

"I'll grab some of those, then."

"Okay, thanks."

It took only a couple of minutes for Shelby to locate the books and stick them in her canvas bag. "By the way," she said casually as she walked back to the counter, "have you given any more thought as to what I was saying about Barry Pellen?" Might as well take advantage of running into her.

Edie nodded. "I was thinking about that, so I gave Trudy a call last night."

"And?"

"She said he's been in to the store a couple of times."

"I wouldn't have thought him a big reader."

"Well, I guess as a developer, he's trying to get more information on the area. It's mainly local books he was looking at, she said, and then, of course, he asked a lot of questions."

"Questions? About what?"

Edie sat back and stretched out her knee. "She said he started out by asking a lot of questions about me, which she didn't answer, and then he said he was interested in knowing about running a small business in Alex Bay and also on the island. He wondered if it was profitable to have that second location."

"She didn't find that odd?"

Edie shrugged. "She did, and she told him he'd have to talk to me about anything to do with the business. I guess that ties in with his wanting an introduction. Why do you ask? Do you think he could be running a smuggling operation?" Edie's eyes danced as she asked this, and Shelby found herself laughing.

"You never know. He told me you were 'unusual and charming.' I think you have a fan."

"I don't need a fan. I have thermostat control every place I go. Anyway, I'd think he has enough on his hands trying to sell the village and the council on his hotel and casino, which should keep him too busy for anything else, illegal or otherwise."

Shelby nodded. "I guess you're right. Just checking all the possibilities. But I'd better get going. It's a long swim to the island if I miss that shuttle."

She just made the shuttle boat and spent the entire trip thinking about Barry Pellen. She was still curious about him, and even more so when she noticed him walking toward the grotto later that day. He hadn't stopped by the store, so she'd had no idea he was on the island until she caught a glimpse of him on the path. She debated only a second and then followed him at a distance. If he turned around, he'd see her for sure, but she could always say she was taking a break, which was true, and always took a walk around the island, which wasn't. He didn't turn around but veered off the path and over to the fence that edged the island. He seemed to be very interested in the coastline and even stopped to duck under the rope and peer over the edge a couple of times.

Shelby felt a hand on her arm and almost cried out. She spun around to face Matthew, who put his finger to his lips, indicating she should be quiet, then pulled her back to the trail.

"What are you doing?" he asked in a soft voice.

She wasn't sure what to say. She didn't want to look too silly. "Just taking a break, and I noticed Barry Pellen."

"So you followed him. I watched you. What do you think you're doing?"

"It's a long story."

"Well, why don't you go to the Sugar Shack and buy us each a coffee, and I'll join you shortly. Then you can tell me all about this long story." He pulled a ten-dollar bill out of his pocket and put it in her hand. "Now."

Shelby was torn between asking what he was up to and wanting to finish tailing Pellen but decided to do as Matthew suggested. She nodded and made her way back to the main trail. When she turned around, both men had vanished.

Totally intrigued and hoping Matthew would have some useful information, she bought the coffee and wandered over to a remote picnic table nowhere near the trail to the grotto. She had just checked her watch for the third time when Matthew showed up. Finally. She'd have to get back to the store soon.

He took the coffee she slid over to him, pulled the top off, and had a long sip after he sat down across from her. She decided to let him take the lead, but he just kept sipping and looking around like he was enjoying the scenery. She followed suit and immediately felt some of the tension in her shoulders start to leave her body. The setting was that beautiful. A perfect sunny day with a few puffy white clouds, a surprisingly calm river up close to the island with some choppiness farther out in the channel, and an immaculately tended green lawn with pops of color in the occasional flower beds around the grounds.

She couldn't hold back any longer and finally asked, "What's going on?"

"You know I like to keep an eye on things around here; in fact, that's part of my job. This Pellen guy has been over here quite a bit in the past week, and he's been walking the property, taking it all in. So, whenever I see him, I keep an even closer eye on his movements."

"What do you think he's doing?"

"Since he's a developer, you never know. I'm thinking it might be something to do with the hotel and casino, but I can't figure out what it would be."

"Do you think it has to do with smuggling?"

"Are you still on that? Listen, Shelby, I know those stories add a certain charm to Blye Island, but that was a long time ago. There's no way that could be happening these days, not with modern technology and law enforcement all over the place. I think you should give it a rest. Who knows, maybe he wants to develop the grotto as a wedding destination. With the right lighting, it could be pretty romantic in there. And scenic, too."

"What? How could he do that?"

Matthew smiled. "I don't know if it could be done, but I'm just throwing out a suggestion. You want some reasons for his being here."

"What if we ask him outright?"

"That's not going to happen," Matthew said, standing and picking up his cup. "Leave that to the town council,

Shelby, and leave the murder investigation to the police. Your aunt would be inconsolable if anything happened to you."

Shelby felt as if she'd been doused by a cold bucket of water. She was still shivering when she walked back into the store.

# Chapter Thirty-Four

She didn't realize, until it was time to start closing up, that the rest of the day had flown by in a blur and she hadn't had a chance to think much about what Matthew had said earlier. The store had seemed about to pop its seams around midafternoon when a group of seniors, on a Knights of Columbus tour that had originated in Florida, swarmed the small space, all talking and laughing at the same time. That had netted Shelby her best sales day yet at the store, along with a bare shelf where the local authors had been displayed.

She called the main store and asked Trudy to put aside what copies they could spare, promising to pick them up the next morning on her way to work.

Then she dashed around the bookstore, straightening book displays, shelving a book that had been left out on a table, and counting the cash. She'd just finished that task when the phone rang. Much to her surprise, the caller ID displayed Felicity Foxworth.

"I'm sorry for bothering you at this late hour," she said,

"but I was hoping you could stop by my store when you get back to the village. Can you do that, or do you have plans?"

"Sure, I can do that. Is anything wrong?"

"No . . . yes . . . well, I just need to talk to you."

"Okay, I'll come straight from the shuttle."

"Thanks, Shelby." And Felicity hung up before Shelby had a chance to ask anything else.

Shelby spent the final few minutes making sure things were ready to go in the morning, and then on the shuttle ride back, she puzzled over what Felicity wanted to see her about. Was she still upset about their last talk? If so, Shelby had no idea how to deal with that. If it was something else, well, she'd just have to wait and see.

When she reached the Gallery on the Bay, she could see Felicity sitting behind the counter staring into space. *Maybe not such a good start.* Shelby hesitantly pushed the door open, and the bells above it startled them both. Felicity turned to look, but her expression relaxed when she saw who it was. She looked every inch the businesswoman today. Her hair was artfully styled in a chignon, her glasses were propped on her forehead, and the crisp stand-up collar of her white cotton shirt peeked above the line of her collarless navy suit jacket.

"Thanks for coming, Shelby. I've been giving our last talk a lot of thought, and I think I should tell you something."

*Uh-oh.* Shelby prepared for the worst, which in her books would be a lecture from Felicity. She looked around but couldn't spot another stool, so she just leaned against the counter.

"I don't think anyone will interrupt us at this hour of the

day," Felicity said, looking out the store window. Then she took a deep breath and turned back to face Shelby.

"I wasn't entirely open with you when we last spoke. In fact, I have to admit I've been in a bit of a snit, and also fooling myself about the relationship between Loreena and Duncan. I'm pretty sure it was getting to be more than friendship, even though I'd always hoped he and I would be together, if you know what I mean. That's why I was snapping at you. It wasn't your fault. It was just hard to face up to the truth. But Loreena had also recently been dating Barry Pellen, of that I'm sure, so I told Duncan. I know it was mean of me, but he did have a right to know, what with acting so loopy about her, and also, I hoped he'd drop Loreena and finally realize he had feelings for me. So foolish, right?"

Felicity looked so forlorn and yet hopeful, her blue eyes watery and the corners of her mouth turned down ever so slightly.

Shelby silently agreed but knew that wasn't what Felicity wanted to hear. She patted Felicity's arm instead.

Felicity carried on without acknowledging Shelby's touch. "I don't know what, if anything, went on between the two of them, but I did hear Loreena and Barry arguing a couple of days later. They were sitting on the outdoor patio of the Ice Cream Shoppe, and I happened to pass by, but then I ducked into the doorway of the Clockworks store, right next door, and unabashedly listened in as well as I could. Loreena was saying something about that she knew why Barry was dating her."

"Did she say anything else?"

"No. The store door opened and I managed to squeeze inside without being seen. A few minutes later I saw Loreena stomp past, but I don't know where Barry went. That's actually the last time I saw Loreena. Do you think it's connected? Do you think Barry's the killer?"

Shelby's mind was racing, and that's exactly what she was thinking. But even though the exchange made it sound like Pellen had a motive, she still had no idea what he was up to and why he'd have to stop Loreena from doing whatever it was she'd planned to do.

What should Shelby do? She realized Felicity was waiting for a reply.

"I really have no idea about any of this, but I do think you have to tell the police."

"I guess you're right, but I do feel sort of foolish, about Duncan and all. I didn't want Tekla Stone to know how silly I've been. And now I've waited too long to tell anyone. What will the police think?"

Shelby really did feel badly for her now. "Why not call the State Police. Ask for Lieutenant Guthrie. He'll probably think you were confused about what to do, that's all. I'll stay here with you while you explain it to him, if you'd like."

"Would you?" Felicity looked relieved. "You're right. But I think I also have to tell Tekla. And tell her first, or she'll have it in for me. She always liked being the one in charge." Felicity picked up the phone and dialed, listened to a message, and then hung up. "It's closed for the day. She always did think I was a bit of a twit. Now this will confirm it."

Shelby dug into her purse and pulled out her iPhone.

"Here, I have her home number. You probably shouldn't wait." She dialed the chief and handed her iPhone over to Felicity when Stone answered. Shelby listened while Felicity quickly explained everything, although she was certain the chief wouldn't be able to untangle all the information.

She was right. The chief was on her way over. Felicity didn't waste any time chatting with Shelby but rather finished her closing process while Shelby wandered around the shop, eyeing the stock.

Finally, she leaned against the counter and said to Felicity, "I saw you having dinner with Barry Pellen the other night."

Felicity stopped in her tracks. "You saw us? Uh, I was sort of hoping nobody had."

"Why?"

"Because I was being really silly, that's why. Barry made a play for me and I thought he really liked me. We went out a few times. But then I found out he was also dating Loreena and, after her, some young thing who works at the Inn on the Bay. I realized then what an idiot I'd been. What would he see in someone like me, anyway?"

"Did you break it off?"

"Not yet, not really, but I haven't gone out with him lately. He still sends me flowers. Silly, huh?"

Fortunately, Shelby didn't have to answer because Chief Stone arrived just then.

When Chief Stone arrived, Shelby felt some of her own nervousness evaporate.

After Felicity went through it all again, at a slower pace,

Stone frowned, pulled out her phone, and made a call. "I've called Dwayne Guthrie at the State Police. He'll be right over. I want you to repeat what you've said when he gets here."

Felicity looked both tired and like she'd prefer to hide under the counter. But about fifteen minutes later, Lieutenant Guthrie walked in the door and Stone turned the sign on the door to CLOSED, locking the door. Felicity went through her story yet again while Shelby watched Guthrie's face for a reaction.

He finally looked at Shelby and asked, "What are you doing here?"

"Felicity asked me to stop by so she could tell me what she just told you."

"Why you?"

Shelby couldn't tell if he was mad or just unhappy. Maybe it was his dinnertime and he was hungry. She could relate to that. "Because we'd talked about Loreena and Duncan a few days ago."

He grunted. "That must have been before your middle-of-the-night visitor, right?" He didn't wait for an answer. "Okay tomorrow we'll have a talk with those two," he looked at the notes he'd been making—"Barry Pellen and Duncan Caine, and see if any of this means anything. Would you like to sit in, Chief?"

"Damned straight."

"Please don't mention this to anyone else, Ms. Foxworth," Guthrie continued. "And you, Ms. Cox, you are not to talk to any of them before I do, is that understood?"

Shelby nodded, although she thought she was being

unfairly warned. If it hadn't been for her previous talk to Felicity, none of this might have come to light.

"Good. Now, I suggest everyone go on home and have supper."

Felicity followed them all outside and locked the door behind her. "Thank you for staying, Shelby," she said, then picked up her dog who had been surprisingly quiet through everything and hurried off.

Chief Stone put a restraining hand on Shelby's arm. "Guthrie's right, you know. You're in over your head on this, and I'd hate to see a repeat of the other night. I'm going to ask him to continue to send a patrol car around for spot checks overnight. Now, you head home and stay put, young lady. You hear?"

Shelby nodded, suppressing a smile. *Young lady.* Whether she liked it or not, Chief Stone had more in common with Edie than she thought.

# Chapter Thirty-Five

Shelby had just finished washing her supper dishes when she felt someone step onto the deck of the houseboat, followed by a knock on the door. She almost tripped over J.T. as she hurried to the door. She hoped it was Zack, although why he'd stop by now she didn't know.

She saw Barry Pellen standing at the door, and her heart started pounding. Lieutenant Guthrie had said not to speak to him, and yet, she hadn't sought him out. Surely that wouldn't count. She did have a few questions for him, but what if he was involved in whatever was going on? Could she be in danger? He knocked again and pointed to the doorknob. She opened the door but didn't invite him in.

"Hi, Barry. I'm sort of busy right now. What can I do for you?"

"I have some business I need to talk over with you, and it really can't wait. I have some decisions to make tomorrow, so I was hoping to take up just a few minutes of your time tonight. Would that work?"

She hadn't heard him sound so friendly before. Maybe it

would be all right. "Okay, come in. But I really don't have a lot of time."

"Thanks," he said as he stepped through the door she'd pulled open. He looked around the room. "This looks nice and cozy. I've always wondered what it would be like to live on a houseboat."

She almost asked him how he knew where she lived but remembered that this was Alexandria Bay. Nothing was a secret here.

"What can I do for you?"

He turned around to face her. "I have a business proposition for you and your aunt."

"And you need to discuss it tonight? At this hour?"

"Deals are made at any time, day or night. In my line of work, when a decision needs to be made, there's no waiting. As I said, it may affect something I have to decide on tomorrow. Now, I stopped by Bayside Books in the village today and was lucky enough to find your aunt there, so I told her what's on my mind. She wanted nothing to do with it. I'm telling you that outright so you can see I'm not trying to pull a fast one. But I thought you might be more reasonable. You are a partner, after all, and, being younger, I thought you might see beyond the sentiment and measure the business value of what I'm proposing."

Shelby definitely didn't like where this was heading or to be hearing it without Edie present, but she didn't see what else she could do. "Okay, I'm listening." She made a point of not inviting him to sit down but, rather, leaned against the wall and crossed her arms.

Pellen smiled. "Okay, I get it. But this is all very simple and aboveboard. I'd like to take over your lease at Blye Castle."

"You mean like take over the bookstore?"

"No. I mean you shut down the bookstore and I take over the space. I'm offering you two a very, very lucrative compensation package. You can sink the money into the main store and expand, or redecorate, or do whatever."

That was the last thing Shelby had been expecting to hear, and she wasn't quite sure what to make of it. "Why our space? Isn't there somewhere else? And for what purpose?"

"Not in Blye Castle there isn't. The Heritage Society has made that very clear. In fact, Loreena was most adamant that nothing else commercial could be let inside those sacred halls." He snorted.

"Even given your relationship with her?"

For a fleeting moment, Shelby thought he looked embarrassed. "Oh, that. No, she didn't mix business and pleasure."

"But you do." A light dawned. If he was a murderer, it certainly wasn't because of a lovers' quarrel or triangle. But would Loreena stonewalling him about the castle be a motive? It didn't seem likely. What did he want the space for anyway? "That was why you were so keen on meeting Edie. You saw another way into the castle?" Shelby huffed.

And here she'd thought he might have a personal interest in Edie. He'd intimated it anyway, or maybe that's just how she'd taken it.

"Oh, come on now. You were out in the business world before coming here. You know how these things work. So, let's cut the indignation and get down to the business at hand. As I already mentioned, the money I'm offering could go a long way into paying off the bookstore bills and maybe doing some of the renos and expansion that Edie's been wanting for the main location."

That was the first mention Shelby had heard of Edie wanting any of those things. Was he bluffing? It didn't matter; it wasn't her decision to make alone.

"I'll have to talk it over with Edie. Even if I were tempted, I can't agree to it on my own, even if I wanted to. And, just so you know, I don't."

He grimaced, then took a step toward her, and she drew in a sharp breath. "I can make it worth your while. You might just want to give that some serious thought. On the other hand, you need to remember that small businesses can be very tricky. Any number of problems can occur. Customers drop off, supplies don't arrive, accidents happen. And what would happen if your aunt fell and hurt her other knee now that's she's on the mend? Might she then reconsider, thinking it's getting to be too much? My offer would be off the table by then, and what would your options be? Think about it."

He turned abruptly and had the door open before turning back to Shelby. "By the way, I hear that you think Loreena's murder might be tied into some smuggling in the area. That's a nasty piece of business, if it is happening. I'd be careful, if I were you, asking all those questions around town. After all, I want your support for the space in the castle. I'm not interested in getting it over your dead body."

He closed the door, and she felt gentle rocking as he stepped back onto the dock. She couldn't believe he was actually whistling as he walked away.

Shelby sat down on one of the club chairs until her heart stopped pumping so fast. She wasn't quite sure what to do, but she thought she'd just been threatened. That the store had been threatened, too. She stood up and walked over to the phone but didn't pick it up. She went to the refrigerator first and took out a partially empty bottle of red wine and poured herself a glass. After a hefty gulp, she called Chief Stone and sat back down to wait.

J.T. pounced on her lap and started kneading on her leg. Shelby didn't even bother to push him off. She wanted the contact. It felt settling. Finally, she heard Chief Stone's voice at the door as she called out and then knocked.

Shelby set J.T. down on the chair and opened the door.

"Okay, so what's so urgent, Ms. Shelby?" Chief Stone looked like she'd been getting ready for bed. She'd scrubbed her face clean of her usual mascara, blush, and lipstick and had unwound her hair from its usual braiding. It flowed down below her shoulders in a mass of thin waves. Shelby looked down and noticed the clogs on her feet, the gray sweat pants, and the knit sweater pulled over a T-shirt.

"I'm sorry to have disturbed you, but I just had a visitor. Barry Pellen."

Stone's face hardened. "I thought we told you not to talk to him."

"He came here and insisted on talking to me. What could I do?"

"Okay, so what did he want?"

Shelby gestured for her to sit, then recounted the conversation. When she finished, she took another sip of her wine and held up her glass to the chief. "Would you like one?"

Chief Stone shook her head and sat silent for several minutes. Shelby wondered what was going on in her head. She'd love to hear some words of reassurance. Or did the chief think she'd blown things out of proportion? Surely not.

Finally, Chief Stone smiled. "I think we may have finally shaken loose something useful in this investigation. Now, you lock up and don't answer the door again tonight. On second thought, maybe you should stay at Edie's."

Shelby shook her head. "No, I don't want to worry her. And besides, he thinks I'm giving his so-called offer some thought. I don't see why he'd come back or try anything else."

"You could be right. But I want you to call me on my cell phone when you get up in the morning, and then I expect a couple of calls throughout the day, just letting me know that everything's okay. Okay?"

Shelby nodded, grateful for the concern. But also, all of a sudden, a bit terrified.

* * *

Shelby was on the phone to Edie first thing the next morning. She quickly filled her in on the conversation with Barry and waited for a reaction.

"I can't believe he went to you behind my back," Edie

exploded. "I turned him down, on both counts, and expected that would be the end of it."

"What do you mean, both counts?"

She heard Edie sigh and could picture her settling back in her chair. "Well, first off, he just appeared at my front door without an invitation and without checking with me first. He did have a beautiful bouquet of yellow roses for me, though. I thought that was very thoughtful, so I invited him in and we had some iced tea."

"This is getting interesting."

"*Harrumph.* It could have been, but he got very personal very quickly. Oh, he was suave about it, but I don't like being asked to share personal details on a first meeting. Then, he asked me out to dinner."

"He did?"

"Yes, he did, and I said no. He turned up the charm, but I didn't change my mind, so then he changed tactics and made the same store pitch he gave you."

"Ouch. Do you think he'd been buttering you up with the flowers and dinner invitation?"

"Yes, I do, and I don't do business like that. I told him what I thought about the whole thing and showed him to the door. Can you believe the gall?"

Shelby took a moment in answering. "He sounds like a desperate man, but why?"

"I have no idea, but I hope you stay clear of him."

"Oh, I will, Aunt Edie. You can bet on it."

They hung up, and Shelby grabbed her sweater and bag before dashing off to the shuttle.

Taylor met Shelby at the dock and immediately filled her in on the online shopping spree she and Chuck had done the night before. Within the next couple of weeks, deliveries of baby items would be arriving, spurring them to devote the upcoming weekend to painting the room that had been designated as the nursery.

"I know, I'm rushing it a bit, like quite a bit, but I just wanted to leap into the excitement. And Chuck was keen, too. I figure we'll treat ourselves to a mini-spree a month." She leaned against the boat railing, adjusting her collar to block out the wind, looking very pleased with herself.

Shelby reached out and squeezed her arm. "That is exciting. And I think mini-sprees are the way to go; that way you won't have humungous bills all at once."

"Exactly." Taylor turned to face into the wind, letting it blow through her hair, and Shelby did the same.

"How are you feeling these days? You will let me know if the doctor says you shouldn't be working, right? Or if you should just be sitting behind the cash register all day? That would work. Maybe in the village so you wouldn't have to take the boat every day?"

"Listen to you. I'm still so far away from having to even consider lighter work or fewer hours. You can't mother-hen me, you know. Chuck's already taken that roll." She laughed and gave Shelby's arm a squeeze.

Shelby smiled back and relaxed. She hadn't realized until that moment the she'd been worried about Taylor.

By the time they'd reached the store, Shelby was in a

good frame of mind, all thoughts of Pellen's intrusive visit under control. As the day wore on, though, she found the apprehension building. She didn't go for her usual walk around the castle grounds in the afternoon, and she stuck with Taylor after closing, walking down to the shuttle. When they parted back in Alex Bay, Shelby took a good look around the parking lot and street before walking home.

She stopped before setting foot on the dock leading to her houseboat. She could see a pair of feet, crossed at the ankle, resting atop the railing of the upper deck. Her heart beat faster as she ran through a list of things she should do. At the top of it was call the police.

After a few seconds of panic, she took a deep breath and reasoned that anyone lying in wait to do her harm would be out of sight. Not visible to her and the entire community. Although she had to admit, as she glanced around, there wasn't much community in evidence. She waited until her heart rate dropped back to normal and then headed for the houseboat. The feet hadn't moved by the time she boarded, so she put her bags down just inside the door and then took the stairs up.

Zack Griffin looked over at her as she reached the top and grinned.

"I hope you don't mind my making myself comfortable while waiting for you. It's been a busy day." He wore his reflective aviators so she couldn't even guess where his eyes were trained. His CGIS ball cap was pulled down low over his forehead, but he'd discarded his jacket, which lay on the other chair. And the sleeves on his blue shirt were rolled and pushed up over his elbows. In total, he looked relaxed and totally at home.

"I don't mind, if you don't count the heart failure you very nearly caused. I could see your feet all the way from the shore."

He'd planted them on the deck by this point and even stood. "Sorry about that. I didn't think you'd mind my waiting for you up here. Did you think your visitor was back again?"

"Which one?" she asked with a grimace.

"I've heard about two. Have there been more?"

"No. At least, not that I'm aware of. One never knows what happens during the daytime when I'm not here."

It was Zack's turn to grimace. "Tell me about last night."

"There's not much to tell. Barry Pellen stopped by to see me. I thought he was interested in dating Aunt Edie because he asked me to introduce him to her. I was so wrong. It was just a tactic. He actually wants us to vacate the space at the castle so that he can take it over. Edie said no, so he came to me to convince me to change her mind."

"Did he say why he wants it?" Zack had settled back in the chair in a casual sprawl, but J.J. noticed he seemed more alert.

"No, he didn't, even though I did ask him. It just sort of flew out of my mind amid the threats. Is it important?"

"That depends on what his answer is."

Shelby shook her head in frustration. "That doesn't help."

"Did he talk about anything else?" He leaned forward.

"Well, he did say he'd heard I was trying to link Loreena's murder to smuggling."

Zack shot upright. "My point exactly. Everyone around town knows what you're up to. I'd hoped you would have given all that up by now."

"Well, I haven't gone around asking more questions. But I may have mentioned that Loreena's death at the grotto might just add to the legend. But you already know that."

Zack shook his head. "And you still don't think that might get someone to thinking that you know a whole lot more than you actually do?"

"No, I don't see that. What I do see is a Coast Guard Investigative Service special agent who keeps popping up when there's something related to Blye Island, and since Loreena's murder fits that description . . ." She didn't finish her sentence but instead gestured at him.

Zack sat forward and laughed. "You have an extraordinarily active imagination, Shelby. I just wanted to make sure you were okay, and also, once again, although I know it's entirely futile, to warn you off asking any more questions. It seems like it's getting to be an even more dangerous game."

"I know," Shelby said with a shudder. "I'm taking it to heart."

"I'm very glad to hear you say that," Zack said. "And call me immediately if you have any more surprise visitors." He stood and squeezed her shoulder, looking into her eyes for a few seconds longer than necessary. She held her breath and then slowly let it out when he dropped his hand and walked toward the stairs.

He stopped when he got to the stairs and turned to face her. “You know, you were lucky, again. Maybe not next time. Please be careful.”

# Chapter Thirty-Six

Shelby spent the next morning alternating between serving a surprisingly inquisitive group of customers (who had been to the store before, bought some books on local history, and wanted more) and tidying the store. Taylor had called in sick, and Shelby had made the decision to run the store by herself rather than trying to get a replacement on short notice. Cody was working in the afternoon, so she'd just have to manage by herself for the morning.

She decided to move the display of local books closer to the cash register, hoping to attract the attention of customers as soon as they set foot in the store. While she did it, she thought about why Barry Pellen might want the store space. What also struck her was the fact that he'd been dating so many women at the same time. And, even more curious, she realized, was that the ones she knew about were members of the Heritage Society board. Did that mean anything? Could he be so desperate to get the bookstore space that he'd try to influence the board's decision to lease the space to Bayside Books? It sounded far-fetched, but he had sounded very determined the other night. Of course, he had dated the hotel clerk, but if there was a plan, that didn't seem to be a part of it.

She moved over to shelving some books next to the bay window when she noticed Duncan Caine out on the side lawn. He seemed to be headed toward the grotto. *What does he want?* Better yet, what a good time to ask him some more questions. Did he know anything about Pellen's plan? She stuck her phone in her pocket, swapped the Open sign to Closed for Lunch, and slipped out of the castle.

She waved at Matthew, who seemed deep in pursuit of a stray limb on one of the trees. She doubted he noticed her as he struggled to hit his target with his long-handled cutters.

As she approached the pathway to the grotto, she took a minute to look around. There were no tourists within sight, which was good since so much of the area was designated off limits at the moment. She could hear the waves hitting the shore before she actually focused on the whitecaps on the river. She hadn't realized the wind had come up sometime during the morning, and her walk to the grotto had been through the sheltered part of the island. It looked like too stunning a place for a murder to have occurred, she thought, feeling a stab of sadness.

As she approached the entrance, she was surprised to find the gate to the grotto ajar. Her attention was drawn away from the gate by the sound of a small motor approaching the grotto. Who was it? What was going on? Before she had a chance to do anything, Duncan called out to her.

"Miss Cox, Shelby. Just the person I wanted to see next. Do you have a minute?"

Shelby looked around, wondering what to do. Listen to the small inner voice that told her to head back to the store? Or ask him her questions? She moved closer to him, determined to keep the gate between them.

"I do, in fact, I have a few questions for you. But who's in the boat?"

"I don't know. Maybe it's one of your smugglers."

She could tell he was laughing at her, and as tempted as she was to take a look, she stood her ground, fairly certain Matthew would show up soon—that is, if he was still keeping an ear peeled for boats.

"I know now that's highly unlikely," she said, and glanced behind her to look for Matthew. At the same moment, Duncan stepped around the gate and grabbed her arm, pulling her toward the entrance to the grotto.

She screamed, but he clamped his hand over her mouth, twisting her arm behind her and shoving her forward. She stumbled and wrenched free, only to feel a gun jammed in her back.

"Stand up and don't try anything foolish."

She got to her feet and looked back to see if it really was a gun. Duncan waved it in her face. "Yup, it's a gun, and I do know how to use it. Now, get inside."

She stepped gingerly through the opening, pausing to let her eyes adjust to the change in light. When she was able to focus, she saw Barry Pellen stepping out of a small boat and tying its rope around a rock.

"Miss Cox, so sorry you had to join us. You would have been much more useful as an ally," he said, nodding at Caine.

"I don't get it," Shelby finally said.

Pellen walked right up to her. "You don't? That's odd, you seem to be so adept at sticking your nose into everything. Shall we tell her, Duncan?"

"Might as well. She won't be sharing it with anyone."

Shelby felt herself shivering and took a deep breath to calm down. "Does it have something to do with why you're wining and dining the female members of the Heritage Society?"

Pellen sat down on a large boulder and looked thoughtful. "Well done. Yes, you see, I need them on my side when the announcement is made."

"Which announcement is that?"

"The one that I'm intending to buy Blye Island on behalf of my consortium and turn the castle into a hotel and casino."

"You wouldn't." Shelby felt outraged.

"Oh, but I would. Think of what a hit it would be. We'd make loads of money, and who knows, maybe even the good folk of the village would be on our side. After all, they didn't like the idea we first floated of a resort right in the bay. But it wouldn't be in the middle of everything if it was on the island. Isn't that right, Duncan?"

"Exactly. I think I can get the council to give their approval to this plan."

"But what was Loreena's role?" Shelby asked.

"Loreena? She was a romantic old fool. Thought she was still in high school," Caine answered, not sounding at all upset about his old friend. "We needed her on our side because she has . . . had . . . so much influence in the town."

"But both of you dating her?"

"Why not? She was happy," Pellen answered.

Shelby shook her head in disgust. He sounded so smug. "But why kill her?"

"That wasn't the plan. But she stumbled across Barry and me that day. We were pacing off locations on the island for various attractions. We'd come over in Barry's small boat and tied up in the grotto so we wouldn't be spotted. I thought we'd done well to avoid Kessler, and then, there she was. We steered her into the grotto and finally had to explain. She started screaming and pushed me, so I pushed her back and she fell, hitting her head, and then tumbled into the water. It was an accident," said Caine.

"In your version, anyway," Shelby said, eyeing the dark waters and wondering if she could swim to the public dock before they caught up with her. "According to the autopsy, she was struck on the head, fell into the water, and then held under until she drowned. Doesn't sound too accidental to me."

Caine looked ready to strangle Shelby, and she could hear Pellen made a strange sound in his throat. Her mind flashed on the water. She could probably make it. She was a strong swimmer, but first she had to knock the gun out of his hand. And hope they didn't follow in the boat. Where was Matthew? Surely he'd heard the engine.

"It worked the first time. Kessler's still the prime suspect," Caine said. "So, why not go for a second?"

Pellen stood up. "I don't know, Duncan. You can BS about the whack on the head and holding her under if you're caught. But a second drowning?"

"What do you mean *I* can do that? You're in on it too."

"I did nothing to harm her."

"But you watched, didn't you?" Shelby glanced at him. "You didn't even try to help get her out of the water or go for help, I'll bet."

Pellen took a step forward. "There was nothing I could do."

"You were in full agreement," Caine shouted. His attention was fully on Pellen.

Shelby made her move. She ducked behind Pellen, shoved him into Caine, and dove into the water.

The zing of the cold water knocked the breath out of her, and she struggled to get back up to the surface. She swam at an angle, hoping she was heading toward the grotto opening. Maybe she could work the boat loose before either man reached it. She surfaced and saw Pellen stepping into the boat and pulling the cord to start the engine, with Caine close behind. She looked toward the opening. She had about a yard to go but knew she wouldn't make it before they reached her. So she snaked under and swam toward the light, hoping her limbs didn't freeze and fall off before she made her goal. She surfaced again and felt momentarily blinded by the midday sun, but then she heard a motor heading her way. Terror washed through her. She swam even harder but felt her strength giving way to the cold. *Just do it.*

At some point she felt two hands reach down for her

from the side of the boat. She couldn't even put up a fight. She waited to be pushed under the waves but instead felt someone lifting her into the boat.

She heard Zack's voice. He bundled her up in a blanket and pulled her close to his chest, saying things, comforting, nice things, she thought, but she wasn't really focusing.

* * *

Zack, Matthew, and Edie sat in Edie's sun-room later that afternoon, drinking beer and filling Shelby in on what she'd missed when she'd been taken to the hospital to be checked over. Mainly, that Zack had handed her into the waiting arms of Matthew while he went back to head off the two men, force them to shore, and arrest them.

Shelby smiled. "Thank you, thank you." She pressed her hands together as if praying and bowed her head toward Matthew. Then she turned to Zack. "You see, I told you Matthew was innocent."

Zack and Matthew shared a conspiratorial glance.

"What?" Shelby asked. "I saw that. What's going on? I know, I was wrong about the smuggling."

Zack leaned closer to her. "What I'm about to say stays in this room for now, agreed?"

Both Shelby and Edie nodded.

"No, you're right about the fact that there's smuggling going on, Shelby; it's just not tied in to the murder."

"I thought that's why you got involved in the investigation."

Zack smiled. "Right again. But I've been focusing on the

smuggling and I have a suspect in sight. I'm just waiting for him to make his move, and I've been worried your *investigating* would scare him off. So now that the murder is solved, just leave it to me, okay?"

"Okay." She shifted in her seat and glanced at him before asking, "But what does that have to do with Matthew?"

"We've been aware of the operation for some time now but were never able to figure out the schedule or the route. So I asked Matthew to keep an eye on things. He's made note of every time he's heard a boat go by and he's been checking on the grotto, once we guessed that it was a hiding place for the smugglers when they thought they were being chased."

"Seriously?" Shelby turned to Matthew. "That means you were never really a murder suspect?"

Matthew shook his head. "They needed it to look like that, though, so that I could continue keeping an eye on things."

"So," Edie jumped in, "there was no need for me to be so worried about you at all?"

Matthew moved over beside her on the love seat, put his right arm around her shoulders, and pulled her close. "No, but it meant a lot to me. It really did, and does, Edie."

Shelby felt like she was intruding, but she had her own questions to ask Zack.

"And you've been humoring me?"

"Well, maybe a bit, but mainly I've been trying to keep you out of all this. You see what happened today? And believe me, it could have been much worse if Matthew hadn't heard the boat and gone to check it out. He phoned me when he saw you being forced into the grotto."

Shelby thought about it a moment. "I had to do something."

"I know you think you had to. And Barry Pellen did end up confessing, but I stress again, it wasn't really smart to get so involved."

"Perhaps." She wasn't about to give in so easily. "But you—"

Edie interrupted. "I'd say we're at a draw here. Everyone had their own reason for doing what was done. Shelby, honey, I can't imagine what I would have done, though, if anything had happened to you. And, Matthew, you can't believe how relieved I am to hear you're not a suspect or even being hounded. But what about Tekla? Does she know? I can't imagine that she went along with the subterfuge."

"Chief Stone? Yes, she's been read in," Zack answered, "but she insisted that she needed to keep riding Matt so that no one would suspect."

"Really? Well, it worked, and I'm sure she enjoyed every minute of it," Edie said, and then took a long drink from her beer bottle. "I'm going to throw some soup on. After your chilly afternoon, I think that's just what you need, Shelby." She looked at the men. "You're both welcome to stay."

Zack stood. "I have more paperwork than you can imagine to start in on, but thanks, Edie."

Matthew also stood. "And I have to make a statement to Lieutenant Guthrie. He'd like something official for his files. I'll call you later, Edie."

Shelby felt disappointed but stood and turned to Zack. "Thanks for what you did out there today. You saved my life."

He leaned into her as he passed by on this way to the door. "I'll let you thank me properly later." His breath fanned the side of her face.

She felt her cheeks flame and was glad the others had already left the room.

# Chapter Thirty-Seven

A couple of days later, Shelby sat on the roof of her houseboat, soaking in the late-afternoon sun, trying to relax after a particularly busy day at the bookstore. She heard footsteps coming along the dock, then felt a gentle list as someone stepped aboard. She knew she should get up and check it out or, at the very least, call out, but she was hoping whoever it was would think no one was home and leave. She just wanted to be alone. She hadn't had much of that lately.

She heard someone climbing up the stairs and knew it must be Zack. At least, she thought it sounded like him, which surprised her. How had she gotten to recognize his footsteps?

"Aren't you supposed to ask for permission to come aboard?" she called out.

"Not when it's a social call," Zack answered as he walked to where she sat.

She opened her eyes. "If it's social, I should offer you a glass of wine, but I'm afraid I'm too lazy right now. You'll find the bottle in the fridge."

He grinned and gave her a quick salute. When he next appeared, he had the bottle in one hand and two glasses in the other. It wasn't just his black T-shirt and shorts that added to his off-duty appearance. She realized she'd been learning to read his body language over the past few weeks. When he was on official business, he looked more stern and held his body in a more rigid pose. Today he looked relaxed, from the smile in his eyes to the sag of his shoulders. She felt a little pleased with herself for noticing.

"Let's consider this a predinner drink," Zack said, handing her a glass, "and then I'd like to take you out, maybe to Absinthe & Aurum? I hear they have great food."

She looked at him a bit more closely. Did he know about her date with Drew? Time to change the subject.

"I'm glad there won't be a resort either on the mainland or the island. I kind of like it all the way it is."

"So, you're still thinking this feels like home?"

"Oh, it does, and I like taking this slow, easing my way into the community, so I'd rather no dramatic changes were made. Not yet, anyway."

"I sort of got those vibes from you." Zack looked at her and she blushed. He looked back out over the water. "I agree. I'd hate to see the Bay become too busy. If it had come to that, I would have made my feelings known."

"That's always a good thing."

"Yes."

They were staring at each other, and Shelby felt it hard to pull her eyes away. She wasn't sure where this conversation was going, but it made her unsettled, so she tried to bring it back around to where they'd started. "So, anything new about Duncan and Barry?"

"Caine has been formally charged with murder and denied bail, which I think is a good thing. He could be a flight risk, and he does have a lot of connections that could make that happen. Barry Pellen is being charged as an accessory and also not granted bail. Until they go to trial, the police will be trying to tie up any loose ends and making sure all the bases are covered."

"Are you part of that process?"

"To some extent, but I'm still on the trail of the smugglers. I'm really hoping we can wrap that up very soon. But it's up to Chief Stone to finish up this case.

"So, we won't be seeing as much of you around here?" She tried to make the question sound neutral, as if it were of little consequence to her.

He grinned. "I still live here, you know. And I'll have to check on the grotto every now and then. I also think you're bound to keep getting yourself into trouble, if you decide to stick around. I feel obligated to make sure you remain safe."

"Obligated?"

"Well, yeah. I did save your life, didn't I?"

"Well . . . yeah. I guess you did." She smiled, unable to stifle the feeling of pleasure that seemed to be suffusing her entire being.

# Chapter Thirty-Eight

Of course, she would be staying, Shelby mused as she walked over to Edie's the next day. She'd already phoned her boss at Masspike Publishing and resigned. After all, she had a bookstore empire to handle, she thought with a grin. Besides, she still wanted to talk to Prissy Newmarket and Izzy Crocker about her mom. She also had new friends, especially a certain special agent. And she had a loving aunt who needed her. She did believe that.

At some point she might try to track down her mom, but at present it didn't really matter. Edie was the one who was there for her, just as her dad had been for all those years while she was growing up. Sure, it still hurt a bit to think that her mom had rejected her, and maybe the fact that she hadn't tried to make contact was a good indicator that Shelby shouldn't either. But that was a question for another time.

Shelby found Edie sitting outside in her backyard. She paused a moment before walking down the back stairs, wanting to take in the colorful view and also to watch Edie for a few moments. Then she took a deep breath and slowly walked down the steps. Edie heard the creaking and turned to look at her, a look of anxiety on her face.

"I thought we could share some crackers and cheese along with a glass of wine before supper," Shelby explained, setting the tray she was carrying on the wooden patio table.

"That's a lovely thought, Shelby." Edie accepted the glass of wine that Shelby held out to her. Shelby thought of it as a peace offering.

She grabbed her own and sat on a green Adirondack chair set at a right angle to Edie's. Edie helped herself to a cream cracker and a slice of Brie and continued to look at her garden. After a few minutes, Shelby put her glass down.

"I've come to a decision, Aunt Edie. I'm staying in Alex Bay. It's where I belong, and the bookstores are also where I want to be. With you."

Edie turned to Shelby, tears in her eyes. "I'm so very, very happy to hear you say that, Shelby. I've been worried that I messed things up and you'd be desperate to leave."

Shelby reached over and took Edie's hand. "You're family, the only family I have. And I'm going to try not to spend the rest of my life dwelling on the past. I have to admit, I'm still trying to come to terms with you and Dad doing, or not doing, what you did. But the main thing I'm taking from this is that you both love me. So, I figure that's pretty great."

"I'm relieved, honey. And also, I think we'll have a good future with the bookstores. And at some point soon, I'll want to start stepping back a bit from the business, and hopefully, you'll be happy to take over. I think, too, that there may be other aspects of this place, one in particular, that will grow on you even more." She winked and took another drink from her glass.

Shelby thought about that for a few minutes. She wondered what Zack would think about her decision. Then she thought back to his good-night kiss after dinner the night before. She was certain he would approve.

# Acknowledgments

There are so many factors and people that go into the writing and publishing of a book so I should start with an umbrella thank you to all involved. Narrowing that down, my utmost thanks goes to Faith Black Ross, my new editor with a new publisher. That can be a bit daunting along with all the excitement that goes along with a new series. She has been both supportive and understanding and I certainly appreciate it.

My agent, Kim Lionetti of BookEnds Literary Agency also deserves so much thanks for her ongoing guidance and support through what has been a challenging year. To my first reader, my sister Lee, many thanks as usual. Your support is invaluable. Heaps of thanks for your insight and writing savvy, Mary Jane Maffini, aka Victoria Abbott, always helping me find my way.

Thanks also to my fellow amazing authors on Mystery Lovers' Kitchen and Killer Characters blogs. And also, to the many talented authors who read the manuscript and offered comments and cover blurbs. What a great community to be a part of!

And, my sincere thanks to the readers who keep on supporting and reading cozy mysteries. You make it happen!

31901064419601